MW01100494

PETER PUMPKIN
GOES
TO A PARTY

PETER PUMPKIN
GOES
TO A PARTY

Peter Nanra

Copyright © 2018 by Peter Nanra.

HARDBACK:	978-1-948962-15-5
PAPERBACK:	978-1-948962-14-8
EBOOK:	978-1-948962-16-2

All rights reserved. No part of this publication may be reproduced, distributed, or transmitted in any form or by any electronic or mechanical means, without the prior written permission of the publisher, except in the case of brief quotations embodied in critical reviews and certain other noncommercial uses permitted by copyright law.

Ordering Information:

For orders and inquiries, please contact:
1-888-375-9818
www.toplinkpublishing.com
bookorder@toplinkpublishing.com

Printed in the United States of America

CHAPTER 1
MY PARTY

"Happy Birthday to you. Happy Birthday to you. Happy Birthday dear Pashelle. Happy Birthday to you."

That was the song every pumpkin would sing to me in about one months' time. My birthday was approaching. I was turning eight years old.

What a glorious time this was. I was going to have the biggest party that any pumpkin had ever seen. Ever.

It had to be my favorite time of the year. Many pumpkins didn't like to celebrate their birthday. I don't know why. But I did. I have a party every year. It was such a special treat for me. To celebrate this wonderful moment with all of my family and friends.

Ms. Pumpkin promised me she would bake the biggest, most beautiful cake that has ever been baked. She said it would be eight layers, each layer to symbolize a year of my life. It was going to be super tall. And each layer would have a different flavor and taste. It's like eight different types of cakes, all stuck together as one. She hinted there may be chocolate mousse on the top layer, and strawberry shortcake on the bottom.

All my friends would attend the party. Polo, Plato, Pannette. Pavneet and Petrina. My brothers and sisters, and neighbors too. My brothers were taking care of all the details. Because the party was supposed to be a surprise birthday party. I was not supposed to know anything about it. I was not supposed to know where it would take place. Or on what day. It may not even be held on the anniversary day of my birth. This year, I was told the surprise was that it could be held on any day. A few days before my birthday, or after. Or maybe even on the actual anniversary date of my birth too. I don't know. Because it was all hush hush. My whole family was helping to prepare for this momentous occasion. I just knew they were working hard on the preparations for this wonderful moment.

It was all I had been thinking about, for weeks.

I think it was important to have a celebration or momento, to mark the time I became one year older. And I felt that I could only become one year older, when I had a party. Only when I blew out the candles on my birthday cake, and made a wish, did I grow one year older. Not before.

And I love the birthday song. I'm not even sure what it was called. The happy birthday song, I think. Ms. Pumpkin sings it so well. She has such a delightful singing voice. And Mr. Pumpkin too.

The whole pumpkin patch would be invited. Everyone would have a great time. It would be the biggest event of the summer. It must be held in the arena. That was the most spacious building in the patch. Or maybe it would be held outside, in the gardens of the eye. It would be such a nice, glorious and sunny day. It always was that time of year. It could get very hot in the summertime. I could sweat like a pig. When I was inside our buildings, as well as out. Especially if the air conditioning wasn't functioning properly. Like it was two years ago. Someone should have detected the situation sooner. No one said anything. Could you believe it? Until some pumpkins realized that there was no circulating air. By that time, all the pumpkins were inside the dining hall. The tables were setup. The birthday cake was so neatly displayed. In front of everyone to see. But I was sure everyone was thinking 'hurry up Pashelle and blow out the candles, so we can get out and breathe some fresh air'.

But I was not sure where my party would be held this year. It was a surprise. I was not supposed to know when, where, or how it would be held. Or who was even going to show up. I was not supposed to see the guest list. But I was sure everyone would be invited.

Last year, my party was in the lounge. It was a blast. So many pumpkins saw me blow out the candles on my birthday cake and see me make a wish. We played lots of games. And there was music. And dancing.

Mr. Pumpkin said he would film the event this year. Make a movie. A pumpkin party documentary, he said.

And I would receive lots of presents. I always did. Pumpkins could be so generous. Last year, Ms. Pumpkin knitted me seven red bows, which I could wear on my stem. And I received a bracelet which dangles from my wrist. Well, sometimes I wear it. Most of the time, it was just packed up in the jewelry box. I received a cool pair of sunglasses from Polo.

I wished every pumpkin could see the cake cutting ceremony live, and up close. But because of the size of the crowd, many pumpkins would end up in the back, and not be able to see what was truly going on. It would be difficult. Not thru all those pumpkins. Not at the back. With such a large crowd. I mean there were over nine hundred pumpkins that lived in this patch. Not to say they would all attend. But every pumpkin loved a party. I mean, anyone was free to attend. Hopefully the movie would be good, so repeat performances could be shown. And there should be lots of pictures taken.

There would be games, and lots of fun. Last year, Paxton wanted every pumpkin to wear a birthday hat. That would have been a lot of hard work, to make that many hats.

I was born in the middle of summer, as were many pumpkins. We were told the weather had to be warm to allow our seeds to sprout properly. Because I was born when I was, it made me a Pleione pumpkin. The name was based on the pumpkin astrological sign. Or calendar. Or whatever it was called. There were thirteen of these signs. There was Pleione, Peacock, Polaris, Pollux, Porrima, Propus, Proxima, Procyon. I cannot recall all of them, actually.

Pleione was known as an 'active hot star'. The sign was supposed to depict the type of personality a pumpkin had. A Pleione star rotated itself quickly. Maybe that was why I was such a great roller. Not that any pumpkin ever had the need to roll. And I loved to stay active and busy. These stars alternated between three different phases. Maybe this was the reason why I could be so emotional. Sometimes I cried for no reason. Maybe because I was sad or depressed. Maybe. I don't know. But it was weird because I never felt sad. I am always very positive minded. I am always upbeat. But I could get hot quickly. I mean hot, as in mad. Not really mad. But I did find myself being overly aggressive at times. I am also open hearted. I loved to share, and showed my emotions and feelings quite easily. And not just how I felt, but how I felt towards other pumpkins. I tended to pass judgement on others. Sometimes without proper due thought. I would just blurt out something. Anything. The first thought that entered my head.

For instance, last week I overheard Pandora and Pippa talking about how Pippa's sister entered into the beauty pageant this year. And Pandora was telling Pippa about all the things Pippi would need to do, to ensure she looked great for the final voting. But that was bad advice. Why? Because it was. And I jumped in and said 'no'. That Pippi shouldn't enter into the pageant because she would never win. She would have no chance. Mainly due to the uneven grooves in and around her left cheek. They were very noticeable. They were like a blemish. I've seen them up close. And I told Pippa that she should be encouraging Pippi to take up another hobby. Well, neither of them seemed very thankful. Pandora didn't even listen to me properly. I could see the mysterious look on her face. As if she was just waiting for me to stop talking, so she could respond. And she did. Pandora said something like 'excuse me, but this is a private conversation'.

Because of instances like this, pumpkins would think I was too pushy. But I didn't think of it as being pushy. I thought I was trying to be more involved in other pumpkins lives. Maybe I was like this because I needed to be loved, and supported, and cared for. That I needed to be wanted. I was concerned with my popularity. I wanted to fit in. I wanted everyone to like me and to think I was interesting. I don't know.

I share the Pleione sign with so many famous pumpkins. Like Pavlov, who was a scientist. And Purdy, who was a renowned chef. And also Par Pumpkin. He was a golfer.

My thoughts were rambling. I was lying on my bed, preparing myself for sleep. But preparation was taking a long time. I had a pad of paper open to a blank page. I thought I would write down the things my family may have forgotten about my party. So I could remind them. I thought I would accumulate a detailed list of activities.

I decided to take a momentary break from that exercise, and paid attention to what my two sisters were up to. My whole family loved to talk and tell stories. I would characterize our family as very social and outgoing. I mean all pumpkins loved to talk.

"Stop talking. Go to sleep!" yelled Paxton.

Paxton was the oldest in our family. He was sixteen. He was an elder, and volunteered in the supply center. He hadn't slept for days. It was the heat. It was too hot for him. He was running himself ragged the past few days, trying desperately to tire himself out during the daytime, so that he could fall asleep at night. The noise and chatter of our house didn't help.

No one paid him any attention though.

"Why do you keep reading so late at night?" asked Plouffe.

"You always say that. Now you broke my concentration. And that was a good part too," replied Patrice.

"I say it because it's true. It's bad for your eyes," countered Plouffe.

Both my sisters were younger than me. Patrice was the youngest in our family. She was four. And Plouffe was five. Plouffe would be attending full time school this fall. Although it seemed that Patrice was the more eager to learn and study. Plouffe was not looking forward to full time school. Not at all. I loved school. It gave me something to do. Something to focus my efforts. Sometimes the summer could be kind of boring. Plouffe was the opposite of me. She was probably the laziest out of all of us. And I do mean to say lazy.

"But it's so light out. We're in the middle of summer," replied Patrice. "There's enough light."

"What are you reading now?" asked Plouffe.

There was a very large family of eleven that lived in this house before us. They lived in this house for many years. All of them. Because Paxton was the first born in our family, and didn't have any siblings, he moved in here with them. Which must have been really weird for him. I mean he didn't live with eleven other pumpkins. By the time Paxton was born, there were only three remaining from that family. The final two were given as an offering a few years back. I knew them. I don't remember them very much. I mean I was little. And they were old. They didn't really mingle and socialize with us very much. They normally stayed in their own room. The only thing I remember about them, was they used to complain about all the noise. And the loud music. Which I always thought was very odd. Considering they grew up in a family of eleven. One would think they would be used to the noise of a busy household.

My four brothers were all older. So there are seven of us in our family.

We lived in the western most column in the patch. In a big house. And the walls between the rooms were paper thin. The noise traveled fast. It ricocheted around the house, like the air itself. I have heard Payne singing from the toilet, on numerous occasions. We all have.

I could hear Payne at this moment. Singing. I was sure he was in the bathtub. He was the second oldest. He was fourteen. Last year he was a senior, which meant that it was his last year of trick or treating during our Halloween festival. He tried to cool himself off by lying in the bathtub. For hours at a time. Singing. Out aloud.

"Stop singing," begged Paxton.

Payne's voice was belting out the lyrics to a song that I hadn't heard of before. I didn't recognize his beat or rhythm at all. The chatter of my other two brothers wasn't pleasing Paxton either.

"…and she almost fainted." I could hear Paradis in the next room. Loud and clear, if I was focused enough. He was the third oldest in the family. He was the tallest and skinniest. He would have dreams, so he claimed. That he was living in some kind of utopia. In a perfect world, with no one around to cause him trouble. That he was the first and only pumpkin ever born. Living of the land, all by himself. Which was very strange.

He was close friends with Paris. Which irritated me. Because Paris was friends with Portia. And I didn't like Portia. So I didn't like it when Paris paid a visit. Especially when it was unannounced.

I hardly ever had dreams. Especially like that. I was more practical. I realized that pumpkins could never live by themselves.

'Who?' I wondered.

"It must have been because of the heat," said Paradis.

"Who fainted?" I asked them, raising my voice.

"Hey. Pashelle." That scream was too loud for Paxton.

I had to find out. I got up from my bed and scurried over to the next room. I jumped on their bed, head first. I made sure I didn't move any of the checker pieces on their game board. I could see Paxton's face down and buried in his mattress, with a pillow over his head, thru the open door. He was in his room. He had his own room. So did Payne.

"Who fainted?"

I wanted to know. Patrice was always reading, and didn't always like talking. And Plouffe had been moody recently. Probably because of school. So it wasn't always fun hanging around with either of them. And I didn't think I could possibly have come up with something new to say to them. Something that would interest them. And I doubt I would need to remind my family about how to throw a party anyways. My brothers were experts.

Paradis was explaining that Panda was dancing, and hopping around in the lounge the other day. And then all of a sudden, she lost all energy and just collapsed to the ground.

"Seriously? Then she shouldn't party so much," I said.

"I'm not getting any air," interrupted Paxton. Probably. Since he had his pillow suffocating his own face.

"Go. It's your turn," instructed Pascal.

They were playing checkers. They didn't seem too interested in my inquisition. As if they thought their story was too boring. I didn't think it was boring. I loved hearing gossip about pumpkins.

Pascal was two years older than I was. Paradis was three years older.

Panda didn't faint. That was hardly what I called fainting. Well she did, I guess. But not like Pandria, I thought to myself. Pandria dropped like a sack of cement a few days ago. She was jogging. I saw her from a distance. I was playing golf, and I was standing at the edge of Star River on the tenth hole. She stopped running and just collapsed to the ground. She fell face first. She hit her cheekbone right on the grass. It was the heat that caused her to faint. I'm sure of it.

"It is hot, isn't it?" I asked of no one in particular.

"How hot is it?" asked Paradis.

"It's so hot that all our bread has turned to toast," blurted Payne.

I chuckled. That was funny. Payne had just come out of the bathroom. He didn't even bother drying himself off, after getting out of the tub. I saw him coming down the hall. I'm sure he liked the cool moisture on his soggy skin. And he playfully took a leap onto my sisters' bed in the next room. My room. He must have landed in between them. Plouffe would have had her back turned, and wasn't expecting the sudden bed shake. But it wouldn't have alarmed her, as Payne makes that jump almost on a nightly basis.

"Hey!" shouted Patrice. Payne was giving her a difficult time. I'm sure of it. She could have been concerned that he had damaged the book she was reading, with his oncoming elbow.

"It's so hot that the sun asked for a water break," he quipped.

"It's so hot that the air conditioner asked the pumpkin to turn on the fan."

Payne loved telling jokes. I thought that last one was funny.

"Are you ever going to stop reading?" he asked Patrice, after he had run out of one liners.

"This is a fascinating book. It's about Frankenstein. I can't put it down yet. Let me finish reading this chapter at least," she begged.

I've seen Payne make a motion, as if he was going to snatch the book away from her hands, but always decided against it. It never mattered anyways, because Patrice always saw his hand coming, and clutched the book tightly against her chest every time. He has managed to take hold of the book on occasion, but there was never any real positive end result. Patrice would try to grab it back, and they would fight over it, until sometimes the book got damaged. So Payne never actually takes it from her anymore.

Patrice, unlike Plouffe, was very eager to go to school. She was very quick, and sharp. She seemingly had a quick retort to anything. She probably takes after me. I mean, I could be sharp and witty as well. Patrice and Plouffe share one bed. I used to sleep with them. But when the last of our roommates were given, that freed up a room for us. And a bed. And I was adamant to claim it. After all, it was us three girls on one bed.

Payne had now entered into the room I was in. With Pascal and Paradis. They also shared one bed. Payne seemed especially bored. He always tried to stay busy. Always had something going on. He was the most social of us in the family. And he could be very impatient. He knew a lot of pumpkins, and was very popular. And he was always inviting them over. Our house could be jam packed, even more so than the lounge at times.

"Let me play too," he inquired.

"There is no such thing as three pumpkin checkers," replied Paradis. Paradis was a spring time pumpkin. The rest of us were born in the middle of summer.

"Last game okay. Your big brother is getting annoyed. We should do him a favour and blow out all the candles," advised Payne.

It was good advice. Although we all knew that it was Payne who was doing most of the annoying. Singing in the bath tub. Even before he got into the tub, he was hopping around the house like a kangaroo. Jumping on and off each of our beds. He could be so hyper. So energetic. He loved to party, and socialize, and tell stories and jokes. I'm sure he was looking forward to my party.

"Someone should squeeze his forehead."

"What does that do?"

"I read squeezing a persons' forehead makes them go to sleep."

"Really?"

"Why are you comparing a persons' forehead and sleep habits to ours?"

"That seems kind of silly."

"I thought it might work."

It certainly had been a hot summer. Maybe a little hotter than usual. And my four brothers seemed to be having more issues coping with the heat than us females. I wondered why that was. Was that just a coincidence, or something in the seeds?

I returned to my room and laid back in my bed. I had a look at my pumpkin skin once more, as I blew out the candle that was on my bed side table. It was normally tender and soft, but it seemed to be drying up. And hardening. Maybe my body had turned to toast.

"Put the book away Patrice. It's late," I said.

"Ms. Pumpkin told me that there were some witches poking around the greenhouse earlier today," she replied.

"Seriously? I didn't know this. Who saw them? How many were there?"

"I don't know. I'm just saying," she said.

"Are they still there? Do you think they will come back? They probably saw a werewolf. It is a full moon tonight."

"I don't know. I'm going to sleep."

I began thinking about my party again. My sisters were helping with the invitations. I instructed them to talk to Papyrus. She does such a real nice job of preparing invitations. And packing presents too. Pascal and Paradis must be coordinating the events in the arena. With Mr. Pumpkin. Payne and Ms. Pumpkin were probably helping with the entertainment. Ms. Pumpkin would ensure there was enough food.

The ghouls certainly were loud on that night. The later we stayed up, the louder their noises seemed to be. It was not so surprising that the witches were seen here. They have been sniffing around our patch my whole life. Looking for pumpkins. Werewolves. Anything they can get their grubby little hands on. Ghouls were always fighting with us. We lived in dangerous times.

CHAPTER 2

FULL MOON

The witches had been fighting with the werewolves for quite a few years now. We're not sure when this latest war started, or even who started it. It was probably the witches. They crave power. They loved to dominate. And control everyone. They were such egomaniacs. They only cared about themselves. I doubt they even cared about the warlocks.

Wanda Witch, their fearless leader, obtained some kind of power a few years back. She discovered the ability to create a silver lightening, spear like bolt that dropped the werewolves. Whenever there was a full moon. Hundreds died. Maybe even thousands. Instead of werewolves being born on a full moon, they died instead. We were told they were born on a full moon. Some were being born too. Babies. But just as many died. Even the babies. And many of them died on the same day. On their birth day. Imagine that. The witches probably thought this was the best way to control their population. If that was what they wanted.

After the lightning strikes stopped, werewolves began to organize themselves better. They would gather in droves to protect themselves, and eventually started counter attacking. But it was difficult for them to catch the witches. Only the ones who could fly had any success. And even still, catching them was difficult, as witches were so adept at flying on their broomsticks. The witches could zoom in and out on their broomsticks so fast and with so much agility, that they could dance around the werewolves.

Wanda doesn't have the lightening power anymore. The witches cannot shoot them out of the sky. The werewolves have probably figured out that they should stay on the ground anyways. So now the witches come down to the ground to seek them out. More often each day, it seemed. We had to be mindful of their war.

And witches were always chasing after us too. We were never safe.

Pumpkins are not that strong, nor agile. We don't fly. We are a peaceful species. It made me mad to know how some species could be so mean and wretched. Lying in bed at night, thinking about all the terrible things different species have done to each other over the years. The wars they have fought. The countless dead. It was strange how my thoughts had shifted in such a short time. I was thinking of my upcoming birthday party a few minutes ago. And now here I was thinking about war and death.

I could hear the echo of the screams and yells of the witches outside. All ghouls. Patrices' comment cut my curiosity loose. I wondered if the ghouls had made their way into our patch that evening. They sounded as if they were just outside our house.

I wondered if everyone in my family was asleep. I had been lying awake for quite some time. I climbed out of bed and went out of my room. I peered into each of their rooms, and concluded that all four of my brothers were asleep. Even Paxton. After I got a drink of water from our ice box, I thought about going back to my room. But instead I went in to where Paradis and Pascal were. I started searching for my presents. Maybe I was curious. Or bored. Or had temporary insomnia. But I thought I would find something. Anything. I looked under the bed. In the closet. I had to be super quiet. Then I went to Paxtons room to search around. But I discovered nothing. And I couldn't locate any presents in Payne's room either. I checked under their beds. Looking for the tiniest of boxes. Buried underneath other stuff. But nothing surfaced. It always seemed to be a difficult chore finding something each year. I checked a few places in the living room. But they knew not to keep my presents in the house anyways. My attempt seemed futile. They knew I would find them if they were hidden here. And ruin the surprise. They wouldn't want to ruin my surprise.

And then suddenly, I heard a real sharp noise. From outside. Not so much an echo this time. It wasn't the wind. It was more like a growl. Or groan. Or was it a howl? It sounded like a werewolf.

I peered out the window that was next to our front door to see if I could spot anything. Witches or werewolves. Anything out of the ordinary. But there wasn't anything unusual. Nothing noticeable from my viewpoint. But since it was a full moon on that evening, I thought there must be something going on out there.

I hesitated returning to my own room, and into my bed. Instead I stayed near our front door, still looking out the window. And wondered if I should open the door. To see if anything was going on. Anything worthwhile to witness. No harm in that, I thought. I was sure I wouldn't let the door squeak. But there was little I could do to prevent that. I opened the door only a slight at first, to get a better look outside. But all I could see were the bushes across the column. So I opened it further, so I could see down the column. And still there was nothing there.

I wondered if I should go outside. Walk a few steps up the column. Towards the greenhouse. I probably shouldn't have. I mean the full moon curfew was still in effect. We were told that no one should leave their house after eight o'clock when there was a full moon. Like eight? Seriously? I mean I would really be breaking curfew if I went outside at that moment. It had been at least two hours since we blew out the candles. And that was at midnight. But my curiosity got the better of me. It was in my nature. My birthday party had become an afterthought.

I slowly took a few steps, walking along column CD04, peering all around. Even turning around so I could see behind me. It was well past midnight, yet it didn't appear that dark outside. It certainly had been a hot summer day. There was no wind to speak off. A clear night. I could see the stars.

Although I didn't see anyone, I still heard the laughing. And moans. They were coming from the greenhouse. I should have stopped and went back to sleep. Instead I inched closer to the greenhouse. Towards the noises. They became more discernable with each step. I knew it was dangerous. I knew there could only be trouble ahead. But still I moved forward. The curiosity was overpowering. I had traveled quite a distance. The greenhouse was now in full view. I could see it from across Star River.

When I finally decided that I should stop, turnaround, and go back, I saw a werewolf. It was rising upwards, as if it were being pulled up by a string. It had risen over the bushes. What was happening? It looked so strange.

And then witches appeared. Three of them. They came out of nowhere. They took me by complete surprise. Although I'm not sure why, considering I went outside looking for them almost. I didn't even notice them approaching, as I was focused on the werewolf. They couldn't have landed down more than a few feet in front of me. Their brooms still tucked in between their legs. They were studying me. I thought I should run back, but I was frozen. I couldn't move. And there was a fourth still on her broomstick, hovering over me. Watching me, and keeping tabs on the werewolf at the same time.

"Where did you come from?" asked the first witch.

"Hello my sweet little one," said the scariest and meanest looking witch.

"Would you like to play a game? You like to play games don't you," said another.

'No I don't', I thought. I needed to escape.

One of the three witches took a step closer. I took a step back. She had long fingers. She was wagging her right index finger, motioning me to come closer to her. Her finger seemed longer than my whole arm.

"Would you like something to drink?" she asked.

I shook my head, as if to say no. I was speechless. I wasn't thinking about anything, except to find an exit. I thought that one of the witches would grab me at any second.

"I made this back home. This is my own brew. Made in my own, brand new iron cauldron. My own witch crafted, non-alcoholic recipe. Do you want to know the ingredients?"

After a slight pause, she continued.

"I started out by boiling goblin and vampire blood. Then I added in smashed vampire fingernails, and sugar. And then I sprinkled in some paprika, to make it spicy. To give it a little kick. And then I poured in orange juice, pumpkin. Just for you. You like orange juice don't you? Oh don't be afraid of the smoke coming out of it. That's just the powdered dry ice. This drink is becoming very popular back home. Everyone is calling it Winnie's energy drink."

I couldn't believe that it was only the dry ice that was the cause of all that smoke. I knew the whole thing was poison.

"I was going to flush it down that werewolves' throat. Do you see him? Up there? But maybe you would like a taste first?"

She kept reaching the glass out towards me. Her movements were slow. Maybe because she didn't want to alarm me, and have me run away. I'm not sure why I didn't, anyway. I should have done that minutes ago. The witch was trying to lure me into some kind of trap. I was too smart for that though. Even if the drink contained some orange juice, all of those other ingredients made me sick to my stomach.

Winnie Witch started to walk around me. But she kept her distance. She had a slow pace to her steps. Inspecting my appearance with her shifty eyes. She wanted me to take hold of the glass. I mean, as if. There was no way I was going to take a sip of that poison, or whatever it was. Did she call it goblin juice? Pumpkins don't drink goblin juice.

All of them looked scary. Their faces were all green, and ugly. With their sly, devious demeanor. Their big, sharp and pointed noises sniffling the scent around me. And they wore all black. With sharp pointed hats. And funny looking black boots.

"You smell really nice. What is your name pumpkin?" The second witch took a big whiff of the air near me. Everyone loved the smell of pumpkin.

I didn't want to answer. I mean, I was terrified. But I didn't want to give them a reason to get mad at me either.

"My name is Pashelle Pumpkin," I muttered.

"Speak up pumpkin. I didn't hear you," the second witch said. She had lowered her body, so she could stare into my eyes.

"Never mind about that pumpkin," she said, before I had a chance to repeat myself. "Would you like to know my name?"

I didn't really care to, so I said nothing. I thought about running away. Or making noise, so someone could come to my rescue. Instead I noticed the werewolf, who seemed suspended in the air. His arms were flailing up and down. I was sure he would say something again. His howl was probably the sharp noise I heard earlier. I could sense he would say something. Because if he did, someone would surely come to our rescue. The werewolf seemed helpless. He was not able to move freely. I could tell. He couldn't drop to the ground, nor continue flying on his own. He was just suspended in the air. The witches noticed the werewolf had caught my attention.

"Do you want to eat some werewolf too pumpkin?" asked Winnie Witch.

"Sure she does. She can't take her eyes off him," said the third witch.

"Come with us, back to where we live. We'll fix him up real nice for you. Delicious," said Winnie, all the while inching ever so closer to me.

Then the wolf finally did howl. It was loud.

"Aaahhhwwwooooooo," it howled.

The witches seemed annoyed.

"Can't we shut him up Wendy?"

"Why don't we just go? Leave the pumpkin. That werewolf will do just fine. The pumpkin is not worth the hassle."

Then the werewolf belted out another howl.

"Aaahhhwwwooooooo," it said again.

"But this one smells so tasty. I don't think it would be that much trouble. At all."

And just then I heard the pumpkin whistles. Pumpkins came running. They were carrying pales and buckets of water. And when they had arrived onto column CD04, we had the witches surrounded. The army of pumpkins to the north, and me in the south. The witches were forced to take notice. They didn't expect to deal with so many of us. I could see the sudden disappointment on their faces. Their smiles vanished. Their excitement of meeting one pumpkin had turned to an irritation of seeing so many.

Pumpkins were coming out of their houses en masse. Not only on column CD04 but from the adjacent columns as well. I could see them thru the bushes. Paxton snuck up behind me. Darn near gave me a heart attack when he first touched my elbow. He probably noticed I had left my bed, and then came out searching for me.

"We can finish you all, right here, right now," warned Winnie Witch.

"A pumpkin fight. Oh how fun," added the third.

Pumpkins grabbed onto my arm, and pulled me away from the witches.

"Stay back you brutal beast," I heard Mr. Pumpkin say.

"Go home," said Ms. Pumpkin.

"You have no business here. Go away," screamed Paxton.

And as each second passed, I could see more and more pumpkins leave their houses to join the battle. After only ten minutes of first encountering the witches, it ended up being four witches versus over one hundred pumpkins. Probably more. I felt a sudden rush of energy, and wanted to fight them. I was overcome with a new surge of courage. After all, we outnumbered the witches by a very wide margin.

Winnie Witch had left my side. They all backed away to form their own line of defence. The one that was hovering, had touched down. They were pondering their next move, while they made small talk with us. And the werewolf had regained his composure. It had finally fallen to the ground. I could see him shake his body all over. Trying to get the kinks out.

"Don't you go anywhere," said Wendy Witch, staring at the werewolf. The werewolf, himself, was joined by his friends. They must have heard his call for help as well. They had emerged, seemingly from nowhere. The five werewolves who joined their friend seemed ready for battle too. One of them was growling constantly. It sure was mad.

The witches were laughing at them, as if they weren't bothered that their numbers had grown. It was like they were ready to fight a battle on multiple fronts. The battle against us pumpkins and the battle against the werewolves.

"Now look. All these sweet little pies we could bake, after our tasty werewolf dinner," said the third witch. The ugliest one. I mean she looked nasty.

They didn't seem afraid of us, despite our overwhelming numbers. But instead of taking steps forward towards us, as they had earlier, they were taking steps backward.

Just then, yet another witch came flying down. She came out of the night, and stopped. She was hovering over the other four witches.

"There you are," she said. She quickly inspected the dangerous situation. "Oh. It's a pumpkin cook out. How sweet. How come no one invited me?"

Then she leaned into the witches ears and began speaking. They were having conversation. Which was strange. I mean, seemingly, we were preparing for a fight. And they held a meeting instead? Seriously? We all waited. I'm sure the elders were plotting our next move as well.

The werewolves didn't seem to know what to do. To run away or to attack. They all let out another loud howl. A very loud call for help. I'm not sure. I mean they speak such a weird language. With a very distinct dialect. It's English. But this language was almost a mixture of various different species. With different types of words, all mixed in to create one language.

The pumpkins on the other end of the column were crowded together. Hugging and staying close. On this side, Ms. Pumpkin was giving me a hug, and holding me close. She was protecting my whole body from the witches' visual.

"Don't argue with me. Every witch is to attend the meeting Whoopi," said the fifth witch quite loudly. She then left us all and flew away. From where she came.

"Now we have no choice but to let all these pumpkins off the hook," said Whoopi. The nasty looking one. I mean they all looked hideous.

"Yes. And that's exactly what we're going to do. And we will leave the werewolf. Let's go," said Wendy Witch.

"One day I'll be back pumpkin. And I'm gonna be looking for you," added Winnie Witch.

Was she talking to me? It seemed the witch was talking to me, although I disappeared within the mass of pumpkins. I mean, it's not likely the witch could see me. But I knew Winnie was talking to me. It was a threat. I knew it. It made me feel kind of scared. Knowing a creature might be out to get me. But who cares, I thought to myself. I mean witches were always looking for us pumpkins. We had no choice but to get used to the fear. Used to the idea that at any time, we could be snatched up by any ghoul.

And with that sudden message by that late arriving witch, the four of them flew away and left the scene. They left the werewolves intact and unharmed. They left us. They left me.

Did they just get summoned to a meeting? With whom? Why? What was going on? Why did they suddenly leave? A part of me wanted them to come back and fight. I was convinced we could handle them. Especially with more pumpkins arriving to the scene as every second passed. I saw some of my neighbors appear. Pascal had pushed his way thru the crowd to stand next to me. He didn't look too pleased. None of the pumpkins who eventually gathered looked pleased.

The werewolves also left. The one who was suspended in the air seemed scared. He looked so young. I wondered if he was a new born.

Once the ghouls left, and peace had been restored, pumpkins finally got the chance to break their silence. And did they ever. All at once, pumpkins began talking. Most of it was 'what happened?" and 'why was everyone out here?'.

Then the elders started in on me.

"What on earth. Why are you out here?" I heard Ms. Pumpkin say in my left ear.

"Are you crazy?" said Pascal, in my right.

It suddenly became noisy with pumpkin chatter. An explosion of gossip. All at once.

I noticed most of the pumpkins were terrified to death. We all had kept our distance from the witches. None of us dared to venture close to them. Even the pumpkins who had pales of water in their hands. They had thrown their water towards the witches from quite a far distance. I don't believe any of the water hit the witches though. We were told that witches don't like water. That they could suffer an allergic reaction. Or worse. We actually should have used the water hoses.

"What happened?" Mr. Pumpkin asked.

Many pumpkins started talking to me all at once. Asking me questions. Paxton was standing right in front of me. He was practically in my face. But he didn't say anything. Because other pumpkins were in my ear. Screaming. Instead Paxton was giving me a stare down. His eyes never shifted away from mine. He gave me one of his looks. He won't say anything to me, unless he has my full attention. And he wasn't going to waste his time with his lecture, knowing I had too many distractions to ignore him. I had no choice but to listen to the other pumpkins asking me questions. We could be so inquisitive.

"What happened? Why are you out here?" I was asked again.

The chatter had died down enough for me to provide a reply.

"Nothing," I replied. I mean nothing really happened.

"How did you get out here?"

"Aren't you scared?" asked Pascal.

Scared? Was I scared? I don't know. I was. But not now.

"We want to talk to you Pashelle. You're coming with us. Is everyone one ok?"

"She was the only one here, when I came out Pius," offered Mr. Pumpkin.

"Thank you Parse," replied Mr. Pumpkin. Mr. Pumpkin must have been in the greenhouse. He must have seen my interaction with the witches. He was able to single me out.

The pumpkin security guards also started to explain their account of the events to Ms. Pumpkin. They were gathered together in their own group. I couldn't hear all the details though. They had approached Ms. Pumpkin from behind. They better not have said that I was causing trouble. Because I wasn't. Not in the least. They knew it. I wanted to hear what they were saying, but it was difficult. Mr. Pumpkin hadn't finished his rant.

"You didn't answer my question. Why are you out here? Did they drag you outside?" Mr. Pumpkins' eyes suddenly widened, as if to say 'how dare they'.

"Did they come into our house?" asked Pascal.

"No. They didn't come into the house," I replied.

I wasn't able to properly explain myself to anyone. No one really gave me the chance. Ms. Pumpkin started motioning for everyone to return home. And pumpkins began leaving. The show was over for them.

"You too Paxton. Please go back home. We'll get to the bottom of this." Ms. Pumpkin very well knew that Paxton would conduct his own inquiry. His own private investigation and issue appropriate punishment. Ms. Pumpkin seemed satisfied with what everyone had to say, except from me.

"You, on the other hand, are coming with us. You have some explaining to do," Ms. Pumpkin ordered, when she neared me.

And it was like what? I had to go to the office? Why? Seriously? Was I in trouble? Probably. Here came the public inquiry. I realized the full moon curfew was still in effect. But nothing happened. Besides, I actually think I saved that werewolf's life.

While everyone was allowed to go back to their homes, I was escorted to the office. Mr. Pumpkin grabbed a firm hold of my left arm. He was walking really fast. It was difficult to co-ordinate my steps with his. It seemed unnecessary. It seemed overly excessive. It wasn't as if I would get away or escape. So I doubt the tight grip was necessary. Mr. Pumpkin practically dragged me all the way there. He pulled on my arm so hard, it felt like it would pop out of my shoulder socket. I wasn't happy about it. I mean I would have gone willingly. I knew the drill. I had been summoned to the office before. Many times before. Not that I was proud of that, or anything.

Like much ado about nothing. Some elders could make things seem so much bigger than they really were. They over-exaggerate. I think they just misread the situation. They probably thought I was in danger. But really, it appeared the witches were after that werewolf.

"I can walk by myself," I pleaded to him.

He ignored me. He was talking to his friend, Mr. Pumpkin. They were talking about the heat. And how little wind there was that night. Like who cares? 'Just let go of my arm', I thought to myself. He wasn't concerned about how his grip created awkward steps in our travel. My travel. Those two probably wanted to keep pace with Ms. Pumpkin up ahead. She was the one who led the brisk pace.

Upon entering the office doors, I was escorted to a spiral staircase. We climbed these stairs that go around in a circle. Constantly turning left all the way up. We stopped on the second floor. I've never been to the third or fourth floors.

The office was such a beautiful brick building. It was always kept in the most pristine condition. There were paintings and pictures hung up on the walls. Statues of famous pumpkins decorated the tables. It definitely was a tourist attraction, that's for sure. And it was so clean.

We went down the hall and into a room that had nothing except a small bed.

"This is where you are," Mr. Pumpkin barked. "You are not allowed to leave this room. Under any circumstances. We will meet with you in the morning. In the meantime, go to sleep."

I was about to say 'nothing happened' and 'just let me go home'. But it didn't seem to be any point. He wasn't interested in any explanations. When he closed the door, it sounded like he had sealed it shut with a key. I saw the inside door knob slightly move. I heard the rattle of keys from the other side. I mean how childish was that?

Whatever, I thought to myself. My seeds were still bubbling with excitement. That whole scene gave me an energy rush.

And just as soon as I thought I would never fall asleep that night, I awoke. Abruptly. At once. Almost as soon as I had actually fallen asleep. I heard noises again. This time from outside the office. In the dead of night. I overheard pumpkins. And I thought I heard people too. But I couldn't be certain. I wanted to know what was going on. I mean, it was not likely I would have fallen asleep for the second time without knowing anyways. There was quite a commotion outside.

But I couldn't just ask. Security would never let me leave the room. Just by asking. Who knew how many pumpkins were outside the door. Watching me. I needed to create a diversion to persuade the guards to leave the doorway. Because there were no windows in that room to see outside. And I really wondered what the chatter was all about. It was just curiosity.

So I had to think of something. I mean, what would a little pumpkin like me say to a security guard, for him to open the door, and allow me some privacy?

I tried opening the door by myself. And much to my surprise, it opened. It wasn't locked after all. Mr. Pumpkin was leaning against the wall, across the hall. Half asleep. If there was such a thing.

"Mr. Pumpkin? I need to use the toilet," I said.

That seemed to have worked. He got up, and led me down the hall to the public restrooms. And just as I was about to close the door, I turned around. Suddenly. I wanted to catch him by surprise before anything else was said.

"Why? Are you just going to stand out here and wait?" I asked.

The question seemed to have startled him. He wasn't expecting it. I put my hands on my hips and gave him a very puzzling look. As if to say 'I am entitled to my privacy'. And I waited for him to leave, pretending to finally close the door. I saw him and Mr. Pumpkin meet paths and I watched the two of them walk back down the hallway. I ducked inside the restroom door…waited for a few seconds. I never did close the door. Then I went back out into the hallway, and approached the window at the end of the hall. I needed to know what the commotion was all about outside. I mean it was such a late hour.

I could see pumpkins and people outside, on the ground. Pumpkins were carrying crates out of the hospital. I saw Ms. Pumpkin. And Ms. Pumpkin. Mr. Pumpkin was there too. I wondered what was in the crates. I wanted to hear what they were saying, so I opened the window. Just slightly. I even saw Patricia appear from underneath a tree. She was crying. She was quite emotional. I could hear the tears. There were people waiting outside the hospital. And I saw some more in the distance. Three, or four of them. I wondered why they were here.

As the last of the crates had appeared to be placed down outside the hospital, the pumpkins all moved to one side, and started walking out of the Red River Lily garden, and towards the Water Gate Bridge.

"Load 'em up Charlie," I heard a person say. They began placing the crates onto a cart. I wondered what was in those crates. Strange that we would be providing people with something from our hospital. I mean I always thought it was the other way around. Maybe they were medical supplies?

As they were loading the crates onto the cart, I witnessed the most ghastly thing.

Aw! I exclaimed to myself. I was forced to cover my mouth. I didn't want anyone to hear me.

One person accidentally dropped one of the crates. One whole side of the wooden box had popped off. I saw Mr. Pumpkin fall out of the crate. He had rolled out. He laid motionless on the ground. He had lost all color.

Seriously? Are those crates full of...? I had to clamp my hands over my mouth. I didn't want to scream anything out, in error. I didn't even want to think about it.

And poor Mr. Pumpkin. That he fell out of the crate was unfortunate. I was thinking they needed to reseal the crate, and treat him with dignity.

The elders who were outside couldn't see what had just happened. They had their backs turned. They were walking swiftly away towards the Water Gate Bridge. I could still see them from a distance on the second floor. I wondered if any of them heard the noise of the dropped crate. That would have caused one of them to turn their head. But I don't think they ever did.

I knew Mr. Pumpkin was to be given as an offering. He was old. I knew people were going to take him from us. One minute a pumpkin is laughing. The next, given as an offering. Death was so final. So sudden. It made me realize how short life could really be. There were so many things to do in life. I wanted to accomplish and do so many things. I hoped I was never given. I wanted to live until I was two hundred years old. I was getting ready for a birthday party and celebrating my life, while other pumpkins were saying goodbye to theirs. It was so sad.

As these thoughts were rambling thru my mind, I saw a person reseal the broken side board, then pick up Mr. Pumpkin, and quite disrespectfully, throw him back in the box. But before he did, he motioned with his right foot, as if he was going to kick him like a soccer ball. How disgusting. How sad.

I was horrified.

"Too bad the pumpkin fell out," a person said.

"Yeah. They just need to do a better job of sealing these things," replied the other.

I saw a third chuckle. Excuse me, but didn't they just drop the crate? Did they do that on purpose? How nasty. What kind of a morbid, insane person would do something like that? But I wouldn't get it past people to think of that idea. They don't care. All of them had big smiles on their faces. As if the whole episode was some kind of a joke.

At least they held that crate tightly in their hands, when they pulled the cart along, out of the garden. Their trucks would be parked out on Linden road, in Burrowsville. I was sure of it. They would take the offering back with them.

After a few moments, I could hear the blasting of the truck engines. I'm sure they had loaded the crates of the fallen pumpkins onto the truck. And after a few more minutes, I no longer heard the roars of those engines. Not even a sound. All I heard were witches, and vampires, and bats, and monsters. And crickets. They could be rather annoying. Even the crickets. The useless insects.

And the longer I kept looking outside, the more witches and ghouls appeared. They were circling up above, off in the distance where the trucks would be. So many of them. They were desperate. They wanted an offering too. I was sure of it. But our offering is for people, not for the ghouls. We made the offering because people protected us. They realize we need to be preserved. They don't let any ghoul harm us, or take us away. We were a valuable part of their life. They would never let the witches and other ghouls harm us. Some pumpkins were convinced that if we were ever attacked, it would trigger an all species war. I'm sure the ghouls wouldn't want to be the cause of that. The ghouls could never win a war against people. They knew it. Even ghouls had the sense to know that there needed to be a semblance of order in this world.

But then I wondered. Did people give some of our offering to the ghouls? Because if people wanted to maintain order and avoid hostilities, then wouldn't they need to provide an offering to the ghouls? To ensure there was peace? It must be true. People probably didn't keep all our offering. Because if the ghouls didn't get their fair share, they would be more likely to attack us. I don't know.

I stood against the side of the wall for as long as I could. Watching thru the window. When I heard the guards coming, I ran back towards the toilet room. I was barely able to reach the entrance in time. I had to pretend that I was just coming out.

"You should have been back in your room by now," Mr. Pumpkin observed.

"So much noise outside Mr. Pumpkin. What do you think is going on?" I asked.

"I don't know anything about that. I tend to my duties, and that's all," he replied.

"It sounded like there were people outside. What were they doing here?"

I wondered how many pumpkins have seen an offering take place, right in front of their eyes. I wondered how many pumpkins have seen something like that. Has Mr. Pumpkin ever seen that event take place?

"I don't know about that. Here we go. Back to sleep." He was about to close the door, but then he hesitated.

"They're just going to the city. Don't be afraid. Go to sleep." Then he closed the door.

"Goodnight," I managed to say before it was fully closed.

I was forced to spend the night in an office bed. I should say it was a half, make shift bed, with a lumpy old and used mattress. The elders certainly didn't want anyone to feel comfortable in here, that's for sure.

Security awoke me early next morning and told me to prepare myself. Mr. and Ms. Pumpkin were coming. They made their way into the room, and sat down on the corner of the bed. They came right in, right after the guard said to prepare myself. Not sure how I was to prepare myself in those mere seconds.

Mr. Pumpkin didn't even want to be there, that day. He seemed more disappointed in me, rather than be interested about any relevant information I had to offer.

"Why did you go outside? You know it was a full moon. How could you put yourself at risk like that? You endangered your life, and others," he started.

Every time I have done something to upset the elders, Mr. Pumpkin had always been right there. Questioning me. Probing. Scanning me over, like I was a written sheet of paper, to be analyzed and studied. Wondering what type of pumpkin would commit such atrocities. But as the years have gone by, he seemed to have gotten tired of my act. Like he didn't want to ask any more questions.

Ms. Pumpkin was more supportive. I mean she was still upset with me. But she also seemed concerned for my safety.

"What did they do to you? Maybe we should send you to the hospital, to get you checked out," she said.

"No Ms. Pumpkin. I'm fine. Really I am," I replied.

I had to give them an account of the events of the previous evening. But there really wasn't much to tell.

I had to admit to bad behavior, when it was nothing of the kind. I mean I probably shouldn't have went outside. There was really no reason to. But I did live here. I mean, this was my home. Why should

I have to feel guilty if I wanted to go outside, whenever I wanted? Why should I be afraid?

I told them about the werewolf that was there. How it was hoisted into the sky. And it was covered in green smoke. Which was strange. It had been in the back of my mind. I wanted to tell someone. Everyone knew they had been much more effective fighting the witches from the ground. Witches were incredibly agile and quick in their movements on their broomsticks. Werewolves were at a huge disadvantage in the sky. For those that could fly. The werewolves would lunge at the witches, with little success. We have all seen their fights. So why would the werewolf leap into the sky?

Then I realized. It must have been a new born. That would explain why it was in the air. It didn't know any better. It was a full moon yesterday. And it was kind of small. Maybe it was just learning how to fly on its own. But it was weird how it wasn't able to navigate itself more properly.

There was only one realistic explanation. It's called witchcraft. They cast spells. Like magic. And some witches have probably mastered the skill.

Mr. Pumpkin had remarked earlier in the summer, that the werewolf resistance movement was gaining steam in the east. In the mountains. Many witches had been captured. But it was difficult to really verify who was winning this latest war.

"Are you listening Pashelle? This is very serious. What you did was extremely selfish," Mr. Pumpkin added. Just when it seemed the interrogation was over.

Selfish? That was a harsh word. He didn't have to pour salt onto a wound. I was already feeling a little guilty. I understood I put other pumpkins at risk.

"I'm sorry, Mr. Pumpkin. I'm sorry that I put us in a bad position," I finally admitted.

My punishment was that I was no longer allowed outside my house past seven o'clock. For one whole week. Which affected me on many fronts. It meant my party wouldn't be held next week. It wouldn't be likely now. If it was scheduled for next week, it would have to be moved. I mean, the party would have to be at night, with the weather being so nice. Which wasn't too bad because my actual birth day wasn't for another few weeks.

It also meant that after dinner, I would have to stay at home. That to ensure I didn't break curfew, extra guards would be placed on duty at night outside my house. And Paxton wouldn't let me go anywhere anyways. It was like house imprisonment.

Plus I had garbage duty for five days. Sunday thru Thursday. I would have to go around the patch, and pick up any garbage in the columns, and from the gardens of the eye. Great.

I still had to find and meet up with my friends, and tell them everything that had occurred. Of course, this would be after I was escorted around the patch by the guards, picking up all types of garbage and filth. The punishment was to start right away. Like that morning. I hate garbage duty. At least I should have been thankful they didn't order me to clean the toilets. I've had that punishment too.

CHAPTER 3

THE CHILDREN

I was allowed to go home and clean myself up. Have a bath. Security escorted me all the way home. And as soon as I entered my house, I plopped down on my bed. It felt so nice. Sleeping on that lumpy mattress couldn't have possibly been any good for my back. I may have even fallen asleep. If I didn't, I'm not sure why. I stayed an extra-long time in my bath tub too. I didn't want to come out. But I did. It must have been the sense of responsibility I felt, to begin my garbage duty. Or was it the voice of Mr. Pumpkin outside the door. Saying things like 'let's go' and 'hurry it up' and 'today, Pashelle'.

Everyone in my family slept thru the noise. I'm sure they needed the rest, as it had been a long night. It had been quite a night for me, too.

As soon as I got back outside, I was given a glass of apple juice for my morning breakfast. The guard held two bottles of water. That if I was thirsty, I should ask him for a drink.

"Why can't I hold my own water bottle?" I asked.

"Because you will be holding these," he replied.

I was given a stick with a sharp pointed end, and an empty bag.

And away we went. We walked north on column CD04. All of the houses in this column were quite large. Very spacious, with many rooms. Our house has two large sitting rooms. And four bedrooms. And a kitchen, where we keep our ice box. I've been inside some of the houses to the east. And there was no room to move in those ones.

Column CD04 was the westernmost column in the patch. Across from us, on the other side of Star River, there was the greenhouse and farm. With chickens. And all of those types of things. Hens and roosters. And where we grow our vegetables and fruits. There was a golf course further north. And even further north, there was the school. It was a very open area, with lots of grass.

Column CD04 eventually curved to the east, and merged with column CD03. And walking north on CD03 would take us thru the west gate, and into the Rose garden. But we didn't walk that far north. Instead we turned right on column CC01. This column was the only one in the patch that flowed horizontally. And because all the other seventeen columns run north and south, this column intersected with all of them. Well most of them. Some columns didn't stretch all the way south to the border of New Surrey City. I guess the designers of the patch thought it was important to have this east to west column. For food distribution. And emergencies. I don't know. But it sure helped us transportation wise. So we could access most columns, without having to travel north, and onto column CD03. I mean every column kind of merged with CD03 anyways, near the west gate.

The corner of CD04 and CC01 is quite a wide open area. Someone decided to not build any houses there. From that corner, anyone could clearly see the golf course. And the school. And the Water Gate Bridge further north. Near the Tulip garden.

I picked up every piece of paper and garbage that came my way. No matter how tiny and small. Much of the litter was caused by the wind that blew the garbage into our patch from the city. Otherwise, our patch was usually spotless. Pumpkins don't make a mess. We always put our garbage in the recycling containers.

We crossed column CD05, then DS13, then DS14. It was weird how each column was named with a two digit letter, followed by a two digit number. I had no idea who came up with the naming convention.

And then we reached column CD03. This column was by far the widest in the patch. But there was another reason why this column was significant. Further south, there was a bridge that allowed us to cross Star River. And on the other side of the bridge, and on the other side of the trees, there was a park. Not just any park. It was a park in New Surrey City. Where people lived. And they lived in these giant houses that gave us candy once a year. On Halloween. When it was time for us to take part in the long standing pumpkin tradition calling trick or treating.

We stopped to rest at this intersection. We had been walking quite briskly. I was lucky he wasn't paying attention to my garbage collecting. Because after a while, I may have missed picking up several pieces. It appeared Mr. Pumpkin wanted to socialize with the many pumpkins who were sitting outside, near their houses. But I didn't let him.

"Let's go over the bridge. Come on Mr. Pumpkin," I said.

And before he had a chance to agree, he had no choice but to follow me. I raced south on column CD03. Ignoring any garbage. And when I reached the bridge, I leaned over the rails and gazed into the flowing water. I didn't feel it was necessary to cross the bridge. Instead I waited for Mr. Pumpkin. The bridge floor was all bricks. And there were wooden railings on either side for pumpkin safety. When Mr. Pumpkin finally arrived, he sat down on the bricks. He had to. He was tired. It was a hot day.

"It's nice to take a load off," he said. He wiped the sweat from his forehead. He lamented that the bottled water had already turned warm. And it couldn't have been more than two hours, since we left the office that morning.

Mr. Pumpkin told me about the first time he walked over the bridge.

"It was the first time I went trick or treating. And my friends and I were so excited. We were running over this bridge. And we knocked over Porlince who was coming back home, from the other direction. She had her bag full of candy. She couldn't hang onto it, and it all went flying over this bridge, and into the water," he explained.

"Aw! She must have been so mad," I said.

"She was. But I didn't care. None of us did. We were young. It was just an unfortunate accident."

"Why?"

"Because she was a complete snob. An idiot. When word got back to everyone about what had happened, they made me a hero for the day, almost. Even the elders. They would give me extra candy. Accidentally on purpose," he said, as he gave me an eye wink.

"Isn't that kind of mean? I mean it was almost like a joke on her."

"Well she was mean. To everyone. If she wasn't so mean, then maybe pumpkins would have been more sympathetic towards her. And I wouldn't have received so much positive attention."

"Have I ever met her?" I wondered.

"No. She was a heavy alcoholic drinker. She had many health issues. She was given at an early age," he said.

Well, that was too bad. The way the story ended. It was a very interesting story though.

We knew we had to march onwards. That was enough of a rest. And onward we went. I mean I still had to catch up with my friends and tell them everything about the previous night. I had to tell everyone who I met that morning too.

At first, though, most pumpkins introduced themselves by asking me the same question. Like 'why are you on garbage duty?' or 'what did you do this time Pashelle?' It didn't bother me too much. Their judgemental attitude. I mean everyone made mistakes. If we never tried, how were we ever going to learn? I viewed the incident as a learning experience. We have to experience things in life. If not, then we might as well live our life like a vegetable.

"I saw witches last night," I explained to Penny.

And pumpkins were so interested in what I had to say.

"Aw! That is totally unbelievable. Like wow. Like unbelievable." Pom Pom was speechless, almost.

I was explaining the story to Ping and Pong, when we reached column EM01. When out of nowhere, Peekaboo appeared. Right behind me. All of a sudden. He seemed to appear out of thin air.

"Hey," he said.

I hated it when he snuck up on me like that. He did it all the time. Not just to me, but to every pumpkin. I was startled, but only for a second.

"Wow. You scared me. How do you do that?" I asked.

"Do what? What are you talking about? Why are you picking up garbage?"

"Well. Let's see. I broke curfew. I spoke to witches. Drank poison. Slept in the office..."

"You what? You're lying. You didn't drink poison. Or meet with witches."

"Yes I did. I met with witches."

"No you didn't."

"Yes I did."

I couldn't believe that he didn't believe me. Why didn't he believe me?

"Why don't you believe me?"

"And you drank poison?"

"Okay no. I didn't drink poison. I'm not stupid."

"Then why would I believe you met with witches?"

"Okay Pashelle. We must keep moving. Peekaboo, if you don't mind. She is performing her volunteer duties," interrupted Mr. Pumpkin.

What a way to define the exercise. Volunteer duties. I hoped I didn't have to do this for the rest of my life. The sun was starting to take a toll on my head. I was feeling a little dizzy. I thought maybe we could rest again. Just for a minute. We had travelled so far. And there was very little garbage to pick up.

After almost three hours of walking, we had reached the far south east area of the patch. Which essentially was a wooded area. Full of trees. There was nothing much in those woods, except strange creatures. It was considered taboo for us to venture into the trees. It would have been kind of eerie living around there. This was where column CC01 ended. We had reached the eastern most column in the patch. And now we would start walking north. Towards the eye.

"Okay Pashelle. This is where we say good bye," he said.

"Why?" I asked.

But I knew. I knew he wouldn't be with me for the whole day. Mr. Pumpkin appeared. I now had a new escort.

"We don't need to rest Pashelle. We can start our journey." He called it a journey. What happened to volunteer duties?

I had started this exercise so early in the morning. And it was now past noon. Garbage duty would be totally brutal. Every day. The whole week.

"I'm hungry Mr. Pumpkin. Its lunch time. Can we stop now?" I pleaded.

"Well I actually just ate, Pashelle. Besides, lunch is up there." He pointed north. Towards the eye gardens. "So the quicker we move, the sooner we will arrive at the dining hall," he reasoned.

I agreed with him. So I picked up my pace and ignored the pumpkins I met along the way.

"You missed one Pashelle. Over here," he noted.

Seriously? I missed one? Like was he going to be like that for the rest of the afternoon?

I didn't pay any attention though. I just continued to walk at a brisk pace. It seemed to take Mr. Pumpkin by surprise. I even started jogging. I hardly had anytime to greet anyone on column GS05. Nor did I have time to pick up any garbage. I finally stopped running, when column GS05 merged with CD03. I had reached just outside the west gate. Which was the main entrance into the eye. I had to stop, not just because I was tired and fatigued. But I had to wait for Mr. Pumpkin to arrive. So he could confirm I had completed one day of garbage duty. Or else it wouldn't count. It would be a wasted day. I couldn't have that happen.

And when he greeted me with a look of bewilderment, I handed him the stick and showed him how much garbage I had collected. Once he nodded, I dropped the garbage bag and took off. I didn't wait to hear his lecture. I started running again. And I didn't stop until I reached the edge of the Green garden. I collapsed on the grass. It was mid-afternoon. The hottest time of the day. I looked up into the sky, and let the sun beam down onto my body. I needed a minute to catch my breath.

'Oh my aching feet', I thought to myself. After I collected my breath, I closed my eyes, and let out one heavy last sigh.

I'm sure I must have nodded off. Because when I opened my eyes and looked straight into the sky, the sun had moved considerably to the west. And from out of nowhere, a face appeared. It startled me for a second. It was Pavneet. She was blocking out the sun, leaning her face over mine. She was probably waiting for me to open my eyes. Then I noticed all my friends. They were sitting around me.

"Preston said you were picking up garbage? What did you do?" Pavneet started.

"I confronted the witches," I said.

"Were you picking up garbage all day?"

"My goodness!"

"What type of garbage?"

"What do you mean?" I replied.

"There's different types of garbage."

"Garbage smells gross."

"No."

"Yes."

"Paper can be garbage. That doesn't smell."

"Paper is recycling."

"I would hate to be the one who volunteers to take our garbage into the city."

"Yeah. Like Mr. Pumpkin."

"And Mr. Pumpkin too."

"I know right."

"But he likes it."

"Who?"

"Mr. Pumpkin."

"How do you know?"

"Because he told me."

"That would be ugly."

"He didn't tell you."

"Yes he did."

"Rotten food smells really bad."

"Toilet garbage must be the worst."

"Oh my god. Do you have to clean the toilets?"

"No," I replied.

"Let out pumpkin seeds smell nasty too."

"Is that recycling?"

"No way. That can't be. That's real garbage."

"Maybe it is recycling."

"I hope not."

"That stuff must go in different containers."

"I know right. You're not supposed to put plastic in the green container."

"And no rotten food in the grey container."

"Okay stop. This conversation isn't going anywhere," said Plato.

I agreed. I stared at everyone, as if to say, what difference does it make? Didn't anyone hear what I just said? I met witches.

"Witches?" someone finally asked, after a brief silence. It was Pebbles.

"Wait. What? That's interesting. You met witches?" said Pavneet. My friends no longer pretended to ignore me.

I lifted myself off my back and sat on the grass. With one arm in the ground holding my weight, while the other started to whale around the air. I needed to give my legs a good stretch. I had to speak quickly because I knew that even a slight pause on my part could shift the topic. In a moments' notice.

"Some pumpkins are saying the witches made an appearance last night. Did you know about this already?" asked Petrina.

"Yes. I know. I was there," I said.

"What do you mean?"

"That's what I'm saying. There were four, five witches right in front of me," I explained.

"Aw!" they exclaimed.

"In your house?"

"No. I went outside. It was like past midnight. Last night. And I saw witches."

"That seems kind of dangerous. Don't you think? Are you crazy?" asked Pavneet, with a puzzled look on her face. Her eyes had squinted. Her mouth slightly open, as if she was going to say something else. But she was actually waiting for me to further explain myself. I think they all were. At least I finally got their attention.

"Did anything happen to you?" I was asked.

"Yeah. I got garbage duty," I answered.

"No. I don't mean that."

"Before the witches had a chance to do anything, other pumpkins came out. And sent the witches away. We fought them off," I said.

"What do you mean you fought with them?"

"You had a fight?"

"My goodness."

"They were actually attacking a werewolf," I said.

"We know all this already," confessed Prescott.

"Oh. Why did you have to say anything? You should have let her finish. It would have been fun," said Prudence.

"What?" I got confused.

"I told everyone what happened Pashelle," said Plato.

"What? When? How did you know?" I was a little disappointed. I didn't get to tell them the story.

"I was there. Didn't you see me?"

"Why did you go outside in the first place?"

"I don't know. I mean I have no idea. I heard noises. Like howls. And I wanted to know what they were. Besides I couldn't sleep," I said.

Plato took the fun out of my story. If there was any fun to it at all. The topic changed quickly.

"Do you guys want to go sit in the lounge?"

"It's so stuffy in there. It's so hot. The fans are so weak. All they do is circulate the hot air. Who wants to have hot air blown on their face?"

"When are we going to get half decent air conditioning?"

"I know right."

"I'm hungry. Let's go have lunch," I said.

"We just ate."

Oh. That's too bad. I didn't know if I should go eat something, or stay and relax with my friends.

I had to rest my eyes again. For a minute. I could never get comfortable sitting. I would lean on my left arm, then on my right. Then I sat on my rear end. And when it started to hurt, I laid down. On my back. I was tired. I had barely slept the night before. The sun was very strong. I found it easier on my body, to lie on my back.

When the sun hid beneath the clouds for a brief moment, I opened my eyes. I must have nodded off again. I could see the buildings in the eye. There were only a few. Off to the east was a large arena. And next to that was the activity center. Our dining hall was in there. So was the lounge. The hospital and supply center were off to the west. And way off to the west, there was the school on the other side of the Water Gate Bridge.

I had made a full circle around the outer edge of the patch this morning. And with very little sleep the night before, it was no wonder I had no energy. I had no choice, but to lie on my back, with my eyes closed, listening to my friends. And their idle chatter.

We sat in the Green garden for as long as we could. Then we had to prepare ourselves. Mr. Pumpkin was getting everyone up. Trying to ensure we were all active, and that we returned to our homes. We were always supposed to stay near our homes, when the children visited.

"It's very important to be on your best behavior. We want to give them a nice impression," he advised.

And when he left, Pavneet had some more advice for Petrina.

"Don't do anything crazy," she said. She was looking at Petrina. Then she turned to look at me.

"Yeah. Not like last time. Don't get us in trouble again," added Plato.

They were talking about the children visit. They were to arrive at our patch soon. Very soon.

One time, last year, when some children came to visit, we were near my house. The children were getting a guided tour of the greenhouse. So there were lots of children, all up and down column CD04. One child, inexplicably, took off his shoes. I overheard two children talking about what it must be like to live life as a pumpkin. And they realized we didn't wear any shoes. So one child took his off, so he could walk around in the dirt and grass. I don't know. And they went walking up the column, leaving his shoes behind. So I sneaked in closer, hiding in between the bushes as best as I could. I took his shoes and heaved them over the bushes, into the next column. The little boy was beside himself, when he came back, and couldn't find his shoes. The poor little child had to return home without his shoes. That was a riot.

Well I got into trouble for that. Because of Portia. The snitch. She told the elders that I stole the shoes. And so did Plato. Because he was standing right next to me.

The buses would be parked on Linden road. There would be over forty children. They usually came in bunches. All at once. They were here to see us. To see our way of life. And to talk with us. Children visited at various times during the year. In any season. They would come from far off places, such as Fleetwood, and Guildford. And from New Surrey City. From all over.

The elders had announced the children had arrived. Repeatedly. Telling us to go home. That we needed to be in our houses by 4 pm. But they never say your own house. So we all decided to stay at Pannettes house this time. Very few children traveled that far eastward. They enter thru Burrowsville, and for the most part, stay in the west.

We stood outside Pannettes' doorway, occupying the full width of column TY07. If children walked down this way, they would surely stop and talk to us. Patrick and Parson were inside the house. They were her brothers. Peaches and Pillow were outside with us too. And Pacino, who lived close by. Penelope and Piper were there too, even though they lived next to Petrina. On column RY07. And Prospero and Pan, who may have lived close by as well. Most pumpkins were usually outside. Seeing the children was always such a big event for us. And for them.

Even though for the most part, their visits were usually boring. Few pumpkins spent the time indoors.

It being a Sunday, it was not likely this group was from school. I mean there was no school for them in the summertime anyways.

"Does anyone know who these children are?"

"I think from a girl guide group," replied Pamper. "That is what Ms. Pumpkin said."

"What is that?" I asked.

"I don't know. I'm not a girl guide," replied Petrina. She could be quite sarcastic at times.

I noticed Petrina and Pannette had moved off to one side. They didn't seem too interested in talking about the children. They were having their own private conversation. I couldn't resist. I was tired of talking about the children as well. And I moved over, and I listened to what they were saying.

They were talking about the beauty pageant. Petrina had entered. And she wanted to maximize her chances of winning. Last night, during the initial talent show for the pumpkins, who chose singing as their first talent, Pannette had fooled around with the microphone wires back stage. During the singing. To create an unnecessary echo effect. And the plan was to fix the wires just before Petrina would sing. Petrina had faked a cough, to ensure she would sing last. As Pannette would have fixed the wires by then. Well that plan didn't really work. Because the pageant voting committee discovered the problem, while the singing was going on. They announced that pumpkins who had already performed their talent under the faulty conditions, were allowed to come back at a later date to retry. Both of them were lamenting over the failed attempt.

So now they were contemplating another plot. They were planning to trap pumpkins in the greenhouse. On a very hot day. It would give them an extra suntan.

"Their skins would turn all hard Pannette," reasoned Petrina.

"It won't work," countered Pannette. She said this, despite offering up the idea herself. Petrina thought that Peaches and Pannette would

42

round up as many pumpkins as possible. The ones in the pageant who could be a threat to Petrina from advancing into the final rounds. The ones who seemed to be on the bubble. Her primary competition.

Petrina was trying to organize something for the next weekend.

And pumpkins say I could be devious? Seriously?

"Why are you cheating?" I asked.

"This isn't cheating. I'm not cheating. I'm just trying to gain an advantage. Why aren't I allowed to do that? Why wouldn't pumpkins want to visit the greenhouse?" she replied.

"And what are you going to do once you get them all in there? Lock the doors? Seriously? You're going to lock pumpkins in the greenhouse, until their skins dry up?"

"Do you want to win that badly?" asked Pavneet, who was also listening in.

"She seems to be sucking up to Pryanka. Running errands for her, and whatnot. She'll do anything to win this contest," added Pannette.

Pryanka was not a member of the pageant voting committee. But rather, she was a consultant. She helped pumpkins with all types of exercise. And beauty tips.

I didn't think Petrina sang well enough, but apparently she did. Well enough to advance to the second round of talents. And on to the round of twenty. She then started talking about her plans for her next talent, but I had other interests.

While my friends were discussing the pageant, and discussing plotting schemes, I went inside Pannettes house. I thought I would take this opportunity to search for presents. Trying not to be so obvious. But Parson seemed to have noticed me. And he gave me a stare. As if to say 'I know what you're doing Pashelle, and you're not going to find any presents here'. And he was right. There was no point even searching.

I have known Petrina practically my whole life. I must say I enjoyed her company. She could be funny, and kind of exciting to be with. Case in point, her beauty pageant plots. She could be a schemer because she didn't take anything seriously. Everything was a game to her. She thought the beauty pageant was a game. And she could be immature.

And selfish. Sometimes. I mean why couldn't she just compete properly like everyone else? And she was always getting Pannette involved to do her dirty work. Petrina liked to think she was very popular. And in a way she was. But, actually, it was her brother Peter that was very well known in the patch. His popularity almost gave Petrina a type of presence.

Pannette and Petrina were very close. They always hung out together. They seemed to be the best of friends.

I'm not sure I had a best friend. If I did, I would say my sister Patrice, or Paradis. Or Polo. Maybe Pavneet. I don't know.

I have known Polo a very long time. He started to come over to my place when we were both very young. His brother Pimlico was real good friends with Pascal. Sometimes his whole family would come over, and party with us. And I just got to know him very well. I found him to be reliable. He did everything I asked of him. He was very loyal.

Polo had an older brother that was given. He was much older. He had become deranged. He dreamt he turned into a horse, with wings no less. And that he would be able to fly. The notion was crazy. I mean horses don't fly. Pegasus used a ladder to climb up onto a ledge, on the side of the hospital. He was near the top of the building. I wasn't there. So I'm not certain. And I don't ask Polo about it. But Pegasus jumped, and purposely landed right on his head, as he had dove head first. He was expecting to use his hands as wings, and to soar back up into the air. But that didn't happen. He landed hard, and suffered a broken neck. He died almost instantly. In honor of their lost brother, Polo and the rest of his family have come to have a liking for horses. Pimlico is two years older than Polo. Pony, and their sister Preakness are younger.

I was also very close to Pavneet. She may have been my first truly, really good friend. She used to live a few houses from me. She lived with strangers. She had no siblings. She had always lived with strangers. We used to play in column CD04. But then she moved to another column. Then she moved again. And again. She lived in column TY07 for a little while, a few houses north of Pannette, until we found out her roommates were using rat poison in the house. No one knew for what purpose. I would trust her with my life. She was very reliable and dependable. She was very athletic. We played golf together almost every weekend. She and I qualified to participate in the annual golf match against the Squash. It was on the upcoming weekend. After my punishment was over. Pavneet was very proper. Always trying to be perfect. Always trying to do the right thing. Always trying to excel, at any act she performed. To try to meet the high standards she had set for herself. She was a perfectionist. Thinking everything could always be better.

Plato was also a very close friend. He was very smart. Always reading, and learning new things. Plato was expecting two siblings any day. Which he was very excited, and nervous about.

Almost an hour had passed and no children had ventured this far east. As was usually the case. But then, out of nowhere, we heard them.

"Let's go this way," we heard a child say. Their voices could be so loud. They must have big lungs. I mean children were so much bigger and taller than we were.

"I think they are coming this way."

"I wonder how old these children are."

"I hope one of them takes my picture."

"Oh. Sssh. Here they come."

We saw them enter the column. Lumbering towards us, with their long strides. They were walking slowly, bending down, searching for windows to peer into houses. When they neared us they stopped, as we knew they would. They didn't come all this way, just to see inside our homes. They wanted conversation.

They looked anywhere from four to eight years old. But it was really hard to tell though. I mean, people looked all the same.

One of them came a bit closer to me. She bent down, and leant forward. She was almost in my face by the time she asked a question.

"What's your name?"

"Pashelle Pumpkin," I replied.

"Would you like a cookie?"

"No," I said. We were told to never accept any gifts from children. Certainly not food. Their intentions were not always honest.

"You're so small."

So? Why did she care how tall I was? Why did that even matter? Conversations with children could be so repetitive. And boring. They asked the same questions. All of them. All the time.

"And you're so tall," I replied back sarcastically. But children were not that quick to realize that I was teasing her, in a way. Making fun of their tall, long and slender bodies. They could be slow to catch on. She began to explain that she wasn't tall, as compared to her friends. Then the girl straightened up and moved away from my face.

"What do you like to do pumpkin?" another asked.

"Lots of things," I said.

"Let me see you roll. Roll down a hill."

Was he stupid? Like why would I roll down a hill? Just so that the little child could see me roll? Don't be ridiculous.

"I don't want to roll down a hill today. Sorry. Besides, we're not allowed. We have to stay here."

"How old are you?"

"Seven. Eight," I said.

"Don't you know how old you are?" another said. He was mocking me. I could see his ridiculous grin. A few of them started laughing at me. As if I didn't even know how old I was. I felt like telling them to be quiet. Or better yet, kicking them all in the leg.

They asked the same boring questions to all of us. And we asked some too. Pluto asked one of them to provide a demonstration on dog language. They just laughed at him. They are encouraged by their elders to learn about us. To acquire knowledge. They probably learnt about us in their species class. Even though there was no school for them during the summer months. They must have been members of some kind of summer camp. I think Prima mentioned they were part of a girl-guide group. Or was it Pamper? I couldn't recall. I was about to ask one of them, but then the next question came.

"Can you open your front door? Can we see inside your house?"

I looked at Pannette. I wanted to say 'no'. Don't open the door.' But she knew. She wasn't going to open the door. Not for children.

Then they had to go back. Their elders were calling for them. They had been here long enough. And off they went. They wandered back up column TY07 in no time at all. They all left. Except for one girl, named Crystal. She continued to ask me questions.

"Do you like being a pumpkin?" she asked. What kind of a question was that? So I replied with the only thing I could think of.

"I don't know. Do you like being a person?" I asked.

"What a stupid question pumpkin," she said.

Just as she was about to go back, she leaned over. Which I thought was strange. At first, I just thought she wanted to look into my eyes. She had huge eyes herself. They were blue. Her skin was yellow, or beige.

"Can I touch you pumpkin?" she asked.

No, I thought. You cannot touch me. She couldn't even remember my name, and then she wanted to touch me? But she seemed kind of nice. Very peaceful. And I had to think about it for a second.

But that was how they all were, at the beginning. People were trained to give a good first impression.

Then suddenly, she flung her hand forward, and grabbed onto my red bow. That was tied to my stem. She used her fingers to try to rip it right off. The sudden, unexpected pull, caused me to lose my balance. I fell. The next thing I knew, she was standing over me, waving my red bow in my face. It had only taken her an instance to rip the bow off my stem.

"That's mine. What are you doing? Give it back." I was mad.

"Aw!" pumpkins exclaimed.

"That's not yours," my friends said, as they came to my defence.

While I was laying on the ground, I saw my friends grabbing onto her legs. But she shook them off so quickly. She was swinging her feet towards us. Polo had latched onto her leg so tight, that Crystal had to fling her leg numerous times to release him. Polo went flying. He ended up landing between nearby bushes. And as soon as she was free, she ran back up towards the eye.

That stupid Crystal. She stole my red bow.

I got up, and started running after her. But she was too fast. By the time I had passed the west gate, I had lost sight off her. I ran thru the gardens of the eye, towards the Water Gate Bridge. And by the time I crossed the bridge, I realized it was no use. I was sure the children had boarded the buses, and were preparing to drive away. Besides, I would not have been able to recognize Crystal anyways. I mean people looked all the same. There were some whose skin colors were darker, and some taller. But they still looked all the same. How did they even tell themselves apart? They had such an amazing, almost eerie like ability to distinguish themselves. They must have some sort of sixth sense. Like extra sensory perception, or something. I don't know what it would be called. People must have a computer on their foreheads. Which helped them recognize who they were speaking to. I mean how else did they do it? They had a computer for everything else.

Each pumpkin looked so unique. Each and every one of us. I could identify a pumpkin from a mile away. I saw Palmer standing on the other side of the bridge. And Peshi and Piatti talking with Mr. Pumpkin near the farm. And I could recognize Pablo, who was even further away. And Portia.

Polo had caught up with me, as I had stopped chasing when I reached the entrance to the school.

"Did you find her?"

"No. I cannot believe she just stole from me. How can they do that and get away with it? It's not fair."

"Did you tell Ms. Pumpkin? She could have said something. Maybe searched all of them."

"I hadn't thought of that. That's a good idea."

But at that time, it was too late. It had taken me over twenty minutes to reach this spot, and would need another twenty minutes to reach Linden road, further south. Near the greenhouse. There was no chance. They would have left.

Well that was not fair. Not right at all. That Crystal girl cannot just take something from me like that. That red bow belongs to me, not her.

I walked back over the bridge with Polo. We reached out to Ms. Pumpkin, and told her what had happened. But there was little that she could do, she said. She explained the procedure we would need to follow. Which would be to order, obtain, and then to complete people made forms. And then... She explained, but I concluded there was no way I was going to retrieve my red bow. Children could be so mean and inconsiderate. I mean, that childish prank made no sense. She could have obtained a red bow from wherever. She could have just asked me. Children should grow up, and be more mature.

I looked back in the direction of Portia. She was smiling. Why? Was this her scheme? I bet it was her idea. Portia probably put the child up to it. I thought I should confront her about it.

But I thought no. I was too upset with that Crystal. We were supposed to greet them with smiling and happy faces. To ensure we maintained good relations with them. We had to act as if we were happy to enjoy their company. As if we wanted to be with them. But why should we behave so nicely, when they act so mean and cruel? Maybe I won't be so nice next time.

I thought that even if Crystal was questioned about the incident, how would she respond? Would she admit to stealing? Who knows? And even if she did admit to it, what would be her punishment? Probably just a slap on the wrist? I decided to let the incident go. It wasn't worth the aggravation. I was just happy they all left. I mean good riddance to them all.

CHAPTER 4
SQUASHLAND

That week, I spent each and every day walking around the patch, picking up garbage. For six hours per day. It was so boring. A different security guard escorted me every few hours.

On Monday morning, I spent time cleaning the office. And then spent the afternoon picking up the garbage from the gardens of the eye. On Tuesday, I helped the pumpkin volunteers in the dining hall. Wiping tables and picking up dirty dishes, and mopping the floor. I never thought I would say this, but pumpkins were messy eaters.

That afternoon, I noticed Persus doing the same thing as me. And when we found ourselves cleaning the same table after some pumpkins had eaten lunch, he inquired why I was there.

"Why are you here?" he asked.

"None of your business," I replied. I mean it wasn't.

Why was he here? What did he do? I was going to inquire, but then I thought, who cares. I've never liked him. He was such a ruffian. He fought with Polo once, a few years ago. He could be rude and inconsiderate.

For the final two days, I helped the grounds crew fix up the golf course. But that wasn't really garbage duty. Not really. I spent time working on my game. I would help them to even out the sand in the sand traps. Then practice a shot. Over and over again. On any hole that had a sand trap. I needed the practice to sharpen my skills. I had qualified for the team competition. I was part of the team that would compete against the squash.

"Have a nice time in Squashland Pashelle," said Mr. Pumpkin. And with that statement, my garbage duty was finally over. That was very nice of him to give me encouragement.

Mr. Pumpkin, who was also there on that early Thursday evening, instructed all the participants to meet early the following morning. We were to meet near the Farm Exit. That we should be relaxed and ensure we had a good night sleep. And to drink lots of fluids. It was a pep rally of sorts. Everyone was kind of congratulating each other. And we hadn't even left the patch yet. What I loved about golf was that it was a game, and skill that anyone could learn. It was up to the individual on how much time and effort they wanted to put into improving. I loved the competitive spirit that pumpkins felt that evening. I was so proud of myself that I had made it this far.

The next morning, Pavneet and I were talking about how excited we were to be going to Squashland. It was the first time for either of us. It was a two hour bus ride to Squashland. Three members of the PGA would also travel with us. That is short for Pumpkin Golf Association. They were Mr. Pumpkin, Mr. Pumpkin and Mr. Pumpkin. They would settle disputes, organize our trip and set the rules for the tournament with the squash. Mr. Pumpkin was invited to take pictures. Patricia Pumpkin, the elected elder one, also came with us. She had recently been elected our leader. It had been Pudge for many years. In his later years, he had various ailments that caused his deterioration. He was given as an offering last year. That was a sad day for all of us. I had only spoken with him a few times. During his unhealthy years. I never knew him prior. He was remembered for being a jovial and caring soul.

But our trip did not start out so well. We were loading all the equipment onto the bus that morning. The different golf clubs that we would need and a good supply of golf balls. And other golfing necessities. Plus we had presents for the squash. As Parker was loading the last of the bags, he hurt his right wrist. He had done a lot of the heavy lifting, getting us ready. And it was so unfortunate, because he was our best player. He won the individual tournament two weekends prior. So he was chosen as our team captain.

As soon as he picked up that last golf bag and held it up, he knew something bad had happened. He immediately let go of the bag and screamed in pain.

"Ouch!" he said.

Something was wrong. He had injured his wrist quite badly. He tried moving it around, but he couldn't. He couldn't move it at all. We feared it was broken.

Parker was still pleading his case, even with tears of pain dripping from his eyes. His participation in the tournament suddenly became in doubt.

"I think it will be okay. I think I can just use one arm. That's all I need to defeat the squash," he said.

"It's not about that Parker. It's only going to get worse," advised Mr. Pumpkin. "Can you move it around?"

"It's only sprained. If we put some ice on it, I think it will be fine," responded Parker. He was in denial. He looked so dejected. He had to hold his right wrist steady using his left hand. He was in so much pain that he could not allow his right wrist to drop free. He had no strength in it. At all.

Elders examined his wrist. It was starting to swell. Right before our eyes. It had turned into a dark, ugly purple.

"But even the slightest movement is giving you pain Parker. It could be broken."

Mr. Pumpkin was on the cell phone. He was talking to Dr. Pumpkin.

"Send someone. Right away," he ordered.

It wasn't going to happen for Parker. He was out of the golf tournament. It was a disappointing blow to our team. We needed to find a replacement. Because not finding a substitute meant that we would essentially forfeit every match that Parker was scheduled to play. None of the PGA members could participate, as that would constitute a conflict of interest. The rules stated they were to remain neutral.

Where would we find an injury replacement at the eleventh hour? So early in the morning. I mean it couldn't have been past seven o'clock.

"I'm going to find someone," I said.

"No Pashelle. We don't have time. We need to go," I was warned.

But I didn't listen. I didn't want our team to forfeit any of our matches. So I left the group and re crossed the trees, and entered our patch again. And as soon as I came out the other side, the first pumpkin I saw was Peter. He was lingering. Why was he there, anyways? I didn't know. And I didn't care.

"Peter. Peter." I yelled out. There was no way we would forfeit and purposely lose any of our matches. Not against the squash. I bolted towards him. He had just crossed over the Water Gate Bridge, and was heading in my direction. I couldn't imagine that I would find anyone else awake in the patch, so early in the morning. I mean there were security guards visible. But elders could not be playing participants either. I raced to meet Peter, grabbed him by the arm, and dragged him back to the bus with me. I didn't have time to respond to his 'where are we going?' and 'why are you walking so fast?' questions. We barely had time to settle into our seats before the bus driver pulled away from Linden road.

"Welcome to the team Peter," said Paisley.

"You made it after all," said Pavneet.

Peyton gave Peter a solid pat on his shoulder, as we sat down in our seats. The hard smack darn near knocked the glasses of his nose. Peter was nervous. I could see it on his face. He realized that we were on our way to Squashland.

"I'm not very good at golf. I have co-ordination issues sometimes," he said.

"Like we know. Everyone knows you have issues. Golf is easy Peter. You just need a little focus," I said.

I ended up sitting next to Peter on the bus. He could be very quiet. Most pumpkins were social, but not him. He tended to keep to himself. I mean, it's a wonder why he was so popular. Peter was the same age as me. He was Petrina's brother. He was the only pumpkin who wore glasses in the whole patch.

We passed Burrowsville, then Allentown, and then Charlottetown. We arrived in two and a half hours. Squashland was a very small patch of farmland sandwiched between Charlottetown, Fayetteville and Williamsport.

When our bus parked near what seemed like an open, unprotected tract of land, we exited. We seemed to be out in the middle of nowhere. My initial excitement of wanting to see Squashland had dissipated. Somehow I was expecting more. I don't know. But I was still nervous to meet with them. I hadn't the chance to speak with many of them during my life. I did speak with a few of them when they visited the patch last year. I could recall a conversation I had with Scarlett.

They showed up to greet us, right when we exited the bus. Hundreds of them. Just waiting for us.

"Welcome. Hello Patricia. How are you?" said Mr. Squash.

"I'm fine Sammy. And how are you? Wow, you're looking especially green today," said Patricia.

I assumed that was a complement, because Mr. Squash started to blush. His orange started to show. Most squash were green, but they could be orange. As far as I knew, all of them in Squashland were green. We were told their orange color could appear. At times. Like when they blushed. All pumpkins were orange.

Patricia and Mr. Squash shared pleasantries. It was mostly small talk. I'm sure of it. I mean it could be difficult to have an intelligent conversation with a squash. They were not the smartest species, that's for sure. Paticia had to keep it simple.

Their faces and bodies tended to sag. They looked out of shape. All of their weight seemed to accumulate near their waste. And that was because they were out of shape. I have not met many squash in my life. But I have not met a single one, who seemed fit and muscular. Squash were primitive. They were probably the least advanced species in the land. It was a wonder why people could think that pumpkins and squash were related. I mean we were nothing alike.

That was not to say that I was overly athletic. I'm not. Compared to Pavneet anyways. I was shorter than the average pumpkin, as I was less than two feet tall. But I did exercise. A lot. Apart from playing golf, Pavneet and I tried to go jogging at least once per week. I loved exercising. And staying fit. My energy level was always high. It must be due to my astrological sign that gave me the extra boost.

Pumpkins lived longer lives than squash. That had been documented by Pavlov Pumpkin.

Squashland looked very much like our patch. Lots of greenery, with flowers and bushes. The columns were separated by shrubs and bushes. But there were no flower gardens, like we had in the eye. The houses were also made of brick. And there were many other brick buildings. And Squashland was all inland. Whereas our patch was right on the coast, next to the water. On the edge of Burnaby Bay.

After greeting with a few squash, we were escorted to our tents that would serve as our home for the weekend. We were situated in an area called the center village. It was near the golf course. There were numerous tents erected. Some for us to sleep in. Some to hand out food. Others used for games. And tents were set up for squash too, for those who wanted to stay in the village during the weekend tournament. It was a party like atmosphere before we even arrived.

We quickly settled into our tents. Penelope, Pavneet and I shared one tent. We had arrived to Squashland in good time. We were even able to take a short rest. Then we grabbed our equipment and headed out to the golf course. It seemed like the whole squash population was waiting for us there.

It was mid-afternoon by the time we started golfing. The squash had many elders take ceremonial shots off the first tee. So many of them. And so many speeches. That seemed to delay the start time considerably. I mean, I took them forever to finish all the rituals.

It was day one. We would play one ball on this day. Meaning we were in pairs of two. My playing partner Panama and I would use one ball. As if we were one golfer. And we would alternate turns at hitting our golf ball. So there were eight groups of pumpkins versus eight groups of squash. We played against Snoopy and Scooby. We were in group number three.

All the pre=tournament ceremonies and the delayed kick off, made me even more nervous when I took our first shot. I was never interested in golf until my friends and I went for tryouts during spring break a few years ago. I remember that time because that was when the witches and werewolves started their current war. Then I started watching people play golf on television, and I became more interested. I started watching all the drama unfold on a Sunday afternoon.

My first shot off the tee travelled almost to the green. When Snoopy hit their first shot, all it did was roll off to one side. Snoopy slammed his club down into the grass in disgust. It took two more shots before their ball reached the green. Then Panama took our second shot, and it rolled slowly, near the hole. It took the squash pair six shots to put the ball in the hole. I missed putting the ball in the hole on our third shot, but Panama tapped it in on the next. It took us four. We won the first hole.

And that was how our day went for us. It was not stressful. Not in the least. The pace was very slow. We never seemed to be in a position where we would lose the match. And when Panama tapped in on the thirteenth hole, we had concluded and won the match. Which was absolutely great.

I shook Panama's hand after our match.

"Good game," I said.

"For sure," he replied.

And to show good sportsmanship, we shook hands with Snoopy and Scooby.

I noticed sweat coming down from Panama's forehead. It wasn't because he was nervous. It wasn't because he was relieved we had won. He was sweating because it was hot. It was probably the hottest day of the year. In the patch, there was always a cool wind coming in from the water. But not in Squashland. There was no wind to cool us off. In that aspect, we were at a disadvantage. Squash were used to the dry heat. Parker mentioned they purposely tried to hold the competition during the hottest week of the year, to gain this advantage.

But it made no difference on day one. All eight pumpkin groups defeated each of the squash groups. And after day one, the score was Pumpkins 8 Squash 0.

Their golf course was only thirteen holes. Ours was eighteen.

Par Pumpkin designed our golf course. He was the architect. We all love it. I've even heard people comment that our course was first class. Par practiced and practiced, perfecting the course. And on one of the last times he played the course, he posted his best score. He said it was the best he could do. So when we play, we often compare our score to his best round. If we scored the same as he did, then we say we were at Par. Or we say we were under Par if we did better. Or over Par. Since he was the architect, we followed his standard of scoring. To honor him.

Par designed the squash course as well. But squash don't use the same convention of score keeping. Rather, they just count the number of shots it takes to put the ball in the hole. People use the par convention though. I mean, Par Pumpkin had become famous.

The first few times I played golf, I did not do so well. But I kept practicing. This past summer, I played so well, that I advanced to the quarter finals in our annual tournament. A few weeks ago, I lost to Prospero and was eliminated. But I wasn't worried about that, because since I had made it to the round of sixteen, I had qualified to be a member of the pumpkin golf team. I was so excited that I qualified. I was really excited to be participating in the tournament.

Our first day was a success and went according to plan. Except for Parkers accident. The bus ride was fun. We settled nicely into spacious tents. And I played fairly well. It was nice to visit Squashland. I had never been. I was thankful that I got the experience. I'm glad I was able to meet with squash.

Squash were forced to take many breaks to rest on day one. Because they were seemingly out of breath after every hole that was played. They were so out of shape.

And there was a squash that was coming onto the playing area. Constantly. Providing players with back rubs, and feet rubs. Applying various types of applications and creams onto their skin. Probably so they could gain an advantage. I don't know. He was a qualified doctor. I found out later that his name was Seuss Squash.

I hated to lose. I have a fear of failure. And that fear can have consequences. I could be too aggressive at times. I could appear to be mean and uncaring. I was yelling at the squash to hurry up, all afternoon. I was getting frustrated by their inactivity. Golf could certainly test my patience.

And they were still testing my nerves later that evening as well, when we played cards. I yelled at them for their slow play. I mean, I know we were supposed to be having fun, but Samantha and Selma were seemingly playing in slow motion. All of them. It took them forever to decide what card to play. They lacked focus. They had to be constantly reminded when it was their turn. They seemed to be in a daze half the time.

"It's your turn!" I screamed at Snapple for the tenth time that evening.

We played a number of different card games, each one simpler than the previous one. They could never understand the rules. But they were adamant to play. I had to constantly remind them of the rules. Games were repeatedly being interrupted, because of my explanations. One time, I tried collecting all four aces, to demonstrate a poker hand. And I was shuffling thru the deck, trying to locate the fourth ace. And when I realized that there was no fourth ace, I had to question them about it.

"Are you sure you're playing with a full deck?" I finally asked.

All of them were so slow to understand. In everything. A few squash were yelling across the grounds. They wanted the water hose turned on, so they could wash the dishes after our dinner. Sesame was near the water tap, but she was having all kinds of issues understanding. While the squash were yelling 'turn it on', Sesame kept saying 'what? Should I close it?'

I finally got fed up.

"Open, Sesame!" I yelled.

I shouldn't have got so frustrated with them though. We had a party. And a nice dinner. Squash were pleasant and nice. And they treated us with respect during our stay. And they loved to eat food. Sluggo Squash ate so much food, that he had issues getting up out of his seat after dinner. And it became even more of an issue for Sally. Peter, being as clumsy as he was, bumped into Scarlett when she wasn't looking. Scarlett lost her balance. That started a chain reaction. Squash fell down like bowling pins. And just as Sluggo was finally able to get onto his feet, he subsequently got knocked over and landed right on Sally. It was funny at first. But Sluggo rolled up on her leg from behind, and it buckled under the weight. Sally hurt her leg. It was feared she broke a bone. Or two. Dr. Seuss Squash and his three assistants took her to the medical tent. Peter and Scarlett felt really bad about the whole incident. It was a downer, after such a pleasant evening of food and laughter.

The next morning, we started our golfing again. It was day two. We were still in pairs. This time my playing partner was Peyton. And instead of us sharing and using one ball, we played with our own ball. We kept individual scores. This format was called four-ball. Whoever got the ball into the hole in the least amount of shots, would win the hole for their team. Or I should restate. Between Peyton and I, which one of us shot the best, would win the hole for the pumpkin side. Because neither Safari nor Spock was going to win any of the holes.

It was fun, but frustrating at the same time. They took so long in between each shot. On the eleventh hole, Safari had fainted. Probably because of the heat. I was worried when she didn't get up right away. Spock was off to the side, looking for his ball. He lost it. I thought he should find a medical assistant. I would have asked Peyton, but he had to take a toilet break. And I was yelling at Spock over and over, just to get his attention. But it was strange in itself. He had such big ears for a squash, that I thought he should have heard me on my first attempt.

"Are you ok?" I had to ask, when Safari regained her strength.

"I think so," she replied.

I could see the tired look in her eyes. Many squash have green eyes. Hers though seemed to have become a very light yellow. I wasn't sure what that represented though. Whether it meant she was sick, or not. I thought she should take a permanent break for the day. But she refused. She wanted to keep playing. Despite the fact her pairing had lost most of the holes, she still wanted to finish her round. And I admired her resolve. All of them. They were determined to play thru the heat, and the losing. The aches and pains their bodies were going thru. They kept fighting and pressing on. Continuing to examine and study every shot they attempted, as if it was their last.

Peyton played terrific. He won eleven of the thirteen holes. And we tied on the other two holes. He was a more experienced golfer than I was. That is how our pairings were set. One of us was relatively new to the game, with the other having competed in this tournament previously.

Of all the holes that were completed in the first two days, in all the pairings, squash had only won seventeen holes. In total. They were nowhere close to winning any of the matches. It was a complete annihilation. A destruction. A show of power, proving pumpkins were much smarter and more skilled than the squash. We knew anyways. We just proved it.

After day two, the score was Pumpkins 16 Squash 0.

"Congratulations Peyton. You played really well," I offered. I must have told him 'great shot' at least ten times that afternoon.

"And congratulations to you too Pashelle. Your game is improving," he said. That made me feel great about myself. He seemed genuine in his assessment. That complement made my day.

We had a party on the second night as well. We presented them with gifts. We gave them food baskets, full of fruits and vegetables. Plus we gave them blankets. They gave us presents as well. Most of them were golf related. They gave us golf balls and tees. They also presented us with carved miniature statues of famous squash. Some of them were very well made, with lots of detail.

Mr. Squash told us that twenty five squash attended the opening ceremony of the Summer Olympics in New Surrey City last weekend. I thought that was great. The Summer Olympics was a show of power and physical supremacy for people. To show the world how physical and strong people were, versus the rest of the species in the land. Pumpkins were invited to the Olympics as well. To the closing ceremony, on the following weekend. I didn't think it was decided which twenty five of us were permitted to attend. I had submitted my name to the elders. I loved going to the city. It could be so much fun.

We all stayed up quite late that evening. We had a full dinner. The conversation centered on the ghoul wars. Most notably, the current war between the witches and the werewolves. Squash were scared. Pumpkins were scared too. We all knew we lived in dangerous times.

I wondered if people protected squash like they protected us. But from listening to Sofia, it didn't appear so. Not as much anyways. Pavneet and I were invited into a squash tent after dinner. To sleep over. Spend the night.

As the squash were getting ready for bed, I had to chance to talk privately with Pavneet. We were given a bed in the corner.

"Do you think people protect the squash?" she asked.

"I don't know. Probably. But it must be hard for them. There doesn't seem to be many people out here to protect them from the ghouls," I replied.

"It must be difficult. Geographically speaking. Most of the people around here are farmers. They probably don't have time to protect the squash," she reasoned.

"The distance between them is so far."

Sofia overheard the end of our conversation.

"You are right. People do their best, but we are still quite vulnerable here out in the open. We live so far out of the way. It's difficult for us," she said.

Sofia explained how they fear for their lives. All the time. She told us how Siba saw her two best friends get snatched up by witches, right in front of her own eyes. This was only just a few weeks ago. The three of them were playing in a nearby field. And four witches came veering in on their broomsticks, and without stopping, grabbed them. On the fly. They were lifted skywards and taken away. Siba was also grabbed, but she was able to slip from the witches' grasp. She managed to escape before she was taken, because the witch was only able to latch onto her necklace. So when Siba was able to unlock the neckless, at the side of her neck, she fell back down to the ground. Leaving the witch with only the necklace. She said it saved her life.

That must have been a horrific event for Siba. Sofia explained how squash use the bushes to hide. They use them as camouflage. But since they were in the open field, there was nowhere for those three to hide or escape.

Then Sofia got called away. She had to leave the tent and go back to her own.

"Why? Why did she have to go?" we inquired.

"Because she is sleeping with her own friends. In another tent. She only came by, to say goodnight," said Stella.

'Aw' I thought to myself. Her two friends taken away. In the blink of an eye. How things could change so quickly.

"That happens here every day," offered Spam. He too left the tent to go back home.

"Oh don't listen to him. He's just trying to scare you. Never listen to anything Spam says," Stella assured us.

The next morning, Pavneet was still curious. She wanted to hear more about the story. She woke me up quite early to help her. She was hoping to find Siba. Or Sofia. We looked around the camp grounds where we stayed. In the center village. But neither were to be found.

"Excuse me. Have you seen Siba?" we asked anyone.

No one seemed to know. A few squash said that we could try checking around the golf course. And so we left it at that.

We thought it was a good idea to have a healthy breakfast. It was still early for us. We had time to eat plus have time to practice as well. Pavneet filled her tray with fruit. I decided to try the eggs. I was told there was bacon, but really it was only bits of cooked ham. We sat down. Not at a table. They had been removed. It was decided everyone would sit on the floor. Apparently it was a custom on this final day of golfing. Neither Pavneet nor I were aware of this custom. And we didn't ask anyone about it. I guess we were too focused on our game.

Squash were so courteous towards us. As we were sitting and eating, a few of them asked us if we wanted anything else. That they would wait in line for us, so we didn't have to move.

I found myself sitting next to Seuss. Or I should say Dr. Squash. I mean he was an elder. He told me about his medical training. He was able to convince the New Surrey City officials to approve, and to assist with his travel to a different squash patch. Many years ago. Where he studied. After he completed his training and was certified as a doctor, he moved back here. Because this was where all his friends were. And there were no doctors here. He explained the training was rigorous, detailed and difficult. Very extensive. The countless hours of studying and practical training. He specialized in the treatment of skin.

"It took me about eight years to complete all of the training, and be recognized as a medical doctor," he said.

He was currently treating Sahara for excessive dryness. He said her condition had become very serious. He also said that Sally had suffered only a sprain. That she would make a full recovery. That was good news.

Pavneet was still inquiring about that incident with Siba. But few squash were even aware of it. And it was no wonder. There were a lot of squash that lived here. Maybe more than double the population of pumpkins in our patch. Or triple. It was a very spacious tract of land.

"We're not in the safest place. All I know was that it was late at night," said Simone.

"Our green color can look so distinct at night. It's not like the daytime. Where we can blend in with the scenery," explained Spencer.

"Is that why everything here is all green?" asked Pavneet.

"Yes. All the green acts as camouflage. So we can blend in. Then the ghouls cannot spot us, or tell us apart, from a regular bush. Everything has to be green. So we can hide easier," added Stella.

Tell me about it. Our patch was very green too. But in our patch, there were different colors. The brown of the trees. With their different colored leaves. The blue water of Burnaby Bay. And of course, the different colored looking flowers in the gardens of the eye. The pink, red and white roses. The purple tulips.

I found myself talking out aloud. About all the green. I was starting to get tired of it. Maybe I was homesick. I don't know.

"I'm so tired of all the green," I muttered to myself. With a heavy sigh. "Even these eggs are green," wondering if they were properly cooked.

Dr. Squash had been sitting next to me on the floor. He was arising from his spot. He said that he would meet everyone at the golf course. He was off to attend to his duties.

And he had obviously overheard my murmuring. He seemed sympathetic. He leaned closer towards me.

"I know. I don't always like green eggs and ham either," he said.

Pavneet said she had to leave too. She was told to report at the scorers' table before noon. But I didn't feel the need to hurry my breakfast. I wanted to eat slower. I actually wanted to sleep in that morning. But since she had to go, I left as well. We had plenty of time before we started. I mean before I started. It was day three.

"Hey Peter," Pavneet said. We walked out of the dining tent just as Peter had entered. "Make sure you get in a good practice," she added.

Day three of our tournament was called singles. I would be matched up one against one versus Saffron Squash. There was no one to help me this time. I mean I knew I would win. I didn't need any help. But still, there was a degree of uncertainty. I mean anything can happen in sport. If the outcome was pre-determined, then why play the game at all. It is the unpredictable nature of sports which creates mystery and excitement. We were notified of the match up order the night before. Pavneet was in match seven. I was in match eleven.

After we selected our clubs from the golf central tent, I watched Pavneet leave for the practice putting surface. I wished her luck. But I knew she wouldn't need it. She was to tee off within the hour. I figured I had at least two hours for my tee time. I stayed in the golf central tent. At first I thought about mingling with the squash. But decided against it. I didn't need the unnecessary aggravation.

Instead, I re-examined the posted schedule. I had only glanced at it the night before. I knew it was convention to alternate between male and female, if possible. And that the captains' match was to be last. I viewed the full posted listing.

Day three: Singles

Match one: Seven Squash versus Paisley Pumpkin
Match two: Spanky Squash versus Popeye Pumpkin
Match three: Sissy Squash versus Ponima Pumpkin
Match four: Snoopy Squash versus Penner Pumpkin
Match five: Sommers Squash versus Poon Pumpkin
Match six: Spasm Squash versus Peyton Pumpkin
Match seven: Skyler Squash versus Pavneet Pumpkin
Match eight: Scooby Squash versus Pepe Pumpkin
Match nine: Safari Squash versus Pazzy P. Pumpkin
Match ten: Sasso Squash versus Pie Pumpkin
Match eleven: Saffron Squash versus Pashelle Pumpkin
Match twelve: Spock Squash versus Panama Pumpkin
Match thirteen: Scarlett Squash versus Panita Pumpkin
Match fourteen: Snow Squash versus Prospero Pumpkin
Match fifteen: Suzy Squash versus Penelope Pumpkin
Captain Match: Stubby Squash versus Peter Pumpkin

Apart from confirming that I was in match eleven, I couldn't help but notice that Peter was in the captains' match. How was that possible? I turned and said "Peter is our captain?" to no one in particular. No one heard. No one was around. I couldn't believe it. Why didn't we select a new one? Parker was our captain. He was to play in the final pairing.

"What? No...that can't be. Why was he our captain?" That was ludicrous. Didn't anyone even care? I asked again. No pumpkin heard me. I mean I was surrounded by squash. How would they know anything?

I was astonished that we didn't pick a new captain. I starred at the listing for a few more minutes, seemingly with my mouth half open. I mean, what was the world coming to, when we name Peter Pumpkin our golfing captain?

Since the golf central tent was very crowded, I decided to go back outside. I sat down near the first tee. I waited for Pavneet to begin. I watched while she gave the ball a good whack. And I applauded her efforts. It looked like a good shot. Right down the middle of the fairway. That was a nice start to her round. She picked up her clubs and started walking towards her ball.

"Good shot Pavneet!" I yelled. I started clapping for her. But I was not sure she heard. She seemed extremely focused.

Then I spent the next hour or so stretching. And practicing my putting. I was joined by Peter and Prospero. I felt about as loose and ready to go as I could have been. 'No excuses today', I thought to myself.

I decided to return to the first tee. I knew I had to check in at the scorers' table, so I thought I would do that. Mr. Pumpkin was there to help me.

It seemed that the play dragged on. I wish I hadn't woken up so early in the morning. So much idle time before my golf round didn't really help. I tried to stay focused and sharp. I was positive I was going to win. No matter how well Saffron played. I sat down on the grass near the first tee again. Next to Penelope, Pie and Mr. Pumpkin. And waited. And waited.

"Hi," said a squash. She and a few other squash were sitting next to me on the other side.

"Hello. How are you?" I replied.

"How are you?" she asked.

"I'm fine," I replied. I waited for a few seconds, and then added "My name is Pashelle."

"Saraparisa," she said. I think that was her name. She seemed cheerful.

She then turned away from me and whispered something in her friends' ear. They ignored me for a few moments and met secretly. It appeared our conversation was over. Only temporarily though. When they broke their huddle, they turned to look at me again. Saraparisa leaned over towards me.

"You have such beautiful skin," she said. That was a nice thing to say. So I leaned my arm over towards her. Thinking she might want to feel my skin. But she never did. It was like she was afraid to touch me, or something. Then, inexplicably, the three of them jumped up and started running around in circles. As if they were playing some kind of game. A game that I had never seen of before. They seemed to be in such a good mood. Without a worry in the world.

It was such a strange incident right about the time my round was ready to begin. When I saw Pie and Sasso hit their golf balls, I knew I should grab my clubs to get ready. Because finally it was my turn. We must have been behind schedule. It was now after two o'clock in the afternoon.

Any nervousness I had soon disappeared when I saw Saffron hardly make connection with her golf ball on her first tee shot. It just rolled a few yards. She must have just grazed the top of it. Winning was no longer in doubt. It was a foregone conclusion. But I played fairly well, nonetheless. I won the first four holes quite easily. We tied the next two. I had hooked both of my tee shots in the bushes and was penalized for taking the balls out. My mechanics must have been off. It could have been that I was getting impatient with the slow play.

There were so many squash on the golf course. Not just on that day, but all three days. It was a three day festival. So many squash watched me play my round. They were all having a great time. Eating food from the numerous carts all over the grounds. All types of food. And drinks.

However, as we finished each hole, there were fewer and fewer squash watching. I found it eerie almost, that by the time we finished the eighth hole, there were hardly any squash following our match at all. It was like where did everyone go? I could still hear them. They were on the course. There was no doubt about that. But just no longer following me.

By the time we finished the tenth, I noticed most of the spectators were walking backwards towards the early holes. Even the ones who weren't following Saffron and I. No one seemed to care about our match anymore. I mean mathematically speaking, I had already won the match. Any stress I was feeling about competing, if at all, had disappeared. The spectators were more interested in the matches behind me. I knew Suzy was behind me. Suzy and Stubby were their two best players, from the first two days. Squash thought that those two had the best chances to win their singles matches. The only spectator that was following us was Siebel. He was the official scorekeeper of our match.

And Sivonne. She was called an aide. One of the many other squash on the golf course, carrying their golf bags and other equipment. And water. I wondered if that was even fair. I mean no one was holding any of my clubs for me.

The squash who were carrying the manual updated scoreboards had vanished as well.

And by the time we had reached the thirteenth and final hole, I expected to see a large gallery. But there was no such crowd. No roars of applause when I shook hands with Saffron. I did hear a few smatterings of applause from the pumpkins sitting off on the other side of the green. It was anti climatic.

I had won my match seven holes to two. Four of the holes were halved. That means it was a tie. It was an easy victory and I was not even that good of a golfer. Don't get me wrong. With the advice and tutelage of Mr. Pumpkin and Prospero, my game was improving every time I played. But there were many more experienced pumpkins participating in the tournament.

I sat down near a group, next to Mr. Pumpkin. Near the edge of the green. The side closest to golf central. Ponima and Poon were gabbing. I noticed they laughed and told loud jokes in the midst of my putting. I wanted to ask them if they had won their matches, but I wasn't able to interrupt them. I should have asked them what was so funny. They had obviously witnessed something hilarious, and were laughing out of control. They were certainly having a great time. That was for sure.

"Where is everyone?" I asked.

"I'm not sure Pashelle," offered Mr. Pumpkin. He looked up from fiddling around on his cell phone and surveyed the playing area. Almost noticing for the first time, himself, about the lack of spectators, and squash players. He just shrugged his shoulders. As if it was not important.

"Why are Paisley, Popeye and Pepe sitting on the other side of the green?" I asked.

I wondered why they weren't sitting over here. On this side. With us. I mean it wasn't important. There was a big tree on that side offering them shade. I didn't care anyways. At least I had a good view of the action on the thirteenth green.

"I'm gonna go see," announced Pavneet.

"Go see what?" I inquired.

But she got up and started walking away, without responding.

"Where are you going?" I repeated myself.

Again she didn't answer. She was walking back to the thirteenth tee.

"Did you take lots of pictures?" I turned my attention to Mr. Pumpkin, who was taking pictures of all the golfers as they finished their matches. I was glad for that. It could be so valuable. To capture these historical moments. For all to see. For eternity.

"Can I see mine?" I asked.

"Sure," he replied.

And I saw the picture accounted for the sun, which caused the true beautiful color of my orange skin to shine thru. Good, I thought. I had ensured I turned towards Mr. Pumpkin and provided a nice smile after I shook hands with Saffron.

"You're coming to my birthday party. Right?" I confirmed.

Just then, before he had a chance to reply, there was a thunderous roar that exploded from a distance. It sounded like it came from the tenth hole. Or maybe the eleventh hole. I wasn't sure.

A few moments later, I saw Spock shake hands with Panama as they concluded their match. He gave Panama a nice, warm hug of congratulations.

Panama came this way, and opened up a spot between Ponima and I. I see Panama with Ponima and Panita all the time at our golf course. Practicing. Even though their names were very similar, I didn't believe they had related seeds. Or maybe. I don't know. Panita and Panito were related though. I knew that.

Panama laid down facing the sun. With his right forearm over his eyes and forehead. I'm not even sure if he heard me say congratulations. I wondered if he fell asleep. It certainly had been an exhausting three days of non-stop activity.

A considerable time had passed before Suzy was forced to shake hands with Penelope. Suzy wasn't so gracious in accepting her defeat. She didn't want to shake hands at first, but reluctantly agreed. She came close to winning. She lost four holes to two, with seven of the holes halved. That was a close match. She seemed frustrated. Angry, almost. As she left the putting surface, she flung her club away in disgust.

And then we heard another roar. And then another. We knew the crowd was near.

"I wonder what's going on back there," Mr. Pumpkin said, finally taking notice.

As the minutes went by, squash started to make their way towards the final hole. They were arriving in droves. All of them. The players. The spectators. The scoreboard keepers. It seemed the excitement was building for the conclusion of the final match of the day, and for the tournament as a whole.

And all of a sudden, within minutes, a large throng had finally gathered at the thirteenth tee. The squash were boisterous and excited. And loud. It was the final match of the tournament. There was no room to move. Many squash had raced up to where we were, sitting at the edge of the green. So much so, that I no longer had a clear view of the action in front of me.

A squash that was holding a manually operated scoreboard had finally come into my view. And to my amazement, the score of the captains' match was five to five. Their match was tied. Unbelievable. I almost couldn't believe my eyes. I mean I knew Peter was a last minute injury replacement. He wasn't very good. And it was known that Stubby was their best golfer. But to think their match was tied, was to think that squash could fly to the moon.

We all watched both golfers' first two shots of the final hole. They both barely made it to the edge of the green. Then Stubby hit his third shot really close to the hole. That put all the pressure squarely on Peter for his third shot. It had to be well placed, that's for sure. But he kind of flubbed it. As he swung, I could see the face of his club hit the ground before actually making proper contact with the ball. As a result it didn't travel very far. It barely made it onto the green. And since he was further away from the hole, it was his turn again. Things did not look good. He was at a clear disadvantage at that point.

Peter took a heavy sigh. He seemed concerned. Squash were screaming with excitement. Fans were yelling "Stubby". "Stubby". "Stubby". Mr. Squash had to motion to the spectators to quiet down. Peters' ball was at the edge of the green. This was a big put for Peter. This was his fourth shot. Stubbys ball was right near the hole, and he was almost assured to tap it in. And as a matter of fact, since his ball was so close to the hole, it was actually in Peters way. Mr. Squash motioned to Mr. Pumpkin, that at this time, it was appropriate for Stubby to putt first. And he made it in. The squash were cheering excitedly. Stubby had completed the hole in four shots.

And now it was Peters fourth shot. Even if Peter made it in, he would halve the hole. And the match would be tied. And incredible feat for Stubby. An outstanding achievement for the squash species, in general. To think they could match mental and physical prowess with pumpkins. Who could have thought?

Peter walked towards the hole to survey the landscape. Checking the various undulations of the putting surface along the way. He checked the surface on the way back to his ball too. Then he crouched down behind the ball to get an even better look. I've done that too. Getting closer to the ground helped me see more clearly which parts of the surface were elevated.

It was going to be a fast, downhill putt. The ball would move left to right. I knew it. We all did. My ball was in a similar spot. I felt like walking up to him to offer that advice, but it was probably too late. I mean I wasn't even sure if I was allowed. Or even if it was the best plan of action. It might have put more unnecessary pressure on him anyways. The sun was beaming onto his face. It was early evening. I could see the sweat drip from his forehead. He had to take his glasses off to shake the water. Then he had to wipe his sweaty hands against the side of his waist. I was sure the sweat was due to nervousness. I mean day three was the coolest of the tournament.

I felt like saying 'Don't leave it short. Give yourself a chance.' But at that moment, Mr. Squash yelled 'quiet'. I hesitated, and it became too late for me to approach him. There was a buzz amongst the squash ranks. They had moved in front of me and obstructed my view. I had a good view of the green, but not anymore.

Peter stood over his ball. He seemed focused. The pumpkins who were sitting on the other side of the green had moved away. Probably fearing the worst. They didn't want to be mixed in with the elation that was to come.

After a couple of practice swings Peter met his ball. He hit it quite firm. As it was rolling down towards the hole, it was picking up speed. At least it wasn't going to be short. But it was too fast. Way too fast. I knew it. I could tell. He had hit it with too much power. It sped too fast to properly catch the left to right break, and the ball slid past the hole.

As I saw Mr. Pumpkin take a picture, the squash erupted in excitement. They were ecstatic. Overjoyed. They were jumping up and down in a frenzy, hugging each other. Stubby threw his golf club in the air in celebration. Squash jumped on top of Stubby with excitement. He had just won the hole. He had won the match six to five.

All Peter could do was watch Stubby. Amazed that his ball didn't break properly. Like seriously? Peter lost to a squash in golf? I mean losing to any squash, in any kind of competition was an embarrassment. Even if he wasn't very good at golf. Even if he was an injury replacement.

Even if Stubby was their best golfer. Peter must have been embarrassed. I mean, I was embarrassed for him.

The cheering and excitement continued, even when squash allowed Stubby to collect himself off the ground. All the while, Peter had to wait. With many squash standing right next to them, Stubby finally grabbed Peters' hand with both of his, and shook it up and down.

"Good game." "Good game." Stubby said it repeatedly. "Good game." I could see his lips move. I certainly could not hear him, amidst the raucous squash crowd.

That was the first time a squash had defeated a pumpkin in a golf match in at least sixteen years, noted Mr. Pumpkin. The last to accomplish that feat was Star Squash.

It was an amazing end to three full and intense days of golfing.

The final score in the annual golf tournament was Pumpkins 31 Squash 1.

CHAPTER 5
THE LEGEND

I learnt so much about squash and their way of life during the time I spent in their home. I was sitting outside with pumpkins and squash that evening. We were roasting marsh mellows over an open fire. It was such a nice, warm evening. The air had cooled from the hot sticky afternoon.

That evening, we celebrated the partnership and peaceful existence, that squash and pumpkins have shared over the years. Mr. Squash reiterated the continual need for our partnership. But he explained that our history was not always peaceful.

He told us a story. The legend of Sun. Many years ago, in a land far away, pumpkins and squash lived on the same patch. Side by side. They were neighbors. But they could not agree on certain issues, such as volunteer duties, teaching and education methods. And couldn't agree on plans to protect themselves properly.

The issue came to a head when the witches and ghouls attacked the land. They also intensified the power of their evil spirits. People intervened. They felt they had to. To protect themselves. They caught some of the witches that started the battle and held them to trial. They claimed witches were littering the air with unholy spirits. That they were the cause of all the destruction in their city. They wanted revenge. People referred to the question answer period as the witch trials. They declared the witches guilty and burned them at the cross.

People concluded that pumpkins and squash were part of the destruction as well. They demanded answers. Squash blamed pumpkins. Pumpkins blamed squash. They sold each other out. Pontius Pumpkin and Pilate Pumpkin told people, and squash, that Prince Pumpkin was at fault. That Prince was colluding with the witches without their knowledge.

It was the same situation for the squash. They felt they also needed to offer an explanation. They were put in a position that caused them to act selfishly. Mr. Squash explained how they offered up Sun for blame. That he was caught providing the ghouls with sensitive and confidential information. And who knows if any of this was even true? I mean pumpkins and squash feared for their lives. And people were very angry.

At first Prince and Sun denied the collusion. Prince and Sun never admitted to any wrongdoing or guilt. But in the end, they accepted their fate. They sacrificed themselves. And they died as martyrs. They offered themselves to people so that other pumpkins and squash could lead peaceful and long lives.

I've heard this story. Many times. But that was the first time I heard it told from a squash perspective. And it presented me with a different angle to the incident. It was strange how different species could arrive to different conclusions, when reviewing the same facts.

To pumpkins, the story was known as the legend of Prince. Or just simply as The Legend.

It was an incredible story. It was a lesson in unity. From that day onwards, people treated pumpkins with more respect and dignity. Mr. Pumpkin finished the story. He said that pumpkins felt the need to organize better, and be more prepared for events such as that. Pumpkins felt the need for a leader. A voice of reason in a time of madness. But squash and pumpkins couldn't agree on the leader. And slowly our two species drifted apart. It was commonly recognized that our first leader, or elected elder one, was Potus Pumpkin.

Squash held a ceremony to honor all their players afterwards. We watched. And they held a special ceremony to honor Stubby. His victory was a big deal. We had our dinner in and around the thirteenth green, while the ceremony was ongoing. Each squash was given a medal. Stubby was given a plaque for his achievement. The squash suggested naming a tent after him. To properly honor his accomplishment. Stubby Squash had become an instant celebrity.

That evening, for the most part, we left the squash to themselves. To celebrate. And they did so, well into the night. We could hear the hollering all over the grounds.

"Why did you hit it so hard? You just needed to tap it. It would have went in," Pavneet asked Peter that evening.

"I thought I did just touch it. Could it have been the wind?"

"No," I interjected. "There was no wind."

The next morning we all said goodbye. We boarded the bus and headed back home. Being warned that the ghouls came down into Squashland quite regularly, we considered ourselves fortunate that we had a safe trip.

But that feeling of peace soon disappeared. As we entered Burrowsville, driving along Linden road, we saw numerous werewolves lying dead on the side of the road. As we passed, we noticed they not only had been slaughtered, but their remains desecrated. It was a gory sight. The smell was gross. There was blood and guts sprawled everywhere.

"Aw. What a gross picture. Is anyone going to clean this up?" asked Pie.

"Probably not. You know how other species can be. And people don't care," replied Poon.

We saw more werewolves along the way as our drive continued. Ravaged and scoured. And we saw vampires hovering over them, cleaning away their blood with the long sharp tongues. And by cleaning I mean drinking. I'm sure they had sucked the life right out of them. Many ghouls had gathered and witnessed the carnage.

The bus driver, in the name of caution, started to speed up. None of us had any desire to watch the feast. But that proved to be difficult, because further ahead, we could see dead werewolves right on Linden road. They were in the way and blocking the path. The bus had to slow down. We had no choice.

"How are we going to get by, Stan?" asked the bus driver.

"We'll find a way. We might have to speed up. Maybe we could run right over them," replied Stan.

The driver slowed the bus down, and it eventually came to a full stop.

"I think we should speed up," advised Stan.

"Yeah. Maybe."

I could see the bus driver take out his cell phone. He was calling the local police for assistance. He told them that we were in trouble. Like no kidding.

In the meantime vampires approached our bus. The situation was getting scarier as each moment passed. Vampires started peering in the bus thru the windows. They had surrounded us. And then smash. There was a loud noise. I turned to look behind me, to the rear. One of the vampires had rammed something into the window. Maybe his arm or shoulder. I don't know. And I could see a crack had been created. This could not be good. The rear window of the bus had cracked in two. But it was still intact.

"I think we should go Mr. Pumpkin," suggested Peyton.

"Why can't we go around them?" asked Penner.

"Why can't we just run over them?" said Panama.

"Excuse Mr. Bus Driver. But I think we should go. This is not a safe situation for us," instructed Patricia.

And that was exactly our plan.

The bus had to back up first, to gain some momentum. Then the bus started to speed up forward. We seemingly had reached top speed. The bus started weaving its way thru, around and over the werewolves on the road. Treating some of them as speed bumps if necessary. We attempted to leave the vampires behind. But they wanted a taste of pumpkin pie for dessert after the werewolf entrée. And they chased us from behind.

The bus was jumping up and down. Many of us had vacated our seats, and were now crouched down in the aisles.

"Oh my dear," I heard Panita whisper.

"Grab onto something. Anything." We were all giving each other advice. Trying to latch onto anything in order to remain stable. And in one piece. But it was very difficult.

We barely managed to pass the werewolves, when up ahead we encountered a new problem. We were met by witches. We could see them nearing, gliding on their broomsticks.

"Don't slow down now Ollie," said Stan.

"I'm not slowing down. It's hard to maintain top speed. I think something has happened to the left front tire," said Ollie. He was frantic. We all were.

The bus kept moving. And just as it appeared that we were going to clear and make it past all this mess, the craziest thing happened. The front of the bus started to lift up into the air. The bus stopped driving. Out of nowhere we saw green smoke litter the sky. It covered the bus. The driver didn't appear to be in control of the bus anymore. The front end of the bus was suspended in the air. We appeared to be in a complete vertical position.

I saw Pavneet and Peter roll off their seats and land in the aisle. They started rolling down the aisle. Peter zipped right past me. He was unable to latch onto anything to stop his roll. And he slammed into the golf bags at the rear of the bus. Ouch. That must have hurt.

The bus was suspended for at least a minute. And then the front end slammed back down to the ground. The slam of the bus caused me to jump up from my seat. And I landed right back in my seat. I hurt my back. It was a chaotic scene.

Witches were in front of us, with vampires to the rear. It seemed we were waiting to see which species was going to attack first. We were in a vulnerable position. We were trapped. Out in the middle of nowhere.

"What are we going to do now?" asked Ollie.

"Let's keep moving," replied Stan.

"I hurt my head," said Paisley.

"I hurt my hand," said Ponima.

"Everyone. Just stay calm," reiterated Mr. Pumpkin.

I could see the fear in all our eyes. I could see tears of fear. Paisley had shriveled into a ball at the rear of the bus. Her hands and arms covering her face. Poon had her arms around her shoulders. Ponima and Panita were holding on to each other next to me. We were still in our seats.

The engine had shut off. Ollie tried to turn the engine back on, but the motor was not turning.

"Something is wrong with the engine. It's not turning!" he screamed.

The bus became inoperable because of the sudden slam to the ground.

"Don't worry everyone. We have called for help. Someone will be here any minute. Everyone just needs to stay calm," assured Stan.

But there were no assurances of anything. I saw a new batch of green smoke, and again the bus started to rise. But only briefly. Then it slammed back down to the ground again. The green smoke was coming into the bus. It was seeping in thru the cracks of the windows. And the cracks were only widening, due to the repeated slams to the ground.

"What is that smell?" asked Popeye.

"It must be the bus gas," Patricia noted. Those two were seated in the row next to me, across the aisle.

We smelt gas. It was nauseating. We could see Ollie and Stan calling for help on their cell phones. Both of them. We seemed to be the only ones on the road for miles. We were surrounded by farmland. There were no buildings or people anywhere. There were only vampires, witches, and dead werewolves. And other ghouls in the sky. They stayed to watch our terror. Like a good book that they couldn't put down. There were cows in the nearby fields, off in the distance. And scared pumpkins.

Ponima, Panita and I had finally vacated our seats and joined most of the others at the rear of the bus. We didn't want to sit alone any longer.

Vampires had surrounded the back of the bus. The rear window was almost broken. The crack was visible. And now they were attempting to smash in the side windows. There must have been at least five vampires around the bus. They were peering in thru the windows with their bright red, blood shot eyes. I could hear them salivating. With their mouths wide open, I could see their sharp teeth.

The witches were hovering in the air. Watching. Waiting patiently for their turn at us. And laughing at our sad predicament.

The witches and vampires were even bantering back and forth. The witches began antagonizing the vampires, as they neared the bus. They were not willing to wait their turn.

"Those are for us," demanded a witch.

"Shouldn't you be asleep?" asked another. "It's way past your bed time Mr. Vampire."

The witches seemed to have caught the vampires' attention. They left us be, temporarily. The vampires leapt into the air and tried to grab the witches. But witches are too agile to be caught with sudden, unorganized lunges. They moved side to side with so much ease. One daring witch even tried to tempt the vampires, enticing them to come her way. Wanting the vampires to chase her.

"Catch me if you can," I heard her scream out.

Sitting in the aisle near the back of the bus, I could barely see what was going on outside. It was difficult to see anything thru the windows. I was terrified just to keep my wits. We were all huddled together. We were clinging onto each other. Scared to death. Some pumpkins had crawled underneath the seats.

I saw a few vampires focus their attention solely on just one witch. The other witches drifted to one side. It was as if they felt she didn't need any assistance.

"You're no match for us, you little she-devil," said one vampire.

"Don't be stupid," said another.

The vampires were able to surround her. One vampire above her, another below. One in the front, and another behind her back. And they inched closer. The witch couldn't make any more moves. And finally, to her surprise, they were able to seize her broom and rip it away from her. The witch tumbled to the ground. The vampires got a hold of her and held her to the ground. And they ripped her apart, from limb to limb. We all watched with amazement. The whole scene unfolded before our very eyes. Her arms and legs severed. Blood sprayed out from her neck. The vampires ravished on her. The toying game had cost the witch her life. The other witches escaped the scene. They left her to die by herself. It was gory to watch.

Her laughter had turned to screams. 'Let me go' she had begged. But it was no use. No one responded to her plea. It was too little, too late.

"This is called vampire supremacy," I heard.

Meanwhile, our bus was still not operating. And help had not yet arrived. The vampires turned their attention back on us. We were under siege once again.

"We need to fight back!" I screamed.

The vampires were banging their hands on the windows. And one window had smashed to bits. A vampire tried to squeeze thru. I had to do something. Waiting for my own death could be frightening. I got a sudden rush of courage. Probably due to all the anger I felt. I decided I was no longer going to take my death sitting down. I managed to take out one of the golf clubs from a bag. I stood up, and climbed onto the seat to that broken window, and swung the club. I hit the vampire on the hand as it tried to reach its long arms towards me. The windows were too small for them to squeeze thru. So it tried to extend its arms inside. I swung the golf club many times. Almost like a maniac. It tried to grab me, but it failed. I made sure of that.

Peter and Popeye arose from where they were and attempted to do the same thing. Peter swung his six iron. He missed the vampires' hand, though. The club grazed the side of Popeyes' back. That was unfortunate. An accident, I was sure. But our repeated swings could only have scared them away from the windows.

I was so frightened. We all were. We were all scared to death.

Vampires managed to bend the bars near the back window, after the glass had finally fallen apart. We were lucky there were vertical bars preventing them from entering. But they still tried. One vampire ended up half stuck. He was half inside and half outside. The other vampires were bending the bars so he could make it all the way thru. Others were pushing him from behind.

Mr. Pumpkin, Peyton and Pepe were swinging golf clubs at him. Peyton landed repeated blows onto the shoulder. But despite our efforts, it seemed it was only a matter of time before the vampires would break down the bus.

Then we heard a loud, stern voice from outside.

"No!"

Another vampire appeared. I could see him from where I was. His cape was dark black and very long. His teeth sharp. His tongue was long and beet red. He seemed so much bigger and stronger than any vampire I had ever seen. The other vampires seemed like babies, by comparison. All the vampires froze in their spots. They stopped moving and pounding the bus. They stopped talking.

Instead of pushing and propelling vampires inside the bus, they began to pull them out instead.

"Leave those pumpkins alone," the vampire said. His voice was so powerful.

And strangely enough the vampires obeyed. One by one they left the scene. They vacated.

The witches had already left. And now the vampires had left. We were saved.

"They're leaving," I exulted.

"Who was that?" inquired Popeye.

I wondered. Was it Count Dracula? We all thought that was a possibility. The suggestion was stated aloud.

"No. It can't be. Doesn't he live in Transylvania?" asked Popeye.

"Where is that?" I asked.

"Wow. He saved our lives. He ordered all the vampires to go away," Peyton agreed.

"It sounded like Victor Vampire," said Peter.

"How do you know?" I asked.

"I don't. I have only heard his voice a few times. The voice was so familiar," he explained.

Peter had claimed to have spoken with Victor Vampire. He was the leader of the local vampire population. He said the conversations were always terse and short. They were usually about Wanda Witch. Our most feared ghoul. Seriously? But who knows? I mean it could be true.

"Who cares who it was?" said Mr. Pumpkin. "We should just be thankful."

One by one, we all emerged from hiding. We were standing in the aisle.

We had been so concerned about our lives, that we lost track of the two people. Ollie was still on the phone. He had been constantly requesting for help all this time. But Stan was hunched over in his seat. He was not moving.

"Is he dead?" asked Panama.

"No. I think he must have hit his head," said Ollie.

"Let's get out of here," said Penelope.

"How can we? The bus is broken," said Ollie. He didn't seem to know what to do.

There was smoke coming out of the engine. That was not a good sign.

"Then we have to walk," it was suggested.

"Well, I don't know about that. That would be a long walk. Besides the police should be here soon. They are only minutes away," said Ollie. He seemed more concerned with Stan than any of us. I could see him putting his fingers near his throat. Probably checking for a pulse.

"Can't you fix the bus?" asked Peyton.

"Look pumpkin. I really don't want to go outside. At any moment, the ghouls could come back," he reasoned. "Besides. I don't think I can fix the engine."

"Mr. Person, we need to get the bus started. And we need to get out of here. Like right now," countered Peyton.

"Stan? Wake up," he continued. He was shaking his friends' shoulders. Ollie wasn't thinking straight. He was hysterical.

"Never mind about Stan. Can you fix the bus?" we repeated.

"How come no one came to help us? Seriously?" I blurted out. That made me mad. Furious. We had to survive the whole ordeal by ourselves.

It seemed the whole scene took hours. That it was hours since we first made that emergency call. But in reality, it couldn't have been more than a few minutes. Everything happened so fast.

Ollie never was able to restart the bus. He turned the key multiple times. Over and over again. The engine made some noise. But the noise was only brief. It was like a pumpkin trying to speak, but couldn't complete the sentence.

"Okay. I will see if I can get it started. But with that much smoke coming out of the engine, something must be seriously wrong." Ollie gave in. He would try. Great. I mean that was the least he could do.

Reluctantly, he climbed out of the bus. He had to kick on his door repeatedly just to open it. It appeared to have been stuck. Once outside, he opened the hood and started to inspect the engine. We all followed. And I got a clearer view of the shredded witch. And the mess of the werewolves. I could only look for a split second. All the blood and guts splattered over the road was disgusting.

"Can you fix it?" Peyton and Penelope were insistent.

"No."

That was a disappointing answer. I expected him to fix the engine.

"Is everyone okay?" asked Patricia.

Everyone seemed to be okay. We all seemed to have suffered some kind of bruise or another. Paisley was still holding her head. She said she hit it on the large pole, in the middle of the aisle, when she slid down. Poon said she hurt her shoulder. Penner was also holding the side of his face. And Pie was walking around gingerly, testing out his left knee.

Peter said he hurt his shoulder.

"When you slammed into the golf bag?" I asked him.

"No. I think when I swung that golf club at the vampire. I might have popped a muscle somewhere."

"Seriously? You mean when you hit Popeye?"

Peter just shrugged. Popeye wasn't upset though. I mean it was a very stressful time. Who could blame any pumpkin?

The only ailment I suffered was that my rear still hurt. I had slammed down on my seat, after the first crash to the ground. And it was a bumpy ride for a stretch. With all the excitement I just couldn't sit still. But considering the predicament we were in, we all felt lucky that we made it out of that situation alive.

Just then we noticed seeds gushing out of Pavneet. She had finally emerged from the bus. They were seeping out of her left arm and shoulder. She had suffered numerous, severe glass wounds all over her body. There was a huge gash wound on her left arm. Aw. We have to get her to the hospital, I thought. Mr. Pumpkin took some towels out of a golf bag, and wrapped it around her arm. There was still a sharp piece of glass embedded into her left shoulder.

"Hold this tight Pavneet," we all advised.

"Are you in pain?" she was asked.

"No. Not really. My skin does feel weird though. It doesn't look normal, does it?" was her reply.

"Not to worry Pavneet. We just need to have the doctors take a look," she was advised.

"What about this piece of glass?" she asked.

"No. Don't do anything. Let's just wait," advised Mr. Pumpkin.

And finally, after what seemed to be an eternity, the Burrowsville police force had arrived. I mean finally. Where were they when we really needed their help? Why did it take them so long? What were they doing all this time?

They asked the usual questions. They inspected the area. We knew they needed to co-ordinate a clean-up plan. Linden road looked a mess. The smell of the blood and guts was gross. And the aroma of the cows in the nearby field wasn't any better. I wondered what they were up to. I mean, they must have just had a toilet break. Who could blame them? With all of the excitement. I wondered if anyone was going to clean up their mess.

After a few more minutes, two ambulances appeared. The medical staff had to carefully place Stan on a bed. He eventually was rolled into the back of an ambulance, and it sped off without further delay.

We abandoned the bus and we boarded the two police vans. The police helped us with our golf bags. I guess that was the least they could do.

The people medical staff had put fresh bandages over and around Pavneets' arm and shoulder. They didn't take the piece of glass out though. They said that it would be better if pumpkins did that at our hospital. They did their best to prevent anymore seeds from dripping out of her arm.

As we continued onwards on Linden road, we saw more trucks pass by coming from the opposite direction. They were heading towards the scene of the crime. They had a huge cleanup project to undertake, that was for sure.

Pumpkin medical staff were prepared for our arrival. Mr. Pumpkin had called before hand. Alerting them of Pavneets' injuries. The piece of glass looked dangerous. The other gashes up and down her arm were concerning as well. The bandages were holding nicely though. She was rushed to the hospital for treatment. I'm sure she would be okay. She said she was only in slight pain.

I went straight home. And as soon as I got inside, I collapsed on my bed. I was thankful to be alive. That was the second ghoul encounter I had, within a week. It was a relief to be back home. And to lie in my own bed.

I must have been completely in my own thoughts, because it took me a minute to realize there were many pumpkins in the house. Visitors. I could hear the chatter. We were having a house party. I mean why not. You can only have a decent house party on a Monday afternoon when there was no school.

I thought about taking a bath. I needed one. But I felt uncomfortable taking a bath in a crowded house. So I skipped it. Instead I felt the need to tell someone about the events that just occurred.

Neither Plouffe nor Patrice were home. Not in the bedroom, nor anywhere in the house. Our guests were with Paradis, crowded in his room. And when I signalled for him to come out, he was joined by Paris. Well that was not going to work. Because I didn't want to tell Paris. And I didn't really know any of the other pumpkins in the house. So I decided to go find my friends instead. I mean I just had to tell them everything.

And just as I opened the door, there was Patrice. She was coming inside. But I stopped her.

"Hey Pashelle. How was your trip? Did you like Squashland? Did you win at your golf?" she asked.

I wanted to tell her everything. Right then and there. And I also wanted to tell all my friends. I really wanted to tell as many pumpkins as possible, at one time.

"Do you want to go to the lounge?" I asked.

"There's nothing going on. I was just there," she said. She thought it would be more fun at home.

"Come on Patrice. I have to tell you everything." I didn't allow her the chance. I grabbed her by the arm and pulled her with me.

I had the feeling I was going to repeat the story many times over.

"You're not going to believe what happened," I started, as Patrice and I left our house. I found myself walking very quickly. "We almost gotten eaten alive. All of us. On the bus. There were so many witches and vampires on Linden road."

"Aw!" she exclaimed.

"It's true," I confirmed.

"What do you mean? Hey slow down Pashelle," she pleaded. "Why are you walking so fast?"

But I didn't want to slow down. We reached the west gate in no time. And I searched desperately for anyone that I knew. I met Patrick just outside the main entrance of the activity center.

"Do you know where Pannette is?" I asked.

He didn't know. He suggested to look in the lounge.

The lounge was a very cramped sitting area in the activity center building. There had been much discussion about extending this area. But space was restricted. It couldn't be extended north because of the water. There was a larger building to the east right next to the lounge, which we called the arena. So south was the only way it could be extended. But no one would agree to that, because that would mean shrinking the Carnation garden. The flower gardens in the eye were the most beautiful parts of our patch. I mean our gardens were some of the most beautiful in all the land. No one would agree to sacrifice any of that valuable green space. And inside the activity center to the west, was the main dining hall. I mean there were few options of making the lounge roomier. It was always crowded. Pumpkins were always packed in there like sardines in a fish can. It was busy. It was a Monday afternoon. And we had no school in the summer time, so all the younger pumpkins were jammed inside.

At first I couldn't spot any of my friends. But I decided to search around inside anyways. It was frustrating navigating thru the crowd, as I had to push my way thru. I was desperate to tell everyone what transpired on my trip to Squashland. I left the lounge without any luck. My friends must be at Pannettes' house, I thought.

"Come on Patrice," I yelled out, over the raucous pumpkin noise.

During the search, I was telling my story to Patrice. She stayed by my side. She had no choice, as I had a firm grip on her left hand. But I was not sure how much of the story she heard. As we exited the activity center, we saw Pikachu crying, and Patrice temporarily stopped. Why? I thought. Who cared if she was crying? Let's go.

"Why are you crying Pikachu?" asked Patrice. I had to stop too.

While I was waiting for their conversation to end, I spotted Polo. Finally. I mean I could recognize him from seven miles away.

He was on the other side of the eye. Near the Water Gate Bridge. I grabbed Patrice's arm, and yanked it forward.

"Ask her later," I ordered.

We ran to the other side of the eye. And we sat with all my friends. Patrice sat down next to her friend Precious.

And I began talking so fast, that at first I didn't even notice who was there.

"I have to tell you all something. We got attacked by vampires. And Pavneet is in the hospital," I said.

And I was expecting an onslaught of questions. But nothing came my way. My friends just looked at me, and then turned away. It was like I interrupted them.

Pebbles looked at me with her mouth agape. Picasso responded with a 'wow'. And Pekka said 'okay'. Like okay? We were just attacked by vampires, and that was okay? Did anyone even hear what I just said? Or maybe it wasn't interesting enough for them? There must have been over twenty pumpkins sitting in a very cramped spot of grass in the Tulip garden. Idly chatting. I knew they all heard me. Because they stopped their conversations to acknowledge. But only momentarily. Which was amazing, if I really thought about it. That they even stopped to listen. And then their conversations began again. All of them.

"I was in the lounge, and then I walked back home. But then Pashelle wanted to come here," explained Patrice. She was sitting next to me.

"Who else is going to the city?"

"Don't worry about the arrangement of the tables. The guards will take care of them. We don't worry about the food, or the drinks. Or any of that really. We only have one job."

"I asked Ms. Pumpkin, and she said we are waiting for a new shipment of apple juice."

"Puff. Petal. Pauline. Piper, I think."

"And Peter."

"Me too," said Precious.

"But I don't think she's telling the truth."

"How do you know?"

Who? Who's not telling the truth? About what?

"Wanda did meet before a tribunal. Like I told you before. She really does want to hold an all species beauty pageant."

"I saw Pikachu. And she was crying. Why?"

"She lost her pet rodent. She's very upset. She is beside herself. She doesn't know where it is. It escaped from its cage."

"Nobody knows where it is."

"Right. You have mentioned that. Just get the pumpkins serving. And I understand. I agree. The volunteer work at the Tea Party is important. It's such a time honored tradition."

"Like why? Because she thinks she could win?"

"I know right. Has a witch ever looked at themselves in the mirror? With their big sharp pointed noises and wrinkly, ugly, green skin. How could a witch even consider themselves a contender in a truly Miss Universe pageant?"

With so many conversations going on, I didn't know who to interrupt, so that I could begin telling my story. Why wasn't anyone interested in hearing my story?

"I hope Pavneet will be able to go?"

'Go where?' I thought. Where was Pavneet going?

"I thought we made our own apple juice."

"What difference does it matter what type of juice. Just make sure you drink some Pandria. You know how quickly you can just dry up inside. And that's what you have to worry about. Even if you just drink water."

"That's kind of gross. Why does Pikachu Pumpkin have a pet rodent in the first place? Who wants a rodent for a pet? Does she talk to it?"

"Who knows?"

"Does it talk back to her?"

"I'm sure she'll be okay. I'm sure she'll come with us."

"I love the juice right from freshly squeezed oranges much better. But you should listen to Patience. You can't keep fainting like this. You have fainted at least three times this week. Everyone is talking about it now. You could really hurt yourself from a fall."

"I know. That's the part with the street fight."

"No. That comes afterward."

"Oh. Okay. Maybe not then."

"He said he only took pictures. And didn't make a movie."

"There was so much confusion about the draw."

"Did you see the pictures of Suzy Squash? Doesn't she look so different carrying all that extra weight?"

"What movie are you talking about?"

"Heat."

"Why is that person so interesting?"

"Frankenstein is not a person."

"Why didn't you watch the opening ceremony then?"

"Because it was guys' night out in the lounge."

"It is, Pandria. It's the heat that is causing the fainting."

"Maybe my seeds are low."

There were six different conversations going on at the same time. With about twenty pumpkins. All within ear shot. I thought that I would wait for all the conversations to die down. And then someone would ask me about the incident. Besides, I had no other choice in the matter. I sat. Waited. And just listened. I was sitting next to Petrina and Pannette. They were talking about the pumpkin beauty pageant.

"Look Petrina. It's not my fault that it wasn't that hot yesterday. I cannot control the weather."

"You didn't get very many of them inside the greenhouse anyways."

"It's not my fault no one wanted to attend Mr. Pumpkins' day long volunteer seminar. Maybe no one thinks that life in the greenhouse can be rewarding."

"I would hate it, if I didn't make it to the next round."

"You misread so many lines. And there was no emotion in your voice. You were so monotone."

Petrina recited a scene from a play, as her second talent.

"Why do you want to be a participator in the beauty pageant anyways?" I asked Petrina. I was actually jealous. I was going to enter my name. I've always wanted to. But when Petrina submitted her name and made the announcement, I couldn't. Because she would think I was a copycat. That I would be spoiling her fun, on purpose.

"It's participant. Not participator."

"Irregardless. You know what I mean?"

"Do rodents speak English?"

"No. Of course not," answered Plato. "They are not smart enough to speak English. They speak their own language."

"And why do you care anyways?" After responding to Precious and Patrice, Plato gave a stare to Polo. Polo was asking questions about a book that Plato was reading. About Frankenstein. And he wouldn't let Plato read the book in peace.

Plato was very smart. He was always in deep thought. He loved to read books written by a philosopher named Socrates. I asked him about Socrates once. He just ignored me. "I don't think you care about him," was his reply. I wanted Plato to tell me something about him. Like what was his other name? If he had one. He never did elaborate.

Plato was expecting two siblings to be born any day. He seemed stressed about it. He had mentioned many times that he didn't know how to act as a big brother. That the long wait only made him more nervous.

I noticed he had burn marks on the side of his face. I hadn't realized before. I wondered where they came from.

"What happened to your face?" I asked.

Plato looked up at me. He knew I was talking about his face.

"I kind of had an accident over the weekend. I…"

Polo interrupted him, and answered my question. He seemed so hyper and excited.

"He's still trying to replicate and determine how Wanda Witch was able to create lightening out of thin air. He was using this bottle, and…"

"He was trying to create lightening in a bottle," said Petrina. "And it almost worked. But instead of creating lightening, he created a fire that blew up. The bottle exploded, and the fire lashed out. Onto his face."

"That must have been ugly."

"Are you saying his face is ugly?"

"No. I'm saying the situation was ugly," clarified Pannette.

"You've said that already."

"Because she was asking. My goodness."

"I would say your face looks nasty," I said.

Polo began laughing. It was meant as a joke. But no one else was amused. But they knew I was joking. I looked at Plato, as if to say 'Plato, you know I'm joking, right?'

"Not anymore. I'm done with that experiment. I have concluded that it must have been a secret witch spell. That only witches and warlocks were privy to. I've decided to move on to other study material."

"Like what? Of course. Frankenstein. The monster."

"He's not a monster. He's a hybrid," said Plato.

"No. He's not a hybrid."

"He must be. He's made up of different body parts."

"Is Batman a vampire?" I wondered aloud.

"But all the parts are human. You have to be constructed of multiple different species to be classified as a hybrid."

"Who's says."

"Mr. Pumpkin?"

"Well. I don't know if Mr. Pumpkin said so," Plato clarified. "But it just seems common sense to me. He's a different type of human species."

"So why are you reading about him?" I asked.

"Because maybe he wants to construct a new type of pumpkin species."

"No I don't. I just find his character to be interesting," said Plato.

"Where is Pavneet going?" I asked Pannette. Her conversation with Petrina about the beauty pageant was still ongoing. So I had to poke her on the shoulders to get her attention. She hated it, when I did that. She was always complaining about her overly sensitive skin.

"What do you mean? And stop doing that," she said.

Pickle was asking Pepper if Pavneet will be able to go. Like go where?"

"Oh. They did the draw. We get to watch the closing ceremony of the people Olympics," she said excitedly.

Yes. Yes. I jumped up for joy. All right. This was so great.

"I'm so excited." I said.

"I know right."

"It's gonna be a blast."

"How did the elders do the draw?" I asked.

"By random selection."

"What do you mean?" I asked.

"They chose seven pumpkins. My name was drawn. And so I got to choose two others to come with me," announced Petrina.

"Only two? So who did you choose?" I asked.

I sensed a slight hesitation in her voice before replying.

"Um. Well I chose Pannette and Pavneet."

"Well this doesn't make sense. So I'm not going? I'm the one who submitted our names in the first place," I reasoned.

"My name was drawn too. And I chose Polo and you," Plato clarified.

Okay good. So it all worked out. That was a fortunate bit of luck. I looked at Petrina. Why didn't she pick me? I didn't ask. There wasn't a point.

"You actually got double selected."

"What do you mean?" I asked.

"Precious was drawn too. And she picked you."

"Really? Wow. I hardly know her," I whispered. I didn't want her to hear me. She was still talking to Patrice and Porzingas behind me.

Precious was so young. It was amazing that her name was even in the draw. She was real good friends with Patrice. She slept over sometimes. She lived in a large house on my column, with many strangers. She had no related seeds.

"I want to go on some rides in the Amusement park. I hope we're allowed."

"No. Wait. Listen to my story. Seriously." I finally had their attention.

"That's too boring."

"What? What do you mean? I haven't even told you yet. I'm not finished. I have more to say. Come on everybody."

"We know what happened Pashelle."

"What do you mean? How?"

"Peter told us."

"Peter?"

"He and Mr. Pumpkin were just here. Before you. They told us everything."

"So? Now I'm not allowed to tell you?"

"But we know."

"Okay Pashelle. Go ahead. I mean why do you think your bus was picked up off the ground?"

"Yes. Tell us how you escaped."

I explained everything in detail about what happened. I mean I just knew they wanted to hear it from me. I told them how our bus broke down. How it rose in the air. The dead werewolves on and around Linden road. The witches and vampires. How a witch was shredded to pieces. They listened so intently. Pavneet and the broken glass.

"My goodness. That must have been ugly."

"How did you escape?"

"Yeah. Like why did the vampires just go away? If they were in the mood to eat you up, then why didn't they?"

"I don't know. Maybe because it was in the morning. It could have been their bed time. I mean, don't vampires eat at night?"

"Wait. Why did the bus rise?" asked Plato.

"You know witches. They must have cast a spell on the bus. Some kind of new craft. I saw this green smoke at first. Then the front end of the bus lifted upwards," I said.

"That's weird."

"From where?"

"What do you mean?" I asked.

"Where did the smoke come from? How did it get there?"

"I'm not sure," I answered. I mean it just appeared. "And then the bus slammed to the ground. The engine must have damaged. Because it didn't work. Or else, we would have gotten out of there."

"And vampires left you alone, because…"

"I told you. We all heard one vampire. And he yelled out 'No'." I explained.

"And Peter says that was Victor Vampire," Plato concluded.

"Well. Maybe."

"Peter is probably right. Victor is their commander in chief. Who else could it have been?"

"And maybe they left you alone because Peter was there."

"Maybe," I said. I mean it was a possibility.

"Because Peter keeps saying that Victor wants his help. So it would be counter-productive for vampires to harm him."

No one seemed to care that I almost bashed in a vampires skull with a golf club. All they wanted to talk about was how Peter apparently saved the day. By his mere presence. He didn't even do anything. Why were they giving him so much credit? I mean they didn't even know what happened. They weren't even there. So much speculation and conjecture.

I mean Peter never does anything, and it was amazing how popular he was. He was the most recognized pumpkin in the patch. Maybe because of his glasses. I don't know. And I had to try so hard to fit in. Sometimes I think my friends never believed anything I said. I mean I darn near killed a vampire, and they didn't believe me.

I met Wanda Witch and they don't believe me. I have met her. Our most feared ghoul. I came face to face with her. When I was little. We talked at a great length. She was very nice to me. Not like any of the other witches. She even offered me something to drink. And it wasn't poison. I knew. Because she took a sip of the same drink first. She picked me out on purpose. Maybe she thought I was special. Who knows? But strangely, she has never contacted me since. I knew she still watched over me though. I wondered if Victor watched over Peter in the same way. It was possible. In that respect, Peter and I had something in common.

Our conversation stalled. We had all become quiet at once. That was a rarity. All pumpkins loved to talk, and socialize, and tell stories.

"We should go visit with Pavneet."

"We will. But not today. I asked Dr. Pumpkin. He said there was no visiting today. But we could see her tomorrow. They have to take that piece of glass out, and then reseal the holes."

We ended up just relaxing and chilling out for the rest of the afternoon. I took out a deck of playing cards that I kept in my sac. But no one wanted to play with me. That was not a surprise. I mean I always win. And no one likes losing. After a few hours had past, we ate dinner. And we decided to meet at the hospital the following morning, to check on how Pavneet was doing. I hoped she was okay. I'm sure she would be. She was a tough minded individual. A few scrapes and bruises wouldn't stop her from coming to the city with us. I was so tired by the time night fell. It had been a very hectic and eventful weekend.

As I laid in bed, I wondered if my surprise birthday party would be held in the city. I listened intently to my siblings' conversations to search for clues. But they were talking about other things. Even still, that couldn't be true anyways. My birthday party couldn't be held in the city. I mean only twenty five pumpkins would be escorted to the closing ceremony. What about everyone else? All I knew was that it had to be soon. It would be August by the time we returned from the city. It was a very exciting time.

CHAPTER 6
THE OLYMPICS

We left the patch on the next Saturday morning. We would spend a night in a New Surrey City hotel. The Olympics were a huge deal for people. It was a show of their supreme physical talent. An attempt by people to showcase their physical superiority over all other species. It was a series of races and events. The whole world watched. And it was a big deal for the city, as well. They had known the Olympics would be held in the city many years ago. Even before I was born. The residents had been planning for this event for countless years. Mr. Pumpkin explained they had to erect new buildings and renovate other ones. Prepare all of the playing surfaces. They had to upgrade the transportation system. They needed to improve their security levels. And they needed to prepare for many visitors from all over the world. From all species, including pumpkins and squash. It was like a two week party. We were honored to be invited to their event.

People had sent us our invitation quite some time ago. They wanted us to attend. They invited twenty five pumpkins. And twenty five squash. To witness their spectacular display of talent.

The selection on which pumpkins were allowed to attend was quite a dilemma for us. At first, it would be the pumpkins who achieved the best marks in school. Other pumpkins stated that it should be whoever received the most orange ribbons in our games of summer. But both of those suggestions were difficult for the elders to accept. Because many elders no longer attended school, nor participated in our games. They would not be eligible if either of those two options were the deciding factor. So the social committee decided to choose pumpkins by mere random selection. Some kind of drawing of the names from a bowl. From those who submitted their names. It was ironic, in a way. Because so few elders submit their names for outings to the city anyways.

By the time we arrived, most of the events and races had been completed. I mean we were invited to the closing ceremony after all. There were only a few more events remaining. There were swimming races going on in one arena. And there were other events ongoing in the same stadium where the closing ceremony would be held. And that was where we spent our time.

There were so many people attending and watching the games. And we could see so many ghouls flying in the sky. On the first day we were there, we saw people compete in track and field events. Running events mostly. Some athletes raced one hundred meters in less than ten seconds. That was amazing. Viewing the distance, I guesstimated it would have taken me over a minute to race that distance. Maybe more. I don't know.

Everyone in the world watched with such amazement. Even the ghosts made their presence felt. You couldn't miss them, as they were clad in their all-white attire. I overheard some people talking about the ghosts. The famous ones. The ones that had competed in the Olympics previously. That's kind of a weird concept to follow. How a person could change species, and transform themselves into a ghost.

"The ghost of Jesse Owens would be proud," I heard one person say.

Every species must have been amazed at the physical ability of people. But it was difficult for us to see their faces though, to see the glory in their eyes. We were seated at the top corner of the stadium. We were very high up. I had been in this stadium once before. I was invited to watch a football game, a few years back. I remember because it was on new years' eve. And we were much closer to the playing surface. We were able to see everything without having to squint our eyes. I mean this was a very large stadium. Someone had mentioned that over eighty thousand people could sit in this place at one time. Wow. We were in a nice cozy room. Refreshments and dinner were served to us directly in the room. And dessert. Well I won't mention the dessert, actually, because that was a complete disaster. It was a fiasco of major proportions.

During the racing events, my friends and I left our seats to move closer to the playing surface. Using the stadium elevators we moved down three levels. We ended up standing in an aisle, leaning against a railing. We weren't supposed to be there though. The ushers kept telling us to return to our seats. They didn't want us cluttering the aisles. Apparently we were in the way, preventing people from moving up and down the stairs freely.

We often did that back in the patch. We had a bad habit of standing right near the main entrance of the activity center building, watching all the pumpkins come and go.

"Maybe we should move back to our seats?" suggested Pavneet. "It is kind of dangerous standing here."

Pavneet had recovered enough from all her skin wounds. The ones she received during the deadly bus ride the previous weekend. She was one tough pumpkin. The indentation on her left shoulder was still visible.

It was a bit dangerous standing in the aisle. People often could not see us, with their noses so high up in the air. Whether intentional or not, pumpkins have been stepped on and squished by people. And kicked at.

"Mr. Person. It's so difficult for us to see anything sitting in our seats. I mean people are so tall. Even when they're sitting down. It's too hard to see over their heads," I said.

"And some people have such big heads." It was added.

"We're not causing a fuss. Couldn't we just stay here?" added Petrina.

But the ushers wouldn't listen to our appeals. After numerous orders to clear the aisles, we finally agreed. We were told that if we didn't, we would be kicked out of the stadium. I thought that was a harsh thing to say. I mean one minute we were invited here as their guests and the next they threaten us. But we didn't vacate the aisle without having a word or two with the usher.

"What is your problem?" I asked the person. I was getting annoyed with the lack of service being offered to us. I still remembered the fiasco the last time we visited.

"Look pumpkin. I don't want to cause any trouble either. But don't you see that you're in the way? And that people are trying to walk up and down these stairs?"

He did have a point. But he didn't have to be so rude about it.

"Let's just go back. Do you know how mad Mr. Pumpkin would be if he found out we got kicked out of this stadium? Like we would get clean up duty for at least a year," reasoned Pavneet.

"Let me see your ticket?" the usher asked.

"What?"

"Your ticket. To prove you should be this stadium."

"Seriously? I don't have to show you my ticket," I said.

"Yes you do pumpkin. All of you."

"We're allowed to be in this stadium. Okay," I barked. "Let me see your ticket?"

"Pumpkin, I don't need a ticket. I'm not going to argue with you. Do you really want to cause a scene?"

Pannette sensed he was getting upset with us. I mean we really didn't want any trouble.

"Either I escort you back to your seats, or I escort you out of the stadium. It's your choice."

Wow. Some choice, I thought.

None of us wanted that. I mean we were only in the city for a day or two to see the ceremony. And the races and events. And truth be told, none of us really cared which person won any event. We decided to return to our level, which meant we rode in the elevators again. But before we did, we decided to walk around the stadium, peering down onto the field as we walked. And as we did, we could see hundreds of ghouls in the sky. Maybe even thousands.

And periodically, I could see that terrible green smoke again. Or whatever that was. I don't know. The witches were quite far away, though, so it was very difficult to conclude what that smoke was.

Whether some kind of spell or potion, or not. It was weird. It appeared to be spewing out from their mouths. It was the same type of smoke that I saw in the patch two weeks ago. When it surrounded the werewolf. And again, when we were trapped inside that bus on Linden road.

"Do you see that smoke?" I wondered aloud.

"Where?" replied Peter.

"There," I pointed. "Look. Near those witches."

"I can't see. It's too far away."

"Are you that blind? Maybe you need an upgrade on your glasses?"

The ghosts were up to no good. I noticed some of them became visible for a brief moment of time, as they passed by a lady while she was tying the laces on her running shoe. When she arose to her feet, she screamed out "Where's my purse? My purse is gone!" I wondered if the ghosts took her purse.

"What is that ghost doing over there?" Petrina asked.

"I see him. He's recording notes. He must be a ghost writer," replied Pannette.

"A what?"

"A ghost writer. You know, a ghost who writes."

"That's not what a ghost writer does," stated Plato.

"Then what do you think a ghost writer is?"

"What? A ghost writer? What are you talking about?"

"I'm talking about what that ghost is doing."

"Why would the ghost be writing?"

"I don't know. Maybe to record all these events. So he could share with all the other ghosts."

"Yeah. I guess so. All species are so interested in what's going on here."

"No. I mean that's not what a ghost writer is," repeated Plato.

Plato was insistent in making his point. Whatever it was. But it didn't matter. It was quite a day. Tiring and exciting. I loved visiting. There were so many things to do and see. We ate lots of ice cream. We kept going for seconds. And thirds. We had to drag Penelope along with us, as she carried our vouchers.

That evening, when we watched the people news in our hotel room, there was lot of discussion about athletes cheating. The Olympic committee was forced to test every athlete to ensure that no illegal substances were in their bodies. Because it was discovered that so many athletes did have these illegal substances. Far more than usual. They had found so many had cheated to gain an unfair advantage. And all of these athletes were stripped of their medals, it was announced. Too many drugs inside their bodies. They were cheating. Reputations were tarnished. All of them had become a laughing stock. But when the athletes were interviewed on television, so many of them claimed innocence. Some even cried on live television upon hearing the news.

Why would they do something they know was immoral? Just to win a medal at an event? I mean didn't they know they would have been tested afterwards? Why would they purposely do something like that? They trained and exercised their whole lives to compete in these events. To show their ability and physical expertise. The mastery and prowess of a task. Which was so great. But on the most important day of their lives, on the biggest stage, they cheated. It was sad in a way.

"I feel sorry for them."

"Why? It's their own fault."

"Maybe they didn't know."

"Didn't know that they took drugs?"

"How could they not know?"

"Maybe they didn't know which drug was okay to use, and which one wasn't. I mean we take drugs. When you were in the hospital getting treatment from your glass wounds, Dr. Pumpkin gave you drugs."

"But that's different."

"Really?"

"For sure it is."

"How. What do you mean?"

"Well first, I wasn't competing against others in an event. And second they were necessary to help me deal with a physical wound. To help me get better and to deal with my pain."

"I know right."

"But who is to say when it's ok to use drugs?"

"I think its common sense. If you're using them to gain an unfair advantage, like these athletes are, then that should not be allowed. And so I don't have any sympathy for them."

"I agree with the committee. Everyone should be playing by the same rules."

"I think the whole situation is ugly."

"It's not acceptable."

"Didn't they know they would be tested and would get caught?"

"Does anyone know what types of drugs they used?"

"Maybe they really didn't know."

"How could someone be so stupid, and not know what they are putting inside their body?"

"It's possible."

"How?"

"Let's take this cookie."

"I'll take it. I'm hungry."

"No. I'm being serious." Puff was adamant to make his point. "Okay fine. You take it. And you eat it. So do you know what's in the cookie?"

"Well, I see little chocolate chips."

"Okay. And what else?"

"I see where you're going with this Puff. Taking some kind of drug because you have no choice, or it's forced on you, or because you didn't expect a drug to exist in the first place, is different. But I still don't understand how people could go on television afterwards, and claim innocence."

"What a waste."

None of it made sense. It was all over the news. Over forty athletes had been stripped off their medals within the past three days, including twenty seven on this day. And there were hundreds more athletes that tested positive for drugs, even though they didn't win a medal. In a racing hurdles event, all but two entrants tested positive. The committee ended up awarding one person with the gold medal, and the other with the silver medal. Because of the lack of viable entrants, there was no third place winner for that event.

Apparently we were late receiving the news. The issue of positive drug tests had been going on all week.

When the news reported the winners of that days' races for the track and field events, they did so with a caution. The news commentators had to specifically state whether or not that athlete had been tested or not. People wondered if the results were even legitimate. I'm sure all species wondered. The issue had reached scandalous proportions.

By the time it was my turn to take a bath, it was past midnight. The lights had been turned out in the hotel room. I soaked in the tub for quite a long time. It had been a long day, with all the travel. When I came out of the tub, I wondered if anyone was still awake. The reflections of the city lights from the adjacent buildings allowed for enough visibility to look around the room. Mostly everyone had fallen asleep. There was no chatter. Before lying down next to Petrina, I noticed Puff was missing. I wondered if Petrina was asleep.

"Where is Puff?" I asked her.

"He just left. He told me he was going down the hall. He said he saw an ice machine," she whispered back.

"I know. I saw him leave. And that was over thirty minutes ago. That was before I got into the bath tub. Shouldn't he have been back by now?"

"Maybe he got lost."

"We should wake up Popeye. Maybe we should go look for him."

Popeye reluctantly opened his eyes. We were touching his face to arouse him because we didn't want to wake anyone else. He agreed there could be an issue and suggested we go look for him. So Popeye, Petrina and I went out of the hotel room and into the hall to see if we could locate Puff. We found the ice machine but he was nowhere to be found.

"Where could he have gone?" wondered Popeye.

"He told me he would be right back," clarified Petrina.

Popeye suggested we go downstairs to the lobby of the hotel. I didn't mind. It gave me a chance to go for a stroll. And it meant I could ride in the hotel elevator.

"Where are you going?" inquired Pavneet. She had popped her head outside the room. I motioned with my hand, telling her to come with us. And we searched the whole area, in and around the hotel lobby, but he wasn't there either.

"Ask that person. At the front desk," it was suggested.

Popeye moved closer to the front desk. The lady peered over the counter.

"Excuse me Ms. Person. Did you see a pumpkin come downstairs?"

"No. Sorry," she said. And then continued on with her original business. She never gave us a second look.

She wasn't much help. She seemed busy, even though she wasn't really talking to anyone. We decided to go outside to see if we could find him. And there were so many people littered on the streets. I had always thought that people had the same sleeping habits as us. But it was hard to blame them. I mean it was such a warm evening.

At first glance, we could not spot him. But as we continued to walk up the street, Pavneet found him. She pointed, and said 'there'. Puff was standing on a corner up the street. He was talking to children. Unsupervised. That was dangerous. Very dangerous. We were warned to never speak with people. To only engage and communicate with people if the situation was an emergency. We wondered what could have possibly happened.

As we approached we yelled out 'Puff'. And we observed the most ghastly thing. He put a cigarette in his mouth.

"Aw!" we exclaimed.

Was he smoking a cigarette? How could he be so stupid? After all the news about the harm of drugs that we heard and read about. The dangers that it could cause the body. All the terrible medical issues that could result. And he ignored all of that advice, and smoked a cigarette? Seriously? What a senseless act. The children must have given it to him. They must have encouraged him to smoke. Who knows? They may have even forced him. People could be such a bad influence on our lives.

Popeye bolted from our group, yelled 'wait here' to us, and rushed towards him. He grabbed Puff away by his arm and was practically carrying him back towards us. He swatted the cigarette away from his hand.

"What in the world are you doing?" he screamed.

"What? I wasn't doing anything," I heard Puff say.

"You should not be smoking. It's not good for your body, Puff."

"They asked me if I wanted to try. I wanted to see what it was like."

"Why?"

"I don't know."

"Seriously?" I added, when Popeye and Puff had arrived within earshot.

"That is not acceptable."

"Why are you even out here?"

Puff didn't seem to have any answers. His explanations were ridiculous. He said he was hot. But with the air conditioning in the hotel, it was actually warmer outside. He said he wanted to go for a walk. He could have walked around the hotel. I mean he did walk down the hall.

"Actually I do feel kind of sick. My stomach doesn't feel right. And my head is starting to hurt."

"You have broken a lot of rules today Puff. I can tell you there are going to be repercussions from this. First you left the hotel. And…"

"Why were you talking with those children?" I interrupted.

"Are you insane?" added Pavneet.

"They said they were my friends."

It looked like he was going to let out his seeds. He was holding his stomach. We had to hold him steady as we re-entered the hotel. I looked back at the children. I could see the smoke exhaling out of their mouths. Like it was some kind of witch craft.

Once we were back in our hotel room some pumpkins had awakened. It was probably due to the moaning and groaning noises made by Puff.

Patricia was up and made inquiries as to where we had been. Popeye took her aside and told her everything. About Puff talking to children. And smoking. She wasn't pleased. Neither was I. Puff was an idiot. He headed straight for the toilet. We could hear his dreadful sounds. His stomach must be really hurting. The noises woke up everyone else in the room. He must have been in the bathroom for over a half an hour. And when he finally came out, he was about to lay on the bed right next to me.

"Oh no you're not. Not here. You go lie on the floor," I demanded.

The breath odor coming from his mouth was gross. It smelt like burnt fire, if that made any sense. And not just from his mouth. His whole body smelt gross. I mean, the terrible smell from the city can stick to our skin like glue. But this was worse than the usual trash-like aroma from the city. I felt like telling him to go have a bath. But I didn't care. I mean it was his body after all. If he wanted to mess it up, then good for him.

What a day. Coming to the city was never short of moments. Puff finally fell asleep. He had mentioned that his head had stopped hurting. He never did let out his seeds. Not that I know of anyways.

The next morning, we received the greatest news. News that we had been waiting for months. The new babies had been born back at the patch. And this was especially good news for Plato. He was expecting two siblings. Word came to us that Plato had two new baby brothers. Aw. This was incredibly exciting. He was so happy. He couldn't believe that this day had finally arrived. The elders had been trying so hard to get Plato siblings for many years. And after so many years of hard work, and testing, and re testing of birth seeds, they had achieved their goal. Plato had shown incredible patience during this whole time. He could never understand why it was taking so long. He didn't think it would be difficult. But for whatever reason it took us many years.

And as soon as he heard the news, he wanted to go home right away. Without delay. And Puff also wanted to leave to welcome his new baby sister.

That morning, Plato and Puff checked the city bus schedule. The bus would take them to the train that passed by our patch. While those two would go back home, the rest of us would go to the stadium and watch the closing ceremony of the Olympics. Plato and Puff would miss the event, but that had become an afterthought. We were concerned about those two going home by themselves. We were generally aware that we should stay together and travel in groups. For our own protection. It was only one more day, said Popeye. But Plato was desperate. He wanted to welcome his two brothers into the world, as soon as pumpkinly possible.

While we waited in the hotel lobby, Patricia coordinated their travel arrangements with the hotel receptionist. We were told that Plato and Puff could obtain a bus ticket from the hotel. We had to wait quite a long time. I started to get restless. Making the travel arrangements seemed to be taking forever. I decided to go outside. I was curious about Puff, and where he had met those children. The ones that gave him that cigarette. I wondered if they were still there. At that same spot. So I walked up the street and turned at the corner. I found myself in an alley. And even though the sun was shining brightly, it was a very dark, unlit alley way. Even in the morning.

I saw a man. And for some reason he caught my attention. He was drinking straight out of a bottle. I mean it must have been a bottle, even though it was inside a brown paper bag. I watched him from a distance. I didn't want to go near him. He was leaning against a building wall. He seemed to be looking left and right, as if he was waiting for someone. Then he noticed me. He saw me starring at him. It may have made him feel uneasy. Uncomfortable. There was no one else around.

"Are you by yourself pumpkin? I thought pumpkins weren't supposed to be by themselves," he yelled out to me.

He didn't seem uncomfortable any longer. He took a few steps towards me. I thought that I should go back to the hotel.

"I'm not alone. And my name is not pumpkin. My name is Pashelle." I was starting to get annoyed with other species. Why were they always calling me pumpkin? I mean I did have a name. He didn't seem too interested in that. Or too concerned that I was by myself.

"Do you want a drink pumpkin?" He offered me a drink from the paper bag. Strange how species always offered us a drink too, as a first gesture. Witches and people alike. As if it was some kind of ritual.

"Why are you alone?" I asked.

"I'm not alone either pumpkin. My friends are here. Jack Daniels. Johnie Walker. We're all here. We're all having a good time."

"That's it. You only have two friends?"

"Oh I have lots of friends pumpkin. Too many to count. Ummm… Let me see. There's Jim Beam. Glen Fiddich. They're just not with me today. Have you heard of Pappy Van Winkle?"

"I've never heard of any of those people. I mean I don't know any people at all," I said.

He continued to take tiny steps towards me. As if not to alarm me, or to realize that I knew he was getting closer. When he arrived to only a few feet in front of me, he reached out his hand and was ready to give me the brown paper bag. I really didn't want to take it from him. I mean who knows what type of drink it was. I was thirsty. But not that thirsty. I took a few steps backwards. I didn't want him to force it on me. And when he realized I wasn't going to take the bottle, he placed it inside his coat pocket.

"I've got to go," he announced. "Have a good one pumpkin."

And with that goodbye, he staggered passed me and walked towards a parked bus. He must have been tired. He wasn't walking very straight. It was as if he was about to fall over on one side. I followed him, keeping my distance. I needed to get back to the hotel. I saw him climb into the bus drivers' seat, while I joined the rest of my friends outside.

We said goodbye to Plato and Puff as they boarded the bus. I gave Plato a big hug. What a special day it was for him. He was beaming with excitement. I was going to do the same with Puff, but he mentioned that he was still feeling sick. I didn't want him to experience an accident. His stomach must have felt double queezy. So I ensured I kept my distance. Puff claimed he was sick from the excitement. But we knew the real reason why. It was because of that smoking and those sickening drugs. That seemingly disgusting activity.

I remembered when Plouffe was born. I was so nervous to meet her for the first time. And I was even more nervous when Patrice was born. I wasn't sure why. You could never get tired of greeting new pumpkins in this world. I always thought that we would have more siblings in our family. But the doctors say it was difficult to maintain the seeds for redevelopment. They called the process cloning. I should ask Dr. Pumpkin if I will have more siblings. It sure would be nice. It's so cool watching pumpkins learn and grow. Watching them take their first baby steps. Utter their first words. It's like re living your life again, thru another set of eyes. It could be so enlightening.

The closing ceremony was fun. It was a spectacular show. There were actors, and dancers and a band that played music. With lots of instruments. Like violins, drums, and saxophones. Too many instruments to name. On the giant television they showed a movie. It was about the history and culture of New Surrey City. There were gymnasts who performed acrobatic acts, and actors and actresses who performed other acts, each one symbolizing a positive attribute of the city and the country. All of us were in awe. I heard many people comment afterwards how proud they were to live in this city.

And that was that. The Olympics were over. The two week party was finished. I overheard many people comment how sad they were that the Olympics had ended. That it was the best time of their lives. Species had travelled from all over the world to watch.

It reminded me of my birthday party that would happen any week. Maybe upon returning to the patch. I was so looking forward to it. I looked forward to my party every year. And watching all these people have such a good time only fueled my excitement. When we exited the stadium there were people dancing in the streets. Listening to music. Laughing. Having a really great time. They said it brought the city and country together. And it was such a warm and toasty evening. I was sure my party would be just the same. I almost felt like having my birthday party that night. Right there. Right then.

But our feeling of excitement soon disappeared. Almost immediately, when we got back to the hotel. It was the most disappointing news ever. The bus that returned Plato and Puff to the city train was involved in an accident. It was on the news. On television.

"The bus was carrying 26 passengers. And two pumpkins. Four passengers had received only slight injuries. And one passenger was taken to the hospital for further evaluation. We are told, however, one of the pumpkins was thrown out of an open door, and was subsequently crushed under an oncoming vehicle."

"Aw!" we exclaimed.

"Transit is suggesting to take an alternative route away from the Elliott corridor, as both lanes on the route heading north have been temporarily closed off. And also of interest, one of the passengers who was interviewed at the scene, questioned the sanity of the driver. The passenger has requested that tests be conducted on the bus driver to determine if he was driving under the influence. We will have more on this story as it develops."

What? A pumpkin was thrown from the bus? We were in shock. We couldn't believe it. We didn't know what to think. That must have been the bus that was carrying Plato and Puff. We didn't know if it was Plato or Puff that had been crushed. We sat in our hotel room in silence. There was no way for us to contact either of them. Patricia called the local city police to try to get more details.

"Can you please ask the pumpkin? Please ask him to call us," she said.

"What do you mean?" she asked. And then there was silence.

"What is the person saying Patricia?" asked Mr. Pumpkin.

"I don't understand. This accident was hours ago," she noted.

"He is orange. And I don't know his name. It's either Plato or Puff."

"Well I don't know. Because apparently the other pumpkin has died."

We waited for Patricia, as she tried to get more details. Her voice was desperate. It was quivering as she spoke. Tears had already formed in her eyes. It was difficult for her to remain calm.

"I am being calm. I'm just asking you for your help," she said, as she raised her voice. "And my name is Patricia."

She was trying to get as much information from the local police about the accident as possible. And she provided instructions to the local police about where we were staying and our phone number.

Patricia thought she should go to the scene of the accident to find out first-hand what happened. But Ms. Pumpkin advised there was no point. That we should wait for more information.

"They told me the second pumpkin just ran away. Which is really odd," Patricia explained.

"That is strange."

"Witnesses had explained that after the bus was evacuated, the pumpkin ran off," Patricia said again.

"Well. Let's just wait."

And wait we did. We seemed frozen in time. Hours had passed. It was at least a few hours before we finally received a phone call. It was Plato. He was the one that called Patricia.

Plato explained what happened. Puff said he was feeling sick. He got out of his seat and approached the bus driver, while the bus was still in motion. He repeatedly told the driver that he needed to exit the bus to go outside and get some fresh air. And it was during those fatal moments the bus rammed into a parked car ahead. The front doors of the bus inexplicably opened. Maybe because of the collision. And Puff was standing right there, near the door. He was thrown out of the bus and onto the street, in the next car lane. And before he had any time to react, or get out of the way, an oncoming car hit him. The car could not stop in time, and ran right over Puff. He was crushed under the weight of the car. He had no chance of survival.

Plato claimed he, himself, was fine. He hit his head as he rolled onto the bus floor after the collision. But he had escaped near death. He said he asked many people to borrow a cell phone, but no one helped him. And since he was so close to the train, he decided to walk to the train to get back to the patch. He had reached our patch safe and sound. And that was where Plato was calling from.

Patricia explained that Plato was trembling as he spoke, and was in tears. It was tragic. We were all saddened to hear the news about Puff. He was only eleven years old. He was survived by his two sisters. Even though I didn't really know them that well, I still felt sad for them.

Poor Plato. To have witnessed such a horrific event. He was on his way home to welcome his new siblings. Instead of feeling elation along the way, he was dealt with this terrible trajedy. While he was ready to welcome new life into this world, he also saw death up close. It was a contrast of two different states of emotion. He had witnessed death and life, in mere hours of each other. Life and death events could be so traumatic. Death was so sudden. And final. Life was so endless. Limitless. Death so depressing. Life so hopeful. Death could happen to anyone, at any time. Sometimes without any warning. No one could really prepare for it. I mean there was no way Puff could have known of his doomed fate when he boarded that bus. That his death was imminent. It could happen to anyone. Death does happen to everyone.

I was filled with a sudden surge of emotion. So many different feelings were going thru my mind. It was so important to live life to its fullest. To leave no stone unturned. To do the things you want to do. And in order to do this, you must lead a healthy lifestyle. To exercise. Take care of your body. To enhance your mind. To eat and drink sensibly. To think the bus driver may have been under the influence of drugs was to think he was the one who deserved to die. I felt a lot of anger. It was such a careless act. I mean I was glad no person died. But a part of me wished the bus driver died, instead of Puff. He deserved that fate. I could not believe that people could do this random, selfless act, with no regard for anyone else. He failed in his responsibility to take care of those in his care.

We watched the news all evening, to see if they would provide more details. But it was not necessary. We had all the news that we needed. I saw the remains of the accident on television that evening. There were four cars crammed into each other. With the bus at the back. The passengers had spoken to the reporters about what happened. The news said the bus driver had no comment at the time. I mean what was he supposed to say? That he was driving the bus while on drugs? He had lost his awareness. The accident was his fault. He was unfit to drive the bus. The death of Puff was his fault. It made me more furious each time I thought about it.

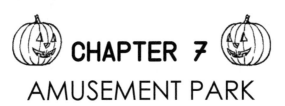

CHAPTER 7
AMUSEMENT PARK

When I awoke the next morning, I expected we would return to the patch. But Patricia presented us with a nice surprise. She had made plans for us to visit the Fleetwood Amusement park.

We all talked about Puff. That if we wanted to go back home instead, we could. But we all decided to visit the park. We thought maybe it would take our minds away from the tragedy. I mean there was nothing much we could do. We didn't need to collect his body. The police had told Patricia that he was unrecognizable. That there was very little left of him. The city had cleaned the streets of his remains.

We all knew many pumpkins would be home, to support his friends and family. There was nothing for us to do at the patch. It was not necessary for us hurry back. That only Patricia would return. And also Petal. He was visibly upset with the news and was very close to Puff. He wanted to return to support his family.

I had always wanted to visit this park. For as long as I could remember. I had mentioned it to the elders numerous times prior to our trip. That it would be a shame to be so close to the park, and not visit. The answer to my request had always been no. Patricia, herself, was convinced that it would be a good outing for us. She had already made the proper arrangements. To stay an extra night in the hotel. And it wasn't difficult. Hotel availability was not an issue, as many guests left that morning to go back to their own homes. The Olympics had concluded. We wanted to take our minds off Puff.

So while Patricia and Petal boarded a bus to return, we boarded a bus that would take us to the park. I was excited.

And when we arrived at the park, the first thing we did was ride on bikes. None of us really knew how. I mean we didn't have any bikes in the patch. We didn't have any need for them. Few pumpkins knew how to ride a bike. We saw children race around a track. It seemed simple. It seemed dangerous, and exciting at the same time. We were provided with bikes that would allow us to reach the pedals. They had two additional wheels on either side, so it wouldn't tip over. They were called training wheels. And we all certainly needed those extra wheels. If it wasn't for them, my bike would have tipped over numerous times during the ride. It was lack of practice. And even with the extra wheels, it was very difficult to keep it upright on its proper wheels, and in balance. The track had twists and turns. There were stretches where the track was downhill and I didn't even need to peddle. I loved going fast. As I came around the final turn, I braked. I slowed to a crawl. And slowly rode to the bike pit.

"Wow Pashelle. That was cool." I was greeted at the finish line by Penelope and Piper.

"That was fun. We should ask if we can get some of these bikes. It would be a riot to do this every day," I said.

"Too bad Peleton didn't come with us. He mentioned to me once that he would love to ride on a bicycle," replied Porter.

We stood and watched as all the other cyclists came to a finish. And all of them seemed to arrive back safely without incident. Except for Peter. He wasn't so lucky. He was racing, ready to make the turn around the final corner. He seemed to be going really fast. Like way too fast.

"Slow down Peter," I heard Peanut scream out from afar.

I was thinking that he needed to apply the brakes.

The final stretch of the track was all downhill. And he was going way too fast. It didn't seem he would be able to slow down enough to make the final turn properly. And the training wheels wouldn't help.

Instead of slowing and making the final turn, he went straight and flew off the track. The bike went flying into a sand pit. And he, himself, flew into a lake.

"Aw!" we exclaimed.

The small body of water was like a swimming pool. It was mentioned that some children did this on purpose on the final turn. As a last adventure. They let the bike fall in a pile of sand, and then took a leap into the warm water. I had seen this with a few children when we first arrived at the track. And I was thinking of jumping into the lake myself. But this was not likely with Peter. I'm certain that was not planned. I mean pumpkins don't swim.

I could see him bobbing up and down in the water. He was trying to stay afloat but it was difficult. He was unable to get himself out of the water. He was floating. He needed help. He was yelling for help. He was desperate to keep his head above the water. I could see him flailing his arms, up and down, in and out. The children who were playing in the lake hadn't noticed this. They didn't help him. Not even the life guard who was on duty.

Porter, Peanut and I ran towards the life guard who was seated atop a tall ladder. We shouted for help. Peter needed his help.

After several yells, the life guard finally took notice. He climbed down from his high chair. He didn't seem to be in a rush though.

"Our friend needs help. He can't swim!" we said.

"Who is that?"

"There. In the water," we pointed. "Peter Pumpkin!" we cried.

The life guard didn't get in the water. Instead, he took hold of a long wooden pole. And reached it out towards Peter.

"Grab this pumpkin," he said.

"Peter! Grab the pole!" we screamed.

The guard was careful to place the pole right near Peters' hands, and after several swings he was able to latch onto it. Probably with dear life. The guard pulled the pole, and Peter, out of the water. None of the life guards seemed overly concerned about the situation. Instead, they were having a chuckle. They seemed amused by the whole incident. For a brief moment I was concerned. But with so many people around to help, my concern was probably over exaggerated. It was actually kind of funny. We all ended up having a moment in the end. When Peter came out of the lake, he was drenched.

"Thank you Mr. Person," he said.

"It's all in a days' work," he guard replied.

I looked at Peter. He still looked frightened, even after he was rescued from the water. His eyes were wide open. Or maybe it was the cold water that made him look stiff. His body and glasses were drenched.

"Don't you know how to use the breaks?" I asked him.

"Why were you going so fast?" Peanut inquired.

The others had arrived onto the scene. We were all gathered around him to ensure he was okay. He was inspecting his glasses. He was concerned they had been broken. But he was calm. I mean he knew he was out of danger.

"I couldn't breathe. I was scared for my life, for a moment there. My finger got stuck in the handle bar. I didn't know what to do. I think I was going too fast. I didn't think I could stop in time. So when I saw the child in front of me jump into the water…I didn't think I had a choice. Instead of crashing into the sand, I jumped too."

We waited for the other pumpkins to complete their bike rides, collected our thoughts, and reorganized. We left the bicycle area of the park, and walked towards the playground section. Where there were rides. We all couldn't wait. I couldn't wait. And the first ride I noticed was the roller coaster. We couldn't miss it. With the tracks soaring into the sky. It seemed dangerous and scary. It seemed like a blast.

"It's the roller coaster. The roller coaster. I want to go on that ride. Come on everybody!" I screamed.

And I raced over to watch that fast moving train, hoping everyone else would follow me. And follow they did. They were just as inquisitive about that ride as I was. I ended up standing right next to a fence, waiting for everyone else to form in around me. I was so excited.

But I saw their fear. I turned and looked into Porters' eyes. They were wide open. His mouth agape. Penelope and Ms. Pumpkin appeared as if their stems would fall off, if they went on that ride. And Paris, Paige and Portia didn't even have the courage to stand near the fence. Peter, still soaking wet, was sitting on a bench cleaning his glasses. It didn't seem as if anyone else wanted to ride on the roller coaster. I watched the train for a few moments. It was at the top of the track. And I followed it, as it raced downhill. And as the train came roaring down, right to where we were standing, at the bottom of the track, it took an incredible sharp turn. It zoomed right by us. I heard the screams of the children. We all did.

"My goodness."

"Oh no. Not for me thank you."

"Me neither."

"Come on you guys. Who is with me?" I pleaded.

No one replied.

"Well I'm going," I said, as I moved towards the starting lineup.

"Pashelle. Are you sure you really want to do this? Why don't we all go on another ride? There are so many of them here."

"Please Mr. Pumpkin. You know I have waited for so long to ride on the roller coaster. For as long as I can remember."

"It might not be safe for you."

"But look at everyone else. They're on the ride."

Mr. Pumpkin knew that there was no way he was going to stop me. I ignored him and waited at the end of the line.

The excitement was building as my turn drew nearer. And slowly but surely, others came to my side, and joined me in line. First Pavneet. Then Polo arrived. Then Popeye. And when it was our turn to sit in a train car, Precious, Patrice and Petrina joined us as well.

A bolt of energy rushed thru me when I sat down in the car. Guards strapped us with extra seatbelts. All seven of us sat in the same car. We managed to squeeze in together. I mean we don't take up very much room.

"Have you ever been on the roller coaster before?" asked a child. There were three girls sitting in the car ahead of us.

"No. This is our first time," replied Patrice.

"Okay. Well hold on tight. It's going to be a fast, furious and bumpy ride," the girl said.

The train started moving. First it took a slow uphill climb. We knew it was going to roar downhill when it reached the top of the track. I could hear the creek of the wheels as the train ascended upwards. The tension was ripping thru the air. I had waited my whole life for this moment. The train slowed to a crawl when it reached its highest point on the track. And I could see the mountains off in the distance. I could see all the people and other creatures on the ground. And the many rides. But that view only lasted a brief moment. Because wow! Did we ever move fast. We flew downhill. My heart stopped on that first descent. I heard the children scream out. And then it swung around a corner so fast, that it seemed like the train was going to fly off the track. I had to do everything I could to stay in my seat. Because if I didn't, it would certainly result in death. I hung onto the front rail with dear life. Even closing my eyes on some of the sharp turns. The feeling was incredible. Speeding along that fast was amazing. My stomach tightened with each turn.

I didn't start breathing again until the train had come to a complete stop. It may have been the most exhilarating two minute experience that we would ever experience.

"My heart almost stopped," said Patrice.

"Wow. I cannot believe we just rode on the roller coaster," said Petrina.

That's for sure. When the ride was over, all I kept thinking to myself was 'wow I rode the roller coaster'. I could hear the children say the same thing, as we exited from the raceway track.

"Let's go again," I said.

"No. No," said Mr. Pumpkin, waving his index finger in front of my face. "We're not going to wait here for another thirty minutes while you go on this ride again."

That made sense. Since we needed to stay together, all the others were forced to wait for us. We decided to move onto other rides.

The bumper cars were fun. And we were allowed to ride in the cars with no children. The security guards reasoned it would be much safer if it was just us pumpkins on the driving surface. So for two races the children watched us. All the bumper cars were full of pumpkin drivers. But it proved to be an exercise in futility, because none of our legs were long enough to reach the foot pedal to move the cars. So we had to use our imagination. We rode two per car. One knelt down and pressed the foot pedal down with our hand, while the other maneuvered the steering wheel. Each of us had one turn at the steering wheel, and a turn at the foot pedal. It was very difficult. But it was fun. Except for one instance, when Pavneet was driving. She rammed our car into the front of another bumper car so hard, that my head jumped up and hit a metal bar.

"Wow. Gotcha Pannette," said Pavneet. I had to climb out from inside the car to see Pannette's reaction. And while we were still gloating in our success, Peter smashed into us. He hit us so hard that his glasses popped up and down.

We ate cotton candy.

We saw a person perform magic tricks with a deck of playing cards. It reminded me the ways witches and warlocks could act, performing their craft. There was one trick where the magician had to guess an unknown card that was in my hand. And how he knew, I will never know.

"Pick a card," he said. "Any card." For some reason, he knew I chose the seven of diamonds. He performed other tricks as well. He pulled out the four queens from the deck and showed them to me. And then he mixed them back in with the rest. He began shuffling them all up. And when he finished shuffling, he showed me the cards again. One by one. And magically there were only three queens. One of them had disappeared into thin air. I couldn't believe it. Where did the queen of hearts go? He waited for a few minutes, looked straight into my eyes, and then he proceeded to pull the fourth queen from out of my sac. Aw. He must have been a warlock.

"Are you a warlock?" I asked.

"No pumpkin. I'm only a magician."

We played games for prizes. Pavneet won a prize. She was able to throw three darts thru a minuscule hole in succession. She won a stuffed tiger. Lucky for her. The rest of us weren't so lucky. The keeper wanted us to play more. He said the more we played, the more money he could claim thru the city. I heard his pleas of 'come back', 'come back', as we moved onwards thru the amusement park.

At another table for a different game, I managed to throw some small rubber balls into open pop bottles. And I needed to bury four in a row in order to claim a prize. But the most I could sink was three in a row. I missed out on a prize. I attempted numerous times. On that one occasion, when I managed to bury three in a row, the fourth had bounced off the rim. So close yet so far away, I muttered to myself. I didn't have very much success in sinking many more rubber balls after that one opportunity. Actually not a single one, after that fateful miss. I guess I lost my touch.

The park was so crowded. So many people. And children. It was such a beautiful sunny day, with a nice cool breeze. We ate lunch at a very crowded restaurant. Everyone was staring at us. Especially the children. It's quite common. I mean we could be so popular when we visited the city. They acted like they had never seen pumpkins before. We could draw such an attraction. I didn't eat much except french fries. They were very greasy. But they still tasted really good. My feet were tired from all the walking around. It was nice to take a rest. We had a chance to watch television in a big crowded theatre, but we didn't think it was necessary. We were told it was a taped showing of the closing ceremony of the Olympics from the night before. So we skipped the theatre movie.

We went on more rides in the afternoon. We rode on the ferris wheel. That was nowhere near as fast and exciting as the roller coaster, but it was just as fun. We reached so high up in the sky that we could see for miles away.

"I see our patch."

"Really?"

"Where?"

"Over there," Polo pointed.

"Are you sure? Because I don't think that's even the right direction."

"You're just making that up."

"Yeah. Actually, I don't know which way it is."

"We should have asked Mr. Pumpkin. He would have known."

I'm sure that if we knew which way to look, we would have seen our patch. I may have been able to see my house. Our patch was close to the water. Burnaby Bay. And we could see the water to our left. But we didn't know to look forward and to our left. Or to look behind us and to our left.

We went on another ride, which took us to a house. It was called the haunted house. We were told that ghosts used to live there. Or still did. And because of that, many pumpkins didn't even enter. They waited outside. I wanted to see inside the house. There were so many children around us, I thought they would protect us if the ghosts did anything. I mean ghosts were always up to no good. We walked around the house, wandering thru the corridors, inspecting the furniture and the pictures hung up on the walls. We could hear the ghosts screaming and yelling. They were trying to scare us. But they never made a real appearance. As we exited the house thru the back door, we wondered if there were any real ghosts inside at all. That maybe it was just a ploy by the amusement park officials to entice visitors to enter the house. Which would seem kind of strange.

"That was kind of boring."

"It would have been more fun if the house had real ghosts."

"The only exciting part was when that child put on that clean white sheet."

"I know right."

It was true. There was a restless child, who had draped a white sheet over his body. He was standing near the exit door, trying to give everyone one last scare as they left the house. 'Boo', he would say. Which I thought was kind of lame. I didn't think the amusement park officials would have been pleased though. I was sure they wanted to present their own ghost like experience. Whatever that was.

By the time we exited the haunted house, it was early evening. The day just seemed to fly by. Mr. Pumpkin thought we should return back to our hotel. We thought that we had time to see the animals in the farm. That wasn't a big deal for us. None of us were interested in seeing the cows and roosters and hens and chickens. But what was really interesting about the farm though, was the chance to see the horses. And to even ride on them. Aw. I was thinking of Polo. He had always wanted to ride on a horse. Or even just to touch one. Or to see a horse up close. He would have loved it. But when we arrived to the barn, where they lived, none of them were present. That was a disappointment. A huge let down.

"Are you sure Mr. Person? How long will they be away? When are they coming back home?" asked Polo.

"The barns are closed for cleaning. The horses are out for their daily washing. You can come back tomorrow," the barn keeper said.

"All of them are gone?"

"Yes. All of them."

He didn't seem too sympathetic. He was very blunt and terse.

"Well you cannot ride on them. But if you come back in about twenty minutes, you can see them. They should be back shortly," he clarified.

"Can we?" begged Precious. She was desperate to see them too.

"It's starting to get dark. We need to get back. We still have an hour long bus ride ahead of us. It's been such a long day. And we really don't know how long they will be away. He is saying twenty minutes, but it could be much longer," said Mr. Pumpkin.

He decided it was too late. That we had to catch our bus. The park was closing for the day. Everyone seemed to be cleaning up. Our day at the amusement park was over.

Polo seemed very disappointed. He wanted to see the horses. He was begging Mr. Pumpkin. I wish I could have joined in to assist in the appeal, but I knew that once the decision was made, it would be final. The elders would not change their minds.

When we were walking back to the entry exit gate, Ms. Pumpkin was consoling Polo. I could hear her tell Polo that we would return to the park. In the near future. Polo wasn't convinced that would happen.

I mean after all, the last time he was at the park, there was no time to see the horses either. He looked really dejected. But then Ms. Pumpkin whispered something in his ear, and that seemed to lift his spirits. I wondered what was said.

Precious was sad too. But not the way Polo was. I mean Polo had wanted to ride on a horse his whole life. Precious was only two years old. Actually she was the only pumpkin born during one fateful summer. The witches sent a shot of deadly lightening into the greenhouse, and it hit the baby pumpkin seeds. The only pumpkin that survived that viscous attack was Precious. She was the lone survivor. She had always had an incredible resolve to her. She never gave up. I admired her tenacity. Not just at that special moment of birth, but her fight and resolve her whole life. The never give up mentality was evident in every action she took.

The sun was starting to disappear. We were all tired. I walked with Precious. We talked about our day. And the whole weekend. I wanted to cheer her up. I also wanted to know if she was really that disappointed that we weren't able to see the horses.

"We'll come back again Precious. For sure we will. The horses will always be here," I said.

And just as I uttered those comments and just as we neared the exit gate, we saw the horses off in the distance. We saw five or six of them. Maybe even up to ten horses. They appeared to be returning back to their homes. That was good and bad timing, I thought. It was good because they were so close to us. Bad timing, because we had just missed them.

"I want to back. To go see them," said Precious.

"We can't," Pavneet replied.

"It's too late now," added Petrina.

"Just for one second. If we leave now, then by the time we get to the barn, the horses will be home."

It was a risky thing to do leaving everyone behind. And I thought even if we got lost, which we wouldn't have, we could always ask for directions to find our way back. Precious started to slow down her pace.

She had fallen behind all of us. So I slowed with her. Pannette and Petrina noticed us dropping back, and they slowed down as well. We all fell behind the others by a good thirty feet. I don't know. And there were so many people between us two groups.

I looked into her eyes, sensing what she wanted to do. There were so many people heading for the exits that by the time anyone would notice we had disappeared, we would have reached the horse stables. And as soon as the elders turned a corner, and were hidden from our view by a building, I whispered "come on everybody."

I bolted. I looked behind me to see if anyone would follow. I mean, I always looked back. I wanted them to follow. Precious was right behind me. And then I saw Petrina and Pannette follow. And after we had reached a point of no return, I saw Pavneet racing faster than any of us.

We raced to the stables. We ran as fast as we could. We knew time was of the essence. I mean we couldn't let this opportunity slip away.

We all managed to squeeze inside the barn thru a half closed door. Everyone was just as excited as I was. And our jaws dropped when we first saw them. They looked magnificent. They were big and beautiful creatures. Their skins were wet. Each horse had their own room. That must have been nice. In my house we were so crowded in. I've never had my own room. I was envious. And I was envious of how big and strong they were.

"We have to go back. Now," said Peter, as he snuck in thru the barn door.

Where did he come from? Why did he follow us? I didn't realize he was even interested in seeing the horses.

"Wait. Just wait one second," I said.

When we saw the trainers appear from the back of the barn, we moved away from the door and hid behind a stack of hay. Since we were so small we didn't think anyone would notice we were there. We watched the trainers do a bit of cleaning around the stables, picked up some of their equipment, and they left the barn. It appeared safe for us to emerge from our hiding spot. We were all alone with the horses. We slowly inched our way to the room of the nearest horse. It was white.

The other horses were brown. We had to be careful. We didn't know if the horses wanted us in their home or not. We didn't want the horses to alert the trainers. I put my fingers to my mouth and whispered 'shh'. Their faces were so big. Especially their noses. The white colored horse stuck out her neck over the gate door, and looked down on us. She was probably wondering what we were doing there.

"Don't worry Ms. Horse. We're not going to hurt you," said Precious.

"Why is this one white? It must be special."

"Maybe it's a girl. Or a boy, and the others are girls."

"Can I sit on one?" asked Precious.

"No. Like no way. What if they don't want you to? Then they're going to call for the trainers."

"How are you going to get up there and sit on one?"

"We can use that ladder. Over there," pointed Precious.

"It must be weird having four legs."

"They have big noses."

"I know right."

"They must have extra sense of smell. What is that called?"

"Extra sense of smell?"

"No. I mean there is probably a word for that."

"That's enough time. We should go back," said Peter.

Peter was getting fidgety. I mean if he wanted to return, then why didn't he just go? Why did he come with us in the first place then?

"I agree. I think we should go back," echoed Pavneet.

But they did have a point. Even though I wanted to stay longer, we did come to see the horses. And we had. Even if it was only for just a moment. So I reluctantly nodded in agreement. We all did.

We moved towards the barn door, while waving bye to them. But just as we were about to open the door, we heard eerie witch like noises outside. We feared the worst. We could hear their conversation. Aw. We looked at each other. None of us dared to open the door at that point. We had to wait in the barn, until the witches left. We didn't want to confront them. I mean it sounded like they were right outside the barn door.

"How long are we going to wait?"

"As long as it takes."

"What if they don't leave?"

"How are we going to get out of here?"

"Let me call for help. I have a cell phone."

Peter took out the cell phone from his sac and started dialing. We waited. He had a blank look on his face though. His eyes were looking downward, while we waited for him to say something.

"It's not working. There's no signal," he finally said.

"Seriously!" I yelled.

I immediately placed my hands over my mouth. That was a mistake. We all knew it. My utterance was too loud. The witches overheard me. They stopped their murmur. They changed their tone.

"Hello my sweet little one. Who is in there?" The voice was very clear. It appeared a witch had come right near the door. I sensed her presence.

"It sounded like a delicious pumpkin Walia," said another.

"Are you inside the barn pumpkin?"

"Try the phone again. Keep trying." Peter was calling Mr. Pumpkin over and over, and he kept repeating the same thing. There was no signal. Why? Did the battery run out? And why did he even have a cell phone? Why didn't I have one? Not that I was jealous or anything.

The witches contemplated entering the barn. They were toying with the idea. They were scaring us with that talk. Talking aloud about the things they would do with us.

"Why is the door locked Wan?"

"That won't stop us. I'm sure we could open it, if we wanted to."

"I have a new idea for a pumpkin pie recipe. Should I tell you? Are you listening pumpkin? Would you like to know my idea?"

"I think we should try your new recipe Woroby. I'm tired of eating this leftover bread. And this cake has too much icing on it. All this artificial sugar couldn't possibly be good for my beautiful, perfect complexion. I would much rather have a taste of natural sweetness."

"What type of cake are you eating?"

"It tastes like cheesecake."

"Now there's an idea. Pumpkin cheesecake."

"I think there are many pumpkins inside. Enough for all of us to share in this pumpkin cheesecake. How many of you are inside?"

"Why don't you unlock the door and come outside, and play with us? What games do you like to play pumpkin?"

The horses sensed their evil presence too. They started talking to each other. 'Whoa', they screamed. The horses seemed to be calling for the trainers. And they got their wish. Because the next thing we knew, people appeared outside the barn. They were instructing the witches to vacate the area.

"This is no place for you. Get out of here," one of them ordered.

We thought the horses would be the ones to cause trouble. But they may have saved us instead. And when a trainer briefly opened the barn door to check in on the horses, it was our chance to escape. We all managed to slip outside. We ran around to the other side of the barn. We didn't want the trainers to spot us either, and for us to get into any more trouble than we were already in.

We waited there. All crunched down together, trying to hide ourselves against the barn siding. And when we heard the conversation between the witches slowly drift further away, and when we saw the trainers leave the area for a second time, we re-emerged. It was time to get out of there. We had to find our way back to the rest of the pumpkins.

The Amusement park had completely cleared. Seemingly in a heartbeat. It was only a few hours ago that there were thousands of people. And now there was no one. Except for the few volunteers doing clean-up work.

That was a close call. The whole incident gave me a rush of seeds to my head.

We walked towards the park exit. I mean I think we were heading in that direction. We had seen a sign saying exit, with a directional arrow. We must have been inside the barn for over an hour, because all of a sudden, the sun had gone down. It was getting dark. I thought we should ask for help. We should have just asked the trainers. We weren't lost. We just wanted to ensure we found the quickest exit route.

"Ask that person, if we're going the right way," I said.

Just then, we heard an owl in a tree. It must have just woken up. It said 'tweet'. Really loud. Which was really strange. It caught our attention.

"Maybe it's not an owl. Don't they say hoot?"

"It looks like an owl."

"Then why is it saying tweet?"

"It must be talking to us. I mean it's staring right at us."

"Maybe he's talking to the stuffed tiger."

"What?"

"Pavneets' tiger. Maybe the owl thinks it's real."

"Why would the owl talk to the tiger?"

"I don't know. Why would the owl talk to a pumpkin?"

"Because we're real."

"Owls are smart. We should listen to what it's trying to tell us. We should do what it says"

"I agree."

"Someone ask it."

"Excuse me. Excuse me Mr. Owl. Are you talking to us?"

We waited for the owl to respond, but he didn't seem to care about us anymore. We could see him reclose his eyes. He must still be sleepy. Not enough sleep during the day. And I can empathize with him, especially with all the noise and clamor in the park that day. How could anyone have slept thru the days' events? Petrina pressed the owl further. I mean we wanted to know what the owl had to say.

"Why are you saying tweet Mr. Owl? We thought other birds say tweet."

Again it said 'tweet'.

"Does the owl want us to tweet?"

"Yes. That must be it. It wants us to try the cell phone again. Try tweeting Peter."

"I don't know how to tweet."

Pavneet let her stuffed tiger fall to the ground and ripped the phone from Peter. She called Mr. Pumpkin herself. And lo and behold, she was able to connect. Thank goodness for that. Pavneet gave us a thumbs up. Help was on the way. She also had to explain why we didn't answer their call from before. Pavneet confirmed that we never received a call. Maybe due to the connection issue.

"It was Mr. Pumpkin. Help is on the way," she said when she hung up the phone. "He told us to stay here, where we are. They're coming to get us."

"It must have been a signal issue. Not the batteries. That happens sometimes," confirmed Pannette.

While we waited, we thought of the things we would say to the elders. To avoid trouble. And while we tried to come up with ideas, we heard the witches again. They were still lurking. They didn't leave. We could hear them off in the distance. And as the minutes passed, their voices became clearer and more lucid. We should have gone back inside the barn, but the trainers had left and they probably locked the door. And we couldn't hide in any of the other buildings. We tried to open a few of the doors, but it was way too difficult for us. The door handles were too high up to reach and turn. I tried jumping upwards to see if I could reach one of them, and possibly turn the handle, but it was no use.

The witches had arrived. There were at least three of them. There was really nowhere for us to escape. It was dark and we were out in the open. With no one to help us. They surrounded us in a heartbeat. They can move so fast. And the first thing I noticed was that stupid green smoke again. I could see it shoot out from their mouths. The smoke had surrounded Precious, as if it had eyes of its own. It was like a thick dark green cloud. And we witnessed Precious rise into the air while the witches hovered over her.

"Help me. What's happening to me?" She was helpless. She couldn't stop herself from rising upwards. Peter and Pavneet tried to grab her feet, but it was too late. Before any of us had a chance, she had risen too far. She was nearing the witches' height, which was quite a high elevation.

"Wow. Look at the little pumpkin," said a witch.

"You're flying. Come to us my sweetie pie," said another.

But they never grabbed her. They seemed just as amazed as we were, that she was rising. Floating aloft in the air. They admired their success. They were laughing as they circled her.

"Please help me!" screamed Precious.

We were helpless. We didn't know what to do. All we could do was listen to Precious' screams for help. She was waving her arms and legs. She was covered in green smoke.

Then luckily for us people arrived. And we saw the rest of the pumpkin group approaching from a distance as well. They had found us.

"Help her Mr. Person," we pleaded.

"Let the pumpkin go, you silly witch," demanded a person.

Another person had a water hose. He was probably cleaning the park grounds. And he started spraying the witches with water. They didn't like to get wet. They started to back off. And in all those delicate moments, they never did make an attempt to grab Precious. Precious just hung, helpless in the air. We were all scared for her, not knowing what was going to happen.

And as the witches backed away, the worst thing possible happened. Precious was at least twenty feet in the air. Maybe thirty. I don't know. The water cleared the green smoke. The result was that Precious took a free fall back down to earth. Her screams became louder, as she was falling feet first. We could see her feet buckle, when she crashed down to the ground. She slammed her knee very hard on the concrete floor.

And her screams turned into cries. "Oh my leg! My leg!" she yelled. She was in pain. She was bawling out. We all rushed to her side. Her hands covered her face. Damn those witches. They were so violent and cruel.

We all encouraged her to calm down. But she couldn't. She was in incredible pain. Something serious had happened to her left leg. And both of her feet. When a person tried to touch her leg, she screamed even more. Any slight movement caused extreme agony. She needed help. Right away. It was very difficult to witness her emotion. The tears were visible. They were rolling down her eyes. She was squirming around on her back, unwilling to attempt even the slightest movement on her left leg. It was disheartening to realize there was nothing any of us could do. The people couldn't do anything either, except to call for help.

"Help is coming Precious," we said.

I held her hand tightly. She held mine even tighter. We were all crowded around her. I couldn't believe what just happened. We waited, and waited, and waited for the local hospital to send an ambulance. It took forever. Not fast enough.

And all the while, Precious was in severe agony. She continued to cry. I felt so sorry for her. It was painful to watch.

The other pumpkins immediately asked questions when they saw Precious squirming on the ground. We tried to explain as best we could. That the witches cast a spell on her. That she ascended upwards, then came crashing down. They soon realized that we could do nothing except to wait for the ambulance. She was in no position to be moved.

The ambulance finally arrived after numerous agonizing minutes. With its loud siren and the flashing lights. I was so mad at them for taking so long. But at the same time, my heart felt a sense of relief. I hoped the medical staff knew what to do. In a way, I wished Dr. Pumpkin was here examining her, and not a person doctor.

"Tell me where it hurts pumpkin," he asked.

"It's her knee. And leg," we replied. "She fell down from the sky. She landed right on her feet."

The doctor said he wanted to touch her leg. And despite Precious' reservations, he proceeded to do so anyways. But only for one second.

"It could be broken," he said.

The medical staff looked at each other, as if to say 'what do we do with her'. And I felt like telling them 'Fix her. Like right now'.

"Okay. Let's get her on the bed. Let's take her to the hospital," he concluded.

"Where? To the pumpkin hospital?" asked the other doctor.

"No. Here. I think we should take some x rays," said the first.

"Maybe."

"Well we can't leave her here. How is she going to get back to the patch?"

"No. We don't have time to take her back to the patch," Mr. Pumpkin said.

The two doctors were extremely careful to place her onto a bed. They moved the bed inside the ambulance. All the while Precious was pleading for help. Piper and Ms. Pumpkin also climbed into the ambulance to comfort her. Before the ambulance drove off, Mr. Pumpkin had a short conversation with the medical staff. I wondered what they told him.

Mr. Pumpkin then turned his attention to us. He was super mad. For leaving the group, for one. Popeye had been livid too, but he didn't say anything. It was very difficult for any of us to hold our emotions back.

"What are you doing out here?" Mr. Pumpkin demanded.

"Why did you have to bring Precious on your misguided mission?" asked Portia. She was starring right at me.

It was difficult to explain why we were there. The whole reason was because we wanted to see the horses. I mean, how did we know that the witches would appear and cast a spell on her?

"How could all of you be so irresponsible?" asked Mr. Pumpkin.

None of us had an explanation. And there was really nothing that we could do about it. We were all so saddened about what had happened. We feared what would now happen to Precious.

The people ordered us out of the Amusement park. They didn't want to listen, nor take part in our conversation.

It was a sombre bus ride back to our hotel. It was difficult to come to grips with everything that happened on our trip. First the death of Puff. And now we didn't know what to think about Precious. What a terrible accident. If I didn't want to go see the horses, then none of this would have happened. Was this all my fault? I could sense Portia staring at me all the way back to the hotel.

None of us felt like talking. We were all thinking of the worst. But I didn't force Precious. She wanted to come on her own. And I didn't make her rise in the air. It was the witches.

"The people think she may have shattered and destroyed her left knee. And may have broken bones in both feet," Mr. Pumpkin finally confessed.

People doctors had told Mr. Pumpkin that this needed to be confirmed with x-rays. That they would let us know the results in the next few days. Only after reviewing the x rays would the doctors know the full severity of the damage.

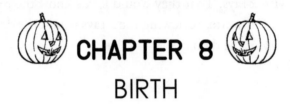

CHAPTER 8
BIRTH

Waiting for the news on her condition was difficult. None of us knew what to think. It was a very stressful time. Many pumpkins had asked numerous questions of me during those few days. The elders wanted to know what happened. All of the details and circumstances of us leaving the group. And how she fell to the ground. They said I showed a lack of judgement in leaving the group. That they doubted Precious would have left the group by herself. That she only did so because of me and my friends.

"You should have known better Pashelle. Precious is not even two years old," said Mr. Pumpkin.

I was expecting a very harsh punishment for my actions. But much to my surprise, I received none. None whatsoever. It was almost as if the elders had taken full responsibility for the incident. That they should have kept proper tabs on all of us, including Precious. I mean that was the only explanation I could think of.

It was difficult to take our minds off the accident. But we needed to carry on with our everyday lives. And one of the first things my friends and I did upon our return to the patch was to visit with Plato and his two new brothers. We went to visit them the first chance we had. There were sixteen new pumpkins born within a three week period. And the elders were expecting another five more births in the coming days. Nine pumpkins were born earlier in the year, during the spring.

It was amazing to see his two brothers. It was amazing to see all of the baby pumpkins.

"My goodness. He looks exactly like you Plato."

"I know right."

"You must be so proud."

"I remember the day Patrice was born, like it was yesterday," I said.

"They look so cute."

"Their fingers are so small."

"I can't believe I was that tiny once," I added.

I noticed the baby's mouth was moving, but I couldn't hear anything due to the constant chatter of talking pumpkins. So I moved my face closer to his, and I thought he said Plato.

"What is he saying? Did he just say Plato?" I asked.

"Plato," the baby said again.

"What?"

"I think he's trying to say Plato."

"What? Why? How does he know your name?"

"Because they know who I am. I don't know what else to say besides 'my name is Plato'. Over and over. Maybe I'm too nervous," Plato explained.

"Don't you think it might be better to say their names instead? What if they think their own names are Plato?"

Plato just shrugged his shoulders. He seemed to not care about that. He looked like he didn't have a care in this world. And I could understand. I mean what kind of dialogue can you have with a pumpkin who is not even a week old?

"What are their names?"

"This little guy is named Pandion," said Plato. He was holding him in his arms.

"And is he Pericles?" asked Petrina. She was referring to the pumpkin that Ms. Pumpkin was holding down the hall.

"Yes. That little one is Pericles," he confirmed.

"My goodness. His stem is so small."

"Pericles is so cute."

"Oh. You're not pronouncing his name correctly. It's Pericles."

"What. Say that again."

"Pericles. As in 'Per-i-kleez.'"

"Oh. My bad."

We spent all afternoon in the birthing center in the hospital that day. And spent most of our afternoons there for several days. Within one week, Pandion and Pericles were starting to speak. At first uttering only single words at a time. Like 'Plato' and 'hello'. But soon they were stringing words together, combining them to make short sentences. They had learnt so much, only by observing others. They were so aware of their surroundings. And after those first few weeks of their lives, we could tell they were very smart. They were learning and picking up things much faster compared to the other new babies. When Plouffe remarked that it was hot, Pandion countered it was due to the sun being so close to the earth. And when Pannette said she was hungry late one afternoon, Pericles wondered why, because it wasn't dinner time yet. I was so amazed at their intelligence level at such an early age.

By the third week, they had taken small baby steps. Plato had missed those first few steps. But he didn't care in the least. He was just pleased that they were healthy. And as each day passed, their skin color grew more orange. Their stems were growing on a daily basis. Their bodies were getting bigger. They were rounding into shape. Plato was so proud.

Pericles, Pandion and all the other baby pumpkins would stay in the birthing center for up to six months. But it varied, as it depended on their own individual development. And also, it depended upon where they would eventually live. Pericles and Pandion would naturally live with Plato. He would be their main caregiver, until they could look after themselves. And Plato needed to be ready for such a drastic life change. And there were other pumpkins who were born from a new and undeveloped seed line. They would be the first in their family, with no brothers or sisters. So they could stay in the birthing center longer, as they would need to be placed with a family who they were not related. I was sure there were a multitude of other factors. I mean I had little experience with any of it.

We were actually in the hospital one afternoon, when we received the sad news about Precious. On the day following the accident, she had lost her left leg. It was amputated. It had become so damaged by the fall that people could not save it. Most of the bones in her knee had been smashed. And they feared the damage to her leg would result in a spread of some kind of body desease. So they contacted us here in the patch, to confirm the amputation procedure should proceed. Since Precious did not have any brothers or sisters, Patricia gave the okay to the doctors, to do whatever was necessary to save her life. She would live but she would never be able to walk again. It was a tragedy. Poor Precious. She had been in the New Surrey City hospital for a few days, receiving treatment while recovering from her injuries. She was scheduled to be released and returned to the patch three days after the accident. People had constructed a special wheelchair that would fit the physical characteristics and size of her body so that she could move around.

It was very quiet in the patch during those few days. Pumpkins were normally a very social species, and loved to engage in active conversation. And laugh. And party. But it was a very saddening time. No one seemed to say anything that was not necessary.

I had overheard Payne and Paradis talk about my party one evening. And I believed it would have occurred in the next day or two. I mean I would turn eight years old in a weeks' time. But it would be cancelled. And rightfully so. I mean the last thing that was on my mind was my birthday party.

Much of our conversation centered on fixing the patch, to make it easier for Precious to move around upon her arrival. The elders held many meetings to discuss the things we needed to change in the patch to make it easier for her in the wheelchair. As far as we knew, no pumpkin had ever been confined to a wheelchair. Not in this patch anyways. I was told there was discussion about whether Precious would be given as an offering. That we may have already seen the last of her. But some elders felt that decision needed to be thought thru, and it should ultimately be hers to make. That if she did come home, we had to ensure that she would be able to travel around in the patch. And to have access in and out of our buildings. It was such a saddening predicament for her.

Pumpkins got to work, without delay.

During those few days she was in the hospital, we began to clear trees and bushes that bordered Burrowsville, in order to create a proper path from Linden road into the patch. A wooden lane was constructed for easy access to and from Burrowsville. That was necessary because Precious could make numerous trips thru that area. Furthermore, work was done to smooth out all the paths in the columns, so the wheelchair wouldn't get stuck anywhere. All the walking paths. Which meant filling up all the dirt holes.

I tried to help as much as possible. I wanted to play my role. Each pumpkin in our column tried their best to smoothen the dirt path. I did feel a bit guilty. I mean there was no real reason to go see the horses. Every time I thought about her predicament, I reminded myself of that. We shouldn't have escaped the group. But it was not just me. It was all of us. Including Precious. I tried to forget about my birthday party. I started to think that if it was her birthday, the best present I could give her was to make her feel at home. To help her.

We all helped out. Seemingly, we all felt this was the most important thing for us to do.

The engineers had renovated the buildings. In the school and the hospital, the entrances was widened. And ramps were built so that the wheelchair could roll up, and into the buildings. In the activity center, the entrance from the lobby into the lounge was widened.

There were other considerations. How would she be able to reach any of the upper levels of the buildings? The higher school years were taught on the second floor of the school. She was still too young for full time studies. But this needed to be thought out more carefully. Precious was actually the only pumpkin in her school class. Would she study with the pumpkins one year older, or one year younger. Or maybe she would receive private lessons. She would probably have to stay on the first floor.

And how would she reach the upper levels of the hospital? It was unclear if elevators would be installed. She could use crutches, if she felt comfortable enough. And although few pumpkins have had issues with physical disabilities in this patch, this could be a more common occurrence going forward. Maybe installing the elevators would be a better and permanent solution. I mean the witches seemed adamant to exterminate all pumpkins. And although there was still a possibility that she would be given as an offering, we wanted to ensure that she was felt welcome in the meantime. I mean this was her home. At this time, she had nowhere else to go. So many questions needed to be asked. So many solutions needed to be found. Every passage way in the patch needed to be looked at. We all had to view the patch from a different light.

The ambulance arrived onto Linden road three days after the accident. It was a sad day for all of us. But we knew that Precious would need to be cheered up. So we all put on our smiling faces that afternoon. I wanted to move closer to the ambulance so I could greet her properly. Give her a big hug. But my friends and I were quite far back. Too many pumpkins in front. I could not even see her sitting in the back of the ambulance when she first arrived.

"It's so sad that she will never walk again."

"She might," suggested Plato.

"I think it's highly unlikely."

"How is that supposed to happen?"

"By using the crutches."

"No. I'm saying she could walk without crutches."

"How?"

"It's possible for people to fit her with an artificial leg. A similar procedure was done in another patch. Far away. Dr. Pumpkin told me," Plato explained. "It would take time. But some people believe that it's possible she could walk again. Maybe one day."

"What would it be made of?"

"How long would it take?"

"I don't know. Probably some kind of iron alloy. And it would be custom made to fit her body. But I don't know how long it would take. Dr. Pumpkin wouldn't say. But people can do almost anything these days."

"But will they really help us? Do they have the resolve to do something for us? I mean the only thing they have done so far is cut off her leg," I said. I know it's kind of a mean and harsh thing to say. But it's reality. All we've heard on the local news was how some company built the wheelchair. They seemed so proud of that. "I bet some of them don't want to help. They don't want to waste their time. They probably want Precious as an offering," I added.

"I don't know. I'm just telling you what Dr. Pumpkin told me. What people told him."

My friends and I watched, as the medical staff took out the wheelchair. They helped Precious out of the ambulance and lifted her into the wheelchair. I could see her wipe the streaming tears from her face, even from this distance.

Once she was wheeled into the patch, the pumpkin medical staff took responsibility for her care. She was pushed to the hospital. It appeared she didn't want to turn the wheels herself. Many pumpkins approached her along the journey and tried to console her. But I didn't think she wanted the attention. I could see she had her head buried in her hands the whole way. Despite the difficulties she would have with her new life, I was thinking the last thing she would want to deal with, was all the attention we were giving her. I was really not sure though. I mean Precious had received extra attention her whole life. Mostly because she was the lone survivor of her birth class.

And she would need constant care. Probably all the time. It was obvious. We all knew it. What would her life be like now? How different would it be?

We were told she was lifted onto a bed on the first floor of the hospital. That was where she would stay for an indefinite period of time. Ms. Pumpkin told me later the doctors and medical staff tried to make her feel as comfortable as possible.

A few days had passed before my friends and I decided to visit her. Dr. Pumpkin said she had been unresponsive. She was very sad. More than sad. It was feared she fell into a depression. She refused to acknowledge anyone who visited her, let alone have a conversation with them. She lost all interest in eating. It was rumored she hadn't said a single word to anyone since her return. Which was so unlike pumpkin behavior. I know it was a unique situation. And no one could really feel what she was going thru. But it was one thing to not be social. It was another for a pumpkin to lose all interest to communicate. So when we did visit her, we wanted to do anything we could, to see if she would say something. Anything at all. I wanted her to interact with me. To respond.

"Hey Precious. How are you feeling?" I asked.

She didn't respond. She was looking off into the distance. She seemed so unattached. In a daze. She pretended like we weren't even there. Almost on purpose. We tried talking about the things that would interest her, in an attempt to cheer her up. But it was difficult.

"I entered into the beauty pageant Precious," offered Petrina. "And I might win."

Everything we said that afternoon was met with unresponsive behavior. She really didn't care. It seemed there was nothing we could say or do, that would interest her. She really was in a depression.

I didn't want to sit with my friends for very long, when we were in the lounge later that afternoon. I was not sure why. I guess I wanted to be alone for a while. Everyone was talking about Precious, and I think I needed to take a break from it all. I left them, and started walking by myself. I walked east thru the gardens of the eye. Past the arena. I went towards a hill on the eastern part of the patch. That hill was amazing. The view at the top was magnificent. I could actually see the tall buildings in New Surrey City. And could look out into Burnaby Bay. And Romo Island off in the distance.

I climbed upwards, manoeuvring thru the jagged rocks. Being very careful not to slip. Because it could lead to a dangerous fall. It was quite a steep climb. I ventured up the hill when I wanted to be alone. And I wanted to be alone.

This area of the patch did not have a name, so I referred to it as Pashelles Peak. Only to myself, because I thought I was the only pumpkin that ever climbed up the peak. And I rarely ever did. Not because I never wanted to be alone. That too. But it was quite a trek from my home. It was really out of my way.

But on that day, there was another pumpkin coming down the peak. The sun was shining in my face and getting into my eyes, so I wasn't able to distinguish who it was at first. I was kind of surprised to see anyone there. I had to stop. I bent down and tried to hide myself behind a big rock. I wasn't sure if I wanted to be seen. But when my eyes got accustomed to peering into the sun, I recognized the pumpkin. And it was Peter coming down. Which was the strangest thing. Why was he there? It was odd running into him like that. I mean it was strange to see any pumpkin there. And I didn't want him to know I was there. I was not sure why. I hoped he never noticed me.

I attempted to move off to one side and out of his path, thinking I could bury myself beneath some rocks and he would not notice me. What in the world could he being doing there? It was the weirdest place for me to find him. I waited for him to come down the peak and pass me. But my body stuck out too much. And since he was moving slowly, investigating every place his foot would land, he noticed me. I knew that he noticed me. I had no choice but to emerge from my hiding spot, and greet him. I didn't want him to think I was some kind of weirdo. Lurking around the rocks. I mean he could think I was following him or something. He must have thought I was being silly, hidden away in the rocks. He probably did think I was following him, and watching him. But I wasn't. Really I wasn't. He didn't say anything about that. He starred at me for a few seconds, his big eyes popping out thru his glasses, as he had stopped in his tracks. He, himself, seemed just as surprised to see me.

"Hey," he finally said.

"Hi. So what are you doing here?" I didn't know what to say to him.

"Nothing," he replied. I found that hard to believe. I mean no one goes up the peak to do nothing. Well that was not entirely true. I mean

I had. He could have climbed the peak for the scenic view. I wondered if he did. I mean, why else would he be there? So I questioned him again.

"Really? Nothing?"

"Oh. Well I came here to see the…" and he pointed up towards the cliff top. But he stopped in mid-sentence.

"You came to see the cliff top? The scenic view?"

"Yes. I came to see the view."

"It's nice, isn't it?"

"Yes. Are you going to see the view too? Because be careful. The witches are here. Circling around. I saw them. That's why I'm coming back down."

I replied okay.

Our conversation stalled at that point. He went into one of his stupors. A daze. I thought he expected that I would walk back down with him. Or for me to make the first move and continue upwards. Maybe he wanted to climb down in privacy. I don't know. But there were a few awkward, silent moments. I decided to continue on my climb upwards.

"Okay. Well I will see you later then," I said. And I took a few steps to move away from him. Conversations with Peter could be very awkward. We didn't really have anything in common. Actually no. Except for one thing. We both knew ghoul leaders. He having an association with Victor Vampire, and me having met Wanda Witch. Not that I was proud of that encounter. I mean, why would I be?

I was careful to watch out for the witches. We were always told that one day the witches would come and invade the patch from the peak. But that was only a myth more than anything. Something the elders would say to young pumpkins, yet have an ulterior motive. The elders just wanted us to avoid the dangers of the sharp rocks and the cliff. A tale told to avoid that area of the patch.

But then I did see a witch. For real. And then I saw more of them. And as soon as I did, I halted in my tracks. I saw that crazy green smoke in the air again. I knew that was trouble. I had to stop and move back down. I heard their laughter. The meanness and evil in their voices. I had always applauded myself for being courageous. And daring. And if I was younger and naïve, I probably would have kept climbing. But I knew to advance any further would be negligent. I had learnt my lesson with the events surrounding Precious in the amusement park.

I only stayed a few more minutes, watching them. I started to sicken by the sounds of their voices. And so I started my descent down the cliff. Their presence would have ruined my scenic view anyways.

And as soon as I reached the bottom of the peak, I was met by Ms. Pumpkin. That was kind of a surprise. She wanted me to come to the office with her. The elders had questions. Like not again. More questions. I had been to the office so many times, it had become my second home.

They had already asked me questions about the horse exploring incident. I admitted my error. I told them I had learnt my lesson. They had asked me so many questions on that day. Why did I leave the group? Whose idea was it? Why I couldn't be more responsible? The elders wanted to know every detail. They wanted to know every thought that went thru my mind. Before, during, and after the incident. I was still expecting some punishment. Nothing was given yet, but I knew it was coming. The elders probably hadn't decided. And I knew what the first question would be when Mr. Pumpkin sat me down in that chair.

"You went up that hill. I thought you had learnt your lesson Pashelle?" he asked.

He was hovering over me, pacing back and forth. After he asked me that first question, he stopped. Right behind me. Waiting for my answer. I didn't have one.

I was seated in a small room on the second floor of the office building. The elders called it the discovery room. It was more like a prison. It was right next to the room that had a bed. The one I had spent in last month. The room was so bland and boring. No pictures on the wall. The bricks had not even been painted over. It was almost as if the elders wanted me to focus on their words, with no distractions. There was one chair. For me. No chair for Mr. Pumpkin. I didn't think he was interested in sitting anyways.

I had been in the discovery room many times. I had been asked numerous questions by many different elders. Seemingly all my life. It was a never ending saga. The first few times, they would offer me a drink. But not lately. I still recall the first time I was there. It was many years ago. I had a run in with Portia. I stuck my foot out and it caused Panic to accidentally trip over. He landed right on his face. Seeds started dripping from his nose. And he hurt his ankle from his fall. We weren't even one year old. Panic complained to Portia. And she informed the elders. And the elders gave me this lecture about the proper behavior that was expected of all pumpkins. Panic was such a cry baby. Portia should have minded her own business.

Anyways, after Mr. Pumpkins' first few questions about my journey up the peak, his tone changed. He became a little more sympathetic.

"Tell me about the green smoke," he asked.

I had mentioned the green smoke that came out of the witches' mouths a few times. When I met them outside my house last month. Near the bus on Linden road. I saw it hovering over the city stadium. And again when the witches put that horrible spell on Precious.

He wanted to know about the green smoke in more detail. All the times I had seen it. Where it came from? From their mouths, I said. How was it created? I didn't know. If I saw it on the cliff just now. Yes. I thought so. If it did originate from their mouths, what was their facial expression before and after it was released? I didn't pay attention. Was it always the same color of green? What difference did that make? More questions about Precious. I told them I felt partly responsible for that incident. But he didn't press me so much on my actions from that day. They knew as well as I did, that each pumpkin who ventured with me came voluntarily. And everyone had the responsibility to look after Precious. He was more interested about the smoke. I mean I really couldn't tell him anymore than I knew. I knew little about most of the questions he asked.

I asked him about Precious. What would happen to her? He said he didn't know. That she was presented the option of becoming an offering. That was a terrible thought. An accident like that could dissolve the will to live. And she was not responding to any conversation. Which was totally unlike normal pumpkin behavior. She was not eating or drinking properly.

I stayed in the office area for a little while, even after I was dismissed. I noticed Peter again. I kept running into him. I overheard him and Patience talking to some elders about a swimming pool project. Not only was swimming a great type of exercise, but learning how to swim may prove beneficial for all of us, Peter explained. Especially since we lived so close to water. And the ability to swim would have helped him when he fell off his bike at the amusement park. The elders seemed to agree. It was a good idea. The issue was the lack of space within the patch. There was nowhere to build a swimming pool. And it was not likely any of us would swim in Burnaby Bay. Who knows what creatures we would encounter in that water?

I left the office. I wondered if any of my friends were still in the lounge. It was nearing dinner time. And I had to walk quickly, because I noticed Portia followed behind me. She was trying to catch up. She wanted a word with me.

"Pashelle, can I talk to you for a minute?" she asked.

No Portia. You can't, I thought to myself. I didn't want to talk to her. I sped up and pretended not to listen.

"Pashelle? Can you stop? I want to say something," she repeated. She was such a pest. Such a nuisance.

"Just leave her," I heard Paige say.

"Why do you even try?" added Paris.

And I agreed with them. Why did Portia want to talk? What did she want? Why couldn't she just leave me alone?

"It's important," she said, trying one more time.

I just didn't want to deal with her. Not now. She probably wanted to know why she was not invited to my birthday party. I mean, she wasn't invited last year. Or the year before. So why was she making such a big deal about it this year? 'Just let it go' I felt like saying. But that meant I would need to communicate with her. I would play right into her hands. That was exactly what she was trying to do. But I was no dummy. I didn't want to be involved in any of her games. I wasn't born yesterday. That was funny. That was a joke. I was born eight years ago. Almost eight years ago. My party was on my mind. It couldn't come soon enough.

I wished I had a better sense of her whereabouts. At all times. Some kind of extra sensory perception, so I could avoid her like the plague. And I didn't like her friends either. Parker. Paige. Paris. Pryanka. Because that was what she was. A plague. She brought so much negative energy to the air, that she could just wear me out. She sapped all the energy right out of me.

One time a few years ago, when we were at the zoo at Burrowsville, she made a terrible situation even worse. And it ruined the whole trip for me. I was playing with a child. We were having a water fight. Using buckets. And just when we were about to go home, I tried throwing one more pale of water at the child. She moved away at the last second. And the water ended up getting dumped on a baby. The baby started crying. The people knew that it was an accident. But Portia budded in. She demanded that I apologize to the family. Well, I didn't feel it was necessary. Portia was insistent. Even the people changed their tone, and also demanded the apology. Not only were they not happy that I refused to apologize, they claimed I used inappropriate language towards them. That I said this and that. I mean I can't even remember what I said. They said they would report me to the authorities. Which was never a good thing. I mean no pumpkin wants to be given as an offering before their proper time. Portia made me apologize. Which I eventually did. Which made me so mad. It wasn't even my fault. The people wouldn't let me get back on the bus until I said sorry.

I could tell so many stories. She was like Ms. Goody=two-shoes. She thought she was so perfect. Her whole attitude could be so annoying.

She stopped walking. She took the advice of Paige. Or was it because I was just walking too fast for her. I reached the steps of the activity center. I knew dinner was being served. I thought I would find my friends. In our usual spot. Near the back wall of the dining hall. The third row from the kitchen. That was our favorite spot. The dinner lineup was long, as usual. Pumpkins could take so long picking out their food. Not sure what the issue was. I wanted them to hurry up. I wanted to sit with my friends before they got tired and decided to leave. 'Hurry up' I yelled out, to the front of the line. No one seemed to care. I didn't think anyone heard me. Except Mr. Pumpkin who was just ahead me. I may have screamed it in his ear. He may not have appreciated that. He turned to look at me, while he used a finger to clear the wax out of his ear.

I saw Pannette and Peaches walk slowly to our table. I knew where they had been. They were checking out the lounge to determine if it was crowded. Because if they could find some places to sit in the lounge, they would instruct all of my friends to go there. And then I would have to eat alone. Instead they sat down. It must be busy in the lounge. It usually was. That was good.

After I was finally able to pick out my dinner, I walked quickly to our table and sat down.

"Hey everybody," I announced.

"Where were you?" asked Petrina. "Where did you go?"

"Nowhere." I didn't feel like telling them I was up on Pashelles' Peak. "Actually I was in the office."

"Really? Wow. What a surprise. So what did you do this time?"

"Nothing. Mr. Pumpkin was asking me about that green smoke again. That smoke I was telling you about. When Precious started to rise."

"We were just talking about her."

"It's so sad. Precious told Ms. Pumpkin that she wants to be given as an offering."

My gosh. We needed to do something to cheer her up. But my friends told me that many pumpkins had tried different things. She never wanted to get out of bed. She didn't talk to anyone. She had become completely unresponsive. She didn't even want to sit in her wheelchair. And she had refused any type of rehab when she was in the city hospital.

"She shouldn't volunteer herself as an offering," I said.

"What would you do, then, if you were in her predicament?"

I didn't know. Would I want to live my life just lying in bed all day? No. No one would. I couldn't imagine anyone would want that by choice.

"We should at least try to encourage her to sit in the chair. I think that would be a great start," I said.

"I brought Pericles with me one day. So she could say hello to my new brother," explained Plato.

"And...?"

"All she did was start crying."

We became quiet. We were all so concerned. I ate my dinner in peace. And the topic changed.

"How is your beauty pageant thing going? Do you have a chance to make the finals?"

"Yes. Of course. You know how beautiful I look."

Petrina could be overly confident in her abilities at times. I knew she had little chance. I was sure she realized that as well. I started to chuckle at the prospects of Petrina winning. It's possible. Anything is possible. I mean squash could fly to the moon too.

"So when do you find out if you made it to the semi-final round?"

"I'm expecting Ms. Pumpkin to notify me at any moment. To pass on the well deserving news."

Plato began telling us all the new words that Pandion and Pericles had learned. He said he had spent all his time with them. Reading mostly. And trying to talk with them. He loved reading books from a dead person named Socrates. He would never tell me his last name.

"And what is his last name again?" I asked him.

He didn't reply. He was too preoccupied. He was holding Pandion in his left arm, with Pericles on his right.

While he was playing with this two brothers, Polo was waving his hands around. He was practicing some kind of martial arts fighting. He still hadn't asked me about the horse incident. He knew we were this close to riding on one of them. He must be so jealous. How we all ran off and saw horses, but didn't invite him along on our getaway.

He had been spending time with Mr. Pumpkin in a summer exercise program. He wanted to win the martial arts competition. Pumpkins were not allowed to enter into the competition until we were in our eighth year. He was telling me there were lots of pumpkins in training. But only four from our class. Including him, there was Panic, Plunder and Perses. He said the one day competition was this weekend. Before the Tea Party.

"Are you entering the martial arts contest? If you do, would you fight against the males?" I asked Pavneet.

Pavneet just shrugged her shoulders. As if to say 'I don't want to win that competition anyways. So why would I enter?' I had the feeling that she could take out all four of them, all at once. Without any training whatsoever. Panic was skinny and scrawny. Plunder was too stupid to understand any of the advised training techniques. Perses was strong though. And he had a mean streak in him. Polo was not as strong or athletic. But he had the desire in his heart to succeed. He liked to exercise and train. He loved to think he was a tough pumpkin. He did resemble one. His skin was not very smooth, but rather bumpy and rough. Uneven ridges. But I didn't think he would win the competition. I mean, he could never defeat Perses. I have known Polo all my life. I would see his brother Pimlico at our house all the time as I was growing up. Hanging around with Pascal. And then Polo started to come over with him, on a regular basis. And we just became friends. I admired his bravery. He liked to stand up for me. It made me feel special. Like someone really did care about me. In a very sincere way.

While I was observing at Polo doing his hand movements, I noticed Pavneet eyes widened. And then they focused. She was looking towards me, but not directly at me. Her eyes focused towards the corner of the dining hall.

"Pikachu!" she screamed. She stood up and glanced the hall, searching for Pikachu. Once Pavneet spotted her, she again yelled out her name. When Pikachu took notice, Pavneet pointed to the far end of the hall.

"There. Over there. Look," she screamed with excitement.

And then Pavneet ran around the edge of the table and bolted. And as she ran past me, a few pumpkins screamed themselves. I turned, and out of the corner of my eye, I saw a small rat like creature scamper across the dining hall, and out into the lobby of the activity center. I turned to look at my friends.

"Don't say anything. I don't want to know what Pavneet just found," said Prudence.

"Neither do I." said Penny.

Both of them had just sat down, with a plate full of food. They didn't want to even look towards the direction of Pavneets exodus. We saw a few pumpkins run out of the dining hall, chasing after that thing, while the rest of us remained seated.

"Pikachu is freaking out. She thought she saw her pet in the Rose garden the other day. And yesterday, under one of these tables," said Prima.

"Aw. That rodent has been in here all this time? Sniffing around our food?" asked Purvis.

"How gross."

"Someone should help her," suggested Pecan.

"We did. But those things move so fast. Pimi and I thought we saw something near the Tulip garden. And we chased it over the Water Gate Bridge. Perkins was there too. He said it crawled into some bushes. And we checked in between the shrubs and everything. But we found nothing. Like magic it was gone. So we gave up. They move like ghosts. Faster than the wind," explained Pebbles.

"I saw it too. Yesterday. It was just sitting there. Not moving. It was like sleeping or something," said Petrina.

"Did you try to grab it?"

"No. I'm not touching that thing. It's not even important."

"Yes it is. For Pikachu anyways."

"Oh. My bad."

I examined my food. I still had at least two more scoops of vegetables to eat. And one more nibble of chicken. I suddenly lost all appetite. I pushed my plate away in disgust. That rat like creature just ruined my dinner.

I didn't even want to eat the small piece of cake that I brought with me to our table for dessert. That was a shame. It looked so delicious. A lemon cake, with icing and cherries on top.

"Let's talk about something else," I ordered. I thought about my party and my birthday cake. And how things kept happening to delay it. They all seemed to be out of my control. I found myself murmuring, aloud.

"But you're already eight," someone claimed.

"No I'm not. I'm not eight until I cut my cake. And blow out my candles. And make a wish. And everyone sings happy birthday. And…"

"I think your party is probably going to get cancelled."

"You're too old to have a birthday party."

"You need to be more mature."

"I know right," remarked Petrina.

Talk about a pumpkin who was mature. Or not. I made up that phrase 'I know right.' I was saying it years ago. As a means of agreeing with pumpkins. Because they remarked I was always combative, and argumentative. So I invented that phrase to indicate to them, that I don't always disagree. But after a while, I found it to be annoying. I grew out of it. I didn't need pumpkins to know I agreed with them all the time. I didn't even know why she continued to use it. It was a sign of her immaturity. Of her vulnerability. She still felt the need to be liked. Like really bad. She had such a big ego. I wanted to be liked too. But only because I felt I was different somehow. I was unique. That pumpkins didn't always understand my good intentions. I discovered there were other ways I could demonstrate those good intentions without having to say 'I know right'.

Pavneet returned to our table after only a few minutes. She shrugged her shoulders. As if to say 'we couldn't find it'. It wasn't necessary for her to say anything. I doubt that thing was ever going to be found. Or captured. Or whatever term was used to describe that scenario.

"Pita said she saw some rats near the arena. But I don't know if it was the pet. How can you tell anyways?"

"Doesn't Pikachu know?"

"Well it's hard. Even for her. You can't compare our species to any other. We all look so different from each other. But it's not the same as other species. It's so hard to differentiate them apart."

"Maybe it wants to run away from home. I mean, would you want to be trapped inside a cage all day?" I said.

"Or maybe it went to be with its friends. It must be strange for it, to be living all by itself. No one would want that."

"If someone does find it, they should just drop it in Star River. Or throw it in the east tunnel."

"I know right. We should get rid of all those things. Once and for all."

The east tunnel was a rat infested passageway for us to leave our patch and enter New Surrey City. It was always very dark. And scary. And there were hundreds and hundreds of rodents in there. All over. They have been known to attack. Pianne was bitten by a rat, when she was re-entering the patch. It clung onto her skin and wouldn't let go. And she didn't even notice it was there until she came out of the tunnel on the other side. She was rushed to the hospital. She spent weeks and weeks getting treatment. But her condition did not improve. The rat dug a hole in her skin so deep that her seeds were falling out. And inexplicably, the hole did not re seal itself back, but actually grew larger. She suffered from some disease. There was nothing the doctors could do. She was given as an offering.

And they have been known to drop down from the roof as well, and land on our hands. Which was totally gross. It certainly was scary in there. And there was very little we could do. The tunnel could not be sprayed with poison, because then we would get sick too, when we travelled thru. They all came from New Surrey City. It could certainly be an adventure travelling thru. Because of Pianne, we were all encouraged to wear plastic jackets over us. But hardly anyone did.

I didn't think anyone in the patch cared if that rodent escaped. I mean many pumpkins were hoping it escaped for good.

CHAPTER 9
ORANGE JUICE

On the next Saturday, my friends and I were in the lounge. We were watching the news. I was bored. The annual Tea Party was in full swing. It should have been my birthday party instead. I was restless. Maybe I thought life should be more exciting. Nothing happened when you're only seven years old. I was wanting more. I wanted to grow up and be an elder. The sooner the better. My party had always occurred before the Tea Party.

Most pumpkins were in the gardens of the eye. The lounge was busy too. It was hot inside. The overhead fans only seemed to be circulating the hot air around the room. They seemed counterproductive. These were the days when we all wished the air conditioning functioned better. I was sitting with Pannette and Petrina. Pavneet had just come back from outside. She looked tired. She flopped down on the comfy couch, and wiped the sweat from her forehead. She was serving food to the elders. That was what the younger pumpkins did during the Tea Party. We served the elders tea. Iced tea. And biscuits. And breads and sandwiches. And cookies. And other appetizers and desserts, while they relaxed and basked in the sun. I didn't feel like serving. I was too depressed because it wasn't my birthday party. I wasn't protesting. I wasn't upset. It was just a disappointing circumstance.

Polo didn't feel like serving either. He was disappointed in his performance in the martial arts competition. He claimed to have slipped during a crucial fight sequence. He had lost to Perses the previous night. And Petrina was upset too. She was notified that she did not qualify for the semi-finals, or commonly called the round of ten. She was hunched over on a lounge sofa. Next to me. And Pannette was to my left. For no other reason than to relax in the lounge.

Pannette was talking about the heat, and the toll it was taking on pumpkins. Excessive heat was never good for our skin. Nor our insides. Our seeds could dry out so quickly. She was explaining that many pumpkins had been admitted into the hospital over the past several weeks. And most were receiving treatment for excessive dryness. That was why it was so important for us to drink lots of liquid. Or else we would dry out completely.

The television was on. We were watching the news from the city, watching and listening to the lady.

"The Olympic committee continues to investigate the unusual number of positive drug violations. It is believed that all athletes have now been tested, the final testing completed in the past two days. And athletes continue to be stripped off their medals. The positive testing is not restricted to any particular country. The results have indicated that many of the athletes who were indoors were not tested positive. For example, only two swimmers have tested positive. The majority of the violations have come from athletes participating in the outdoor events. And rumours continue to circulate that most of the violations were from athletes who competed on day seven, eleven, and day thirteen of the games. Which is an unusual situation, in itself. The committee is expected to release a full report any day now. And joining us live now is Dr. Jones. Doctor, thank you for being with us here today. This situation continues to dominate the headlines. What are now the next steps the committee…"

And out of nowhere, Portia appeared and sat down next to Pavneet. But before she did, she made a sarcastic comment towards me.

"Pashelle, you should be outside helping us. Why don't you help me with these cupcakes? And we can chat for a minute," she asked.

Chat? She wanted to chat? Why? Like as if that would happen. She knew the answer. My body language indicated the answer. I mean she was always out to get me. To get me in trouble. She could be very mean. I made it very clear to Paxton, that neither she, nor any of her friends would be invited to my party.

She didn't even bother waiting for my response anyways. She started chatting with Pavneet. And laughing. I mean what did Portia want now? What business did she have even sitting with us?

Pavneet had become very close to her, in recent years. And I thought 'wasn't that great'. It was such a huge mental stumbling block for me. To have one of my closest friends, befriend an enemy. It was a frustrating situation. I wasn't mad at Pavneet. But I wasn't pleased with the situation either. I've never spoken to her about it. I should, though.

I couldn't stand Portia's eerie witch like laugh. And her silly humor. And her boring stories. I didn't want to stay, and possibly be dragged into their conversation. So I thought about going outside and help serve. I turned to Polo.

"Come on Polo."

"Where?"

"Let's go outside. Let's see what's going on."

On our way towards the exit, I noticed Panic seated at a bar stool. I turned and stared at him, as I walked by. I wondered what devious act he could be contriving up. He caught my eye. He motioned for me to meet him. "Hey," he called out. I was curious as to what he wanted. He was such a character. He could be a goof. But sometimes, he could be fun and exciting to be around. Polo wasn't interested in sitting with Panic though, so he continued onwards. As I saw Polo leave, I thought that I didn't really do him justice. I mean he was enjoying himself, having a relaxing time with our friends. I asked him to leave with me. And now he was out the door by himself. An unintentional cruel ploy. I felt sorry for him at that instance. But I couldn't be bothered with that. And besides, he should be outside serving anyways. I redirected my full attention to Panic.

"What do you want Panic?"

"What are you doing? Enjoying the party? I'm invited to your party, right?"

"Why would I invite you?"

"Don't be like that. You know I would be the life of your party. Do you want it to be boring, like last year?"

"How do you know it was boring? You weren't there."

"So you admit it was boring."

"What do you want Panic?" I repeated myself.

"Mr. Pumpkin isn't here."

"So?"

He was referring to the bartender. He had been in and out of the lounge, arranging for the drinks all afternoon. Some alcoholic. Some not. Apart from Halloween night, this was probably the busiest day of the year for him, and the other volunteers who help out in the lounge.

"Look."

Panic nodded to an opened, alcoholic bottle on the counter. It was left unattended. He leaned his nose over the cover of the bottle and took an inhale. And he widened his eyes and gave me a smile. As if to confirm it was an alcoholic bottle.

"Drink some," he said.

"No. Are you crazy? Why don't you? I dare you too."

"She's scared," said Prime. Prime and Primo were seated next to Panic.

Panic loved daring me to do things. And sometimes I would. Only because I would dare him to do something even more outrageous at a later date. A dare even braver than what he had me do. But I knew drinking alcohol was not a good idea.

I turned and looked at Portia. Wouldn't it be great if I could get her to drink some of it? Seeing her flop all over the lounge would be well worth any punishment I would receive afterwards. Maybe she would say something, and make a fool of herself. Everyone knew that Mr. Pumpkin loved to drink. Perhaps a bit too much. And as a result, he could say some really weird things. He loved to get tipsy. Wouldn't it be great to get Portia to say something stupid?

"Do it Panic. You know you want to," urged Prime.

I didn't want either of them to think that I didn't have the guts. That would have been the worst case scenario in my opinion. Panic would then go around and tell everyone that I was scared. And I didn't want that. So I jumped onto the bar table, lying on my stomach, and was able to grab a glass from underneath the counter, from the opening on the other side. Where Mr. Pumpkin normally stands. Before I did, though, I made double sure no one was watching. And then I landed back on my feet, on the front side of the counter. I poured some of the drink into the glass. It was called vodka. I made sure I moved the bottle back to exactly where it was.

"Now drink it," Panic ordered.

"I poured it. So you drink it," I replied.

It looked like water. It smelt gross. I poured in whatever orange juice I could find, so the smell wouldn't be so bad. And the drink turned all orange. I even put in some ice, thinking it would lessen the smell even more.

We looked at each other. Dared each other. I didn't want to drink it. Apart from getting into big trouble with the elders, I knew the terrible things that could result from drinking alcohol. I mean I didn't want to act the way Mr. Pumpkin did. It was as if he transformed himself into a complete different type of pumpkin. Like a ghost had inhibited his body. Like he had no control over his thoughts and emotions. He said things that he may or may not have meant to say. And I thought about that bus driver. The one that caused the road accident. The one that killed Puff. And almost killed Plato. He had consumed alcohol. I didn't know it at the time when I met him. But he did. All the people witnesses knew it. The police reports confirmed it. He lost all control of his own mind and body. I didn't want to feel that way. I didn't need to be told by anyone. And I thought as much a goof as Panic was, he was probably thinking the same thing. There was no benefit from drinking the vodka. Only bad things could result.

Neither of us ending up drinking the vodka and orange juice. And we didn't know what to do with the vodka drink either.

After a few minutes of unnecessary gamesmanship and idle chatter with Panic and Prime, the bartender returned. So we quickly stood up from our stools. We didn't want him to know what we were doing. Nor what we were thinking. I didn't want him to detect the guilty look on my face. I took a few steps away from the counter. Away from the orange juice and vodka drink. Mr. Pumpkin went behind the counter. He cleared his tray of empty bottles. Then he took out, and placed new, unopened bottles onto his tray.

"I hope you don't mind. I poured myself a glass of orange juice," I said.

He barely noticed me. He was really busy. He was normally a very joyful and social soul. He always loved a good conversation. As most pumpkins did.

He took out another alcoholic bottle from behind the counter. He popped open the lid with some kind of utensil and poured the whole contents into a large pitcher. He then poured in juice. Tomato or cranberry juice. I wasn't sure. It was dark red. He then dumped a bunch of ice into the pitcher, and put the pitcher on his tray. He was certainly very skillful in the art of making drinks. I thought it would be fun to be the lounge bartender one day. I thought I could do that. I would just need a little training, that's all. Then with the help of two others, they picked up the trays and even more bottles, and they left to go back outside. I turned to look at Panic, but he had vanished as well.

I didn't know what to do with the drink. I thought I should have thrown it down the sink. But that seemed like a waste of resources. I thought I should really give it to Portia. But I doubt she would even accept a drink from me, anyways. I decided to return back to where my friends were sitting. Since I didn't know what to do with the drink, I temporarily left it on the counter.

As I walked back to where my friends were, Petrina passed by me, walking the other way. I thought I should ask her what to do with it. But I didn't. Instead I thought what I would say to Portia. But I didn't have to worry about that either. She was rising from the sofa. She was leaving. I was glad for that. At least I could sit down, and relax. Not having to listen to her eerie voice.

And as soon as I sat down, I saw Ms. Pumpkin heading our way. I knew what she would say. So I closed my eyes and pretended to be asleep.

"What are you all doing here? You know you should be outside. You know the Tea Party is an annual, treasured tradition," she said. "A tradition that you need to be a part of."

And when I felt her hand move my shoulders, I even made snoring sounds. Like it would be impossible for her to wake me up.

"We will Ms. Pumpkin. I just came inside to rest for a minute. I was just really thirsty," replied Pavneet.

I waited for Ms. Pumpkin to leave. I had to somehow sense it, because I didn't want to even risk the slightest chance of opening either eye. And have her uncover my secret.

And I listened to my friends talk amongst themselves. I heard Peanut and Peter join us.

"Hey. So what are you guys talking about?" asked Peanut.

"The heat. The Tea Party. What else?" replied Pannette.

"Did Pashelle really walk away because of Portia?" whispered Petrina. She had returned from where she went. Not likely from outside though.

"Probably. Pashelle thinks Portia is very mean to her. So she tries to avoid her," replied Pavneet.

"Take this glass," offered Petrina.

"Talk about the heat. Hopefully this juice will be cold Petrina," replied Pavneet.

"There's some ice in this one. So it should be cold. I didn't find any cold juice containers in the ice box. There were only cartons on the counter. But this glass seems cold. Did you serve the elders outside Peanut?" asked Petrina.

"Yeah. Like is it fun listening to the elders?" questioned Pannette.

"A little. Ms. Pumpkin was singing. I think she is drunk. I came in to bring out some more water bottles. Some cold ones," replied Peanut.

"I don't want to go back outside and serve. I had a tray of sandwiches, and I let the tray slip thru my hands. All of them spilled over and landed on Ms. Pumpkins' lap," explained Peter.

"Aw!" we exclaimed.

"What did she say?"

"She must have been so mad."

"That must have been ugly."

"She was. She became a mess."

They all started laughing. I did too. I was forced to re-open my eyes. If anything, to see the expression on Peters' face. Ms. Pumpkin was so prim and proper. I mean it was mainly due to her efforts that the Tea Party continued. Year after year. She was always instructing us to sit up straight. To respect the elders. To never talk out of turn. She always wanted things done so perfectly. Like she had always done things perfectly. She thought she was the nicest pumpkin on the planet. She viewed herself as the ultimate role model. That if everyone acted like her, the world would be a better place. Nothing was her fault. I could just imagine the look on Ms. Pumpkins face after that accident.

"I feel really lightheaded all of a sudden," remarked Pavneet. That laugh must have taken something out of her.

Pannette felt Pavneets forehead. "My goodness. You're burning up."

"I think I might be sick. My taste buds don't feel right. I couldn't even tell what type of juice that was. I can't even tell the difference between juice, and water, and whatever."

I could see her face turn sour.

"You should be nicer to Portia. She likes you. She is only looking out for you. She can be a great resource," Pavneet said, as she looked straight into my eyes. "She is to me."

Pavneet started lecturing me on how I should try to be friends with Portia. She was talking a mile a minute.

"Portia has helped me with my studies. She has helped me with my housing situation. One time she…"

During her ode to Portia, she let out a big burp. We all started laughing. She had finished all her juice in one gulp. She had suddenly become really energized. First she was talking about Portia. And Paige. Then the spilt tray from outside. Then Mr. Pumpkin. Then Ms. Pumpkin. The heat. The party. My party. And Precious coming to the Tea Party.

And as she continued talking, her speech started to slur. Which was very unlike her. Usually her enunciation was crystal clear. Her words became unrecognizable. She began to slow down. She even got confused as to what she was talking about. And she eventually stopped, seemingly in mid-sentence. It was strange.

Then she closed her eyes. Just for one moment. I starred at her. We all did. I was starting to get concerned. Then she opened her eyes, and gazed at us. But only for a brief moment. She closed them again. She hunched backwards on the sofa. It looked like she fell asleep.

"I think she's sick."

"It's probably the heat."

"Like no kidding. Do you think we should call someone? Like a doctor. I mean it could be serious," I offered.

Then she suddenly woke up. Her head and body had straightened out. She leaned forward. Her right hand was against her stomach. Her face tightened. Her eyes lacked focus.

"Oh my stomach. My head hurts."

Then she let out her seeds.

"Aw!" we exclaimed. We all stood up. In a heartbeat.

All the water and juice, and whatever else she had eaten, had come out of her mouth. Including her seeds. They all splattered on the floor around us. Some of those torpedoes had shot right over the couch, and made their way near the pool table. All we could do was watch.

And it appeared as if she was going to let out more seeds. She was trying to. She was holding her stomach. We could see her mouth open and close. Then she leaned back on the sofa again. She closed her eyes.

"Here Pavneet. Just relax."

"Yeah. Like maybe just lie down for a minute," said Pannette, as she lifted her feet and put them on the couch.

Mr. Pumpkin appeared. He had seen what happened. He came prepared. He had taken out two mops from a nearby closet and a bucket full of water. Mops that are used to clean up split drinks. Not necessarily let out seeds. And he handed me one of them.

"Pashelle. Help me clean up this mess," he instructed.

"Seriously? Why do I have to? This isn't my mess. I mean I don't volunteer in the lounge," I objected.

I mean it was going to be gross. The odor had become unbearable. I reluctantly grabbed the mop, ensured my nose was plugged, put the mop in the water, and then slammed it on the floor. It was a job that would take me not even ten minutes, but one that was going to leave a scar on me for a very long time.

"Let's go to the hospital Pavneet. Can you walk?" asked Ms. Pumpkin.

It appeared she was too dizzy and light headed to even stand.

"I'll go find Dr. Pumpkin," I said. As it gave me an excuse to abandon the clean-up task. He would be outside, somewhere. In the gardens of the eye. I was sure of it.

And just at that moment, when I placed one foot outside the activity center, pumpkins started to scream. Many stood and started to run. There was a lot of commotion. There was a problem. Witches had appeared and were circulating, high up above. Maybe hundreds of them. All laughing and screaming with joy. It appeared to be a planned attack. Seemingly organized and executed to perfection. On a day they knew we would all be outside. Creating a chaos unlike anything I have ever seen.

That terrible green smoke was floating around in the confines of the patch.

Pumpkins were rising. Many were floating in the air. They hadn't risen as high as Precious did in the amusement park. Thank goodness. Most were only in the air for a few moments and they crashed down to the ground. At least they landed on soft grass. Precious had landed on the hard concrete, back in the city.

"Everyone get inside!" pumpkins were screaming out. There was a rush towards where I was standing. To enter the activity center. I watched many squeeze in thru the narrow door way. Three, even four at a time.

The scene was chaotic.

Pumpkins were pulling out the fire hoses, and were spraying the air and witches with water. To see if they could clear the deadly green smoke. And for the most part, the water was successful. The smoke appeared for only a few moments. And it was cleared away. I mean everything happened so fast.

I saw Polka land very hard on her shoulder. Poker fell onto a table. Pompeo had dropped right onto Pablo's lap. I watched with horror as I saw Mr. Pumpkin grabbing onto Ping's leg, and was holding him with dear life. To prevent him from rising.

The smell of the smoke was gross. It was sickening. I wanted to let my seeds out. It was thinly spread out over a large area of the eye. I had seen the smoke much thicker. Like when it surrounded Precious. I mean the witches were much closer to us in the city.

The witches only made a brief appearance, though. When they saw the disorder in our ranks, they began to vanish.

Amidst all the commotion, I was paying attention to Precious. She was sitting on the lawn in the Rose garden. She seemed all by herself. I was watching her. She was trying to stand up on her own. She made numerous attempts, but to no avail. I mean she only had one leg. She first had moved over, to see if she could reach her wheelchair. And she had situated herself right next to it. And she was using her arms, to try to lift herself up off the ground, and onto to her one leg. I was temporarily frozen in my tracks, to try to assist. I thought I should help and do something. But everyone was running around all over the place, all at once. And many pumpkins were in my direct path to reach her.

I could see that no one was helping her. I mean everyone was frantic. I had to do something. I was able to push myself thru the oncoming traffic. I approached Precious. She seemed so scared. So helpless.

"You can do it Precious," I said. I grabbed one of her arms to help her. "Stand up."

"Leave me alone. I don't want to," she said. She had given up trying.

"Come on Precious. You can do it."

She was resisting my efforts. She was pushing my hands away. I didn't know what to say or do, to convince her to stand up. I couldn't lift her up all by myself. Especially if she wasn't cooperating. Like seriously, I thought to myself. What a terrible situation the witches had put us in.

It was the first time I had seen her missing leg up close. I was taken aback. It looked so weird. Her skin was closed right up, where her leg would normally extend out. The color of the skin was a dark orange, unlike the rest of her skin. Like someone had painted the area orange, or something.

Panarin and Mr. Pumpkin arrived to help. But it made little difference. Precious was resisting our efforts. She became fraught with terror. She was crying. Her hands were covering her face. We had to get her out of the garden because we knew the witches could return any second to unleash a new wave of green smoke.

There were still many pumpkins in the Rose garden. Helping the fallen pumpkins off the ground. All the while, others continued to spray the air with water. Up above, only a few witches remained to witness the damage they caused. Wow. Wanda Witch must be loving this.

Two more elders had arrived to help. Precious was forcibly picked up by the three elders and was carried inside. She was still screaming 'leave me alone'.

"Let's go inside Pashelle. You too Panarin," instructed Mr. Pumpkin.

The pumpkins who had risen and fallen were escorted to the hospital. I was sure of it. Some of them landed very hard.

I had made my way back inside the activity center. I took a look back into the gardens of the eye. And it was a mess. The Rose garden was littered with garbage. Bottles and cans. Wrappers. Destroyed food all over the place. Tables were tipped over.

And inside, I could hear outrage.

"Those evil witches."

"They're always up to no good."

"They attacked us."

"We need to exact some kind of revenge. We need to take action."

There were few voices of reason on that day.

"Wow. What a mess," said Petrina, as she suddenly appeared next to me, looking out the window.

"Was Pavneet affected by the green smoke?" I asked.

"I don't know. But it was only outside, so probably not. I think Pavneet let out her seeds because she was just sick. If you know what I mean. Maybe because of the heat. I mean she didn't rise into the air," she reasoned.

"I'm sure glad we were inside." said Pannette.

We waited indoors for hours. The activity center was crammed. We were not allowed outside. No one wanted to go outside. The Tea Party was effectively over. All we could hear was the ranting and raving against the evil witches. How selfish they were. That they did this on purpose. They must have known the Tea Party was that day. They must have planned it all out. Unleashing that venom.

After several hours, the elders deemed the green smoke to have completely cleared. We were encouraged to go home and to stay inside. The clean-up of the eye would occur the following day.

And many of us were in the gardens of the eye that day. With so many pumpkins helping, the clean-up really didn't take us long. Even the elders assisted. In normal circumstances, they wouldn't have. I mean they hadn't helped in the Tea Party clean up in previous years. And the chatter about the evil witches continued. We all talked about the green smoke, and how we all needed to avoid it. The elected elders would have a meeting soon, and discuss the ways we could protect ourselves from it. And how we could detect its arrival. Even before it arrived.

We discovered Prudence and Poker suffered minor bruises. No broken bones. And it was originally feared that Polka suffered a dislocated hip from her fall. But that was a premature diagnosis. It was just a bruise, and she would be okay. Pumpkins were actually quite strong, physically speaking. Our hard skin could protect us.

Pavneet and I were helping the gardeners fix the flowers in the Rose garden. Many of them had been trampled on during the evacuation of the eye. I thought it was strange how she became sick, right about the same time as the smoke arrived.

"The doctors conducted tests on me last night. And they found that I had an unusual amount of alcohol in my body," she said.

"Aw!" I exclaimed. "You were drinking? And you didn't invite me to your social adventure?"

"I'm not kidding. I don't even know how that was possible."

"I guess the green smoke affects every pumpkin differently. Your body could have reacted to it, which caused you to be sick," I explained.

"But so much alcohol?"

"It is strange you got sick at exactly the same instance when the smoke appeared. It must be related. I mean it must be more than just a coincidence."

"But I wasn't even outside."

"But you were outside. You had been serving the elders all day. I mean it's all witch craft. Does anyone really know how that magic works?"

After a heavy sigh, and a complaint about her morning headache, she changed the subject.

"I heard Precious freaked out."

"She did, in a way. I mean everyone was running around. She was so scared. It probably brought back bad memories for her. I was trying to help her get in her wheelchair so that she could escape. But she kept saying 'leave me alone'. She didn't even want to escape the danger. I will never forget how scared and frantic she was yesterday. She was even more scared than when she suffered the accident. Probably because she knew what could happen."

"Wow. I know. I was told the Tea Party was the first time she went outside. And she has been back here for more than a week now. And to experience those same feelings again, would have frightened anyone. To have to relive that moment, and those emotions. I heard she confirmed with the doctors to be an offering."

"It's so sad."

"We should go see her. And find out how she's doing," Pavneet suggested.

And we did. Later on that evening, my friends and I went to the hospital. She was talking to Porter, Peter and Peanut.

"Life isn't fair," she said. "Why me? Why did I lose my leg?"

She seemed angrier on this day, compared to when we visited last week. On that day she was emotionless. She had finally mustered enough courage to sit in the wheelchair and go outside. And meet pumpkins and socialize. And to have that whole incident happen, and blow up in her face, must have scared her. To death. Because that's what she was talking about. She was lying on her stomach.

"I never want to go outside. Ever. I never want to talk to anyone ever again."

Porter turned to us and shrugged his shoulders. He didn't know what to say.

Just then, Ms. Pumpkin wandered in the room.

"Peter, there is a telephone call for you."

"For me? Really? Who is it?"

"Is it Victor Vampire?" I wondered aloud.

"No. It's a person. He says he's from the Olympic committee. Come on quickly. Don't keep him waiting."

I saw Peter stand up from an adjacent bed, where he was sitting. He stumbled as his feet hit the ground. He followed Ms. Pumpkin. What could the person want with Peter? I wondered.

"Do you know why he's asking for you?" asked Ms. Pumpkin.

"No. Well maybe. The committee posted a message online a few days ago, asking if anyone had information regarding all the failed drug tests. And I responded. I wrote something like 'I think we can stop...'"

They're voices grew faint, as they walked out of the hospital room.

"Peter got a telephone call. From a person."

"Who cares," snapped Precious.

"Yeah. Like who cares?" I echoed.

"It was nice you went to the Tea Party," said Petrina.

"No it wasn't."

Right. It wasn't. What a stupid thing to say. I thought we should leave her alone. But then her tears became more louder. And she wanted to talk.

"I can't even go to the toilet by myself. Or bathe. I'm never going to be able to do anything by myself."

Then there was a silence. None of us knew what to say. We were speechless. I mean, what could we say that hadn't already been said to her?

"Life doesn't stop just because of what happened Precious," I said. Hoping it was the right thing to say.

"Not just today. Ever. I'm never going to be able to do anything that I want."

"Then we will help you," offered Peanut.

"But I don't want anyone to help me. I want to move around by myself."

She stopped crying. Her anger had dissipated. I'm sure she was still angry. It just wasn't reflected in her tone of voice any longer. We all wanted to comfort her.

"It's just not fair."

"I know Precious. Life can suck," I said.

"I want this feeling to end."

"What feeling?"

"Of being helpless. Being a burden to everyone. Of being left behind. Not being able to do the things I could do before. Of not being able to live life."

"You have a life. Why can't you use the wheelchair? And the walking crutches?"

"I don't want to. It's too hard. I look stupid. I feel stupid."

"You're not stupid."

"Yes I am," she said. And again she started crying. I thought she had cried all the tears out from her body. But they kept reappearing.

"I'm so bored. I can't do anything."

"Yes you can."

'I don't want to do anything. I look ridiculous."

We waited. And waited. We gave her time to collect her thoughts. And after some time had elapsed, she was able to relax. And be calm. And sensible. She sat up on her bed. She starred at us. She looked so sad. So desperate.

"I want to be given as an offering," she said.

Well, I thought she would be more sensible.

"Do you want to come with us to the lounge?"

"No," replied Precious.

Just then Dr. Pumpkin came into her room. It was time for her daily cleaning. She instructed us all to leave. Another day had passed, and Precious seemed no more interested in living her life. And there was very little that any of us could do about it. It seemed the situation was helpless. Just as much for us, as it was for her.

CHAPTER 10
THE ART OF BEAUTY

A few more days passed, and still no surprise birthday party. I had come to accept that it was not going to happen this year. And no one wanted to listen to my gripes about it anymore. After the terrible events of the Tea Party, I didn't even want to bring up the subject. I began to feel selfish. As if it was for my benefit only. None of my friends cared about it. My friends and I were at Pannettes house on the following Saturday evening, and I didn't even mention it. Instead Pannette had some news for us.

"Petrina has to meet with the elders," she said.

"Why?" we asked.

"The elders think she stole beauty supplies."

"Aw!" we exclaimed.

"I don't want to talk about it," said Petrina.

"You know Pryanka right?"

"Yes."

"Okay well. Everyone knows she gets beauty supplies from the United Way. And she stores them in the supply center. Well she ran out of the supply she keeps at home. And she went to the supply center, and they were not where they were normally kept. They were gone. Well she told the elders. And by coincidence, Portia was there. It was Portia and Pryanka who helped stock them in the first place," Pannette explained.

"Okay. So?"

"Well. On the day before, Portia noticed Petrina coming out of the supply centre. And given Petrina wasn't even allowed in there in the first place, Portia alerted the elders."

"So you stole them?" I asked Petrina.

"No," she replied.

"They found the supplies. After a long search. Petrina is under the suspicion of moving the supplies. Or hiding them."

"Why?"

"What?" replied Petrina.

"I mean why would you do something like that?"

"So Pryanka couldn't apply the proper make up to the beauty pageant contestants," answered Pannette.

"Seriously? You stole beauty products?"

"I didn't steal anything."

I wondered if that was the reason why Portia had been wanting to talk to me. Because she wanted me to provide information. She wanted me to rat-out on Petrina. But that would never happen. I would never go behind my friends' back and get them in trouble. I'm not like Portia.

"Look. Everyone must be going to the arena," said Pavneet.

The front door was open. And we noticed many pumpkins walking north on column TY07. And we could hear lots of chatter outside. Not just in that column, but in the adjacent columns as well.

"The beauty pageant final must be starting."

"That's right. It is. We should go now, if we're going to find seats near the front."

I saw Pavneet give me a wink. And flashed her eyes towards Petrina. Why was she doing that? I squinted back at her and slightly shrugged my shoulders, as if to ask 'what are you trying to say?' And we stared at each other, not wanting to speak aloud. It took me a few minutes to figure it out. And of course. Petrina was a contestant. And regardless of where she finished, she would be allowed to sit near the front. Naturally.

Petrina was notified last week that she did not qualify for the round of ten. She was notified before the Tea Party. Before the third talent contest. She must have messed up on her acting. Or maybe it was due to the supplies incident. I wasn't sure. But anyways, since we all wanted to console her during this time of disappointment, we would be allowed to sit with her. No elder would deny this consolation to Petrina. So it was essential that she came with us. Her presence would allow us to sit up close. The beauty pageant could be very emotional. It was well worth sitting in the front row.

"Yes," I said. We should all go. And I grabbed a hold of Petrina's hand.

"I don't really want to go," she said. She rejected my hand.

Of course she didn't. 'Because she was a sore loser', I thought to myself. The thought of watching a champion be crowned right in front of her eyes, must make her skin crawl. We all took Pavneets hint. I stood up, and prepared myself to leave. We all did. I straightened out by red bow.

"Um. I should lock my door," confirmed Pannette, as she slowly walked towards the door.

"Right," I said. "Come on everybody."

I left the house, and slowly walked up column TY07. Taking baby steps. I turned to see if anyone would follow. In particular, I watched for Petrina. And just like everyone else, she arose. She couldn't resist the temptation. The excitement of the beauty pageant was too much. Pavneet held her hand all the way to the arena, to ensure there was no escape.

As we made our way inside, we noticed the chatter and commotion. I could feel the tension in the air. We should have arrived sooner. But we had been relaxing all afternoon. Being very lazy. Which was totally unlike normal pumpkin behaviour.

We had to push our way thru the mass crowd to get near the stage. Where the action was. We pushed our way thru as far as we could, until Ms. Pumpkin noticed our semi rude behavior. She put her hand on my shoulders.

"Petrina is here with us, Ms. Pumpkin. She wants to sit up close, so that she can congratulate the winners," I pleaded.

She gave a rude stare to Petrina. Probably wondering if a pumpkin who was currently under investigation should even be allowed to sit so close to the other contestants. I mean if the judges had voted her into the final round, then surely she would have been disqualified anyway. And probably wondered if a pumpkin who would have been disqualified would even be allowed to watch the finals. But she agreed. She actually escorted all of us to the third row.

And we were seated just in time. Because Ms. Pumpkin was on the stage. She was asking for quiet, while testing the microphone at the same time. She was tapping it with her finger, creating this eerie witch like echo thru out the arena.

After a lengthy speech about the importance and benefits of the pageant, she instructed the five finalists onto the stage.

"Please give them a warm hand everyone," she said.

That announcement was met by a loud, raucous cheer from the noisy crowd. The beauty pageant had become such a popular event. Even more so lately. Actually, I was sure it always had been. I mean I was never interested in the pageant before. But I was now. Maybe because Petrina had entered. And lost. Who knows?

We watched the five finalists make their way onto the stage. I turned to look at Petrina, to see her reaction. And she didn't have one. I could tell she didn't want to be there. She seemed so disinterested. She was slumped back in her chair, with her arms folded. Her eyes pointed downwards, to the side. She didn't even bother cheering when the finalists appeared on the stage.

The finalists had performed the last of their talents a few days prior. I heard that Prissy juggled four tennis balls for over five minutes without letting any of them drop on the floor. Very impressive. After that talent display, the judges narrowed the field from ten to five. Ms. Pumpkin explained the judges had completed the final voting earlier in the day. After a long, gruelling four week competition, Prissy, Parayka, Pretty, Pixie and Paisley were now finally ready to accept the final outcome. This was their judgement day. They must have been nervous. They were positioned to one side of the stage. They were patiently waiting for the results. They were holding hands. Ms. Pumpkin was still near the microphone providing final instructions to the finalists.

She requested the first envelope from the head judge. That was Ms. Pumpkin. She herself was a multiple winner of the pageant, back in her day. She gave advice to the other committee members. Actually, rumour had it that she exerted considerable influence over the voting members. She still looked great. You could tell she continued to exercise and stay fit. I wish I looked at least half as good as her, when I reached her age.

The arena had quietened with anticipation.

"The fifth place winner is...Prissy Pumpkin," announced Ms. Pumpkin.

Everyone cheered for her. Prissy was so happy. But in reality, she must have been so disappointed. I mean it basically was announced that she was not the winner. After she had given each of the other four pumpkins a heartfelt and emotional hug and turned to face the audience, I could see the tears dripping from her eyes. She tried to re compose herself. She then shook hands with the judges and the elders sitting on the other side of the stage. She was handed some real nice flowers. Then she was escorted of the stage, and sat down in the front row.

"The fourth place winner is Paisley Pumpkin."

Paisley did the same thing. She tried to put on a brave face, but her disappointment was even more glaring. To come so close to being the ultimate winner, and to have fallen short, must have been difficult. So close yet so far away. And to have that rejection announced publicly must have been difficult. But fourth place was quite an accomplishment. She should be so proud of herself. There were over forty pumpkins who had entered into the pageant this year. The field was narrowed down to twenty. Then ten. And after the third talent display, only the top five reached the final stage.

When Pixie was announced as the third place winner, she was unable to hold back any emotion. At all. She began crying profusely on stage. She had her head in her hands. Her moans echoed thru out the arena. Everyone could hear her sobbing. The arena had become quiet.

She was unable to stand. Minutes seemed to have passed. The elders had to assist. They lifted her up out of her seat. Then pumpkins began cheering and supporting her. Calling out her name in unison. That may have cheered her up. I don't know. I mean it may have made things worse. She had to be assisted across the stage, down the steps, and onto the first row. She had to be escorted all the way thru. Elders held each of her arms. And despite that assistance, she still almost fell down the steps. She seemed to have slipped off a step. But did land on her two feet. It was like she didn't realize there were three steps to walk down. She ended up missing the last step completely. That sudden landing on her feet seemed to have snapped her out of her temporary nightmare. Just before she sat down, she waved to the crowd, as if to thank everyone for their support. After she regained her composure, she sat down and wiped the tears from her eyes. I could see her quite clearly. She was seated up ahead, in the first row.

There were only two finalists left on the stage.

The elders remained standing. They actually moved closer to the two finalists. Parayka had come in second place last year. And she fainted. She had stood up, and was consoled by Pretty, then dropped to the ground. They didn't want that to happen again. She was known to faint from time to time. Parayka could lose all the air in her head in an instance, and drop to the ground like a bag of cement. In a moments' notice. Win or lose, the elders wanted to be prepared. But make no mistake. Most of us knew her chances were slim. Pretty looked fantastic. So elegant. And I was told she had sung so beautifully a few days ago.

The arena had become quiet once again with anticipation. Parayka was so nervous that she had to wipe the sweat from her forehead. Not a good trait for a beauty contestant. It was a good thing for her that the voting had already been completed.

Ms. Pumpkin cleared her throat. She was ready to announce the winner. The runner up pumpkin never gets her name announced. Which was quite a strange and sad result from the pageant. She opened the envelope. Her face remained stoic, as she read the name to herself.

"And the winner of this years' beauty pageant is... Pretty Pumpkin!"

And Pretty was so gracious. As she stood, she latched onto Parayka's hand and forced her to stand up with her in unison. She held up both her own and Parayka's hands together up in the air. As if to claim they both had won. Although I wondered if it was really meant to ensure that Parayka wouldn't fall and faint. Parayka looked numb. She was expressionless. Her face became so pale and ashen, that all the orange seemed to have disappeared.

Ms. Pumpkin took Parayka's hand, and escorted her across the stage slowly. Like Pixie before her, she never took hold of her flower basket. But she never fainted either. She just walked off the stage, in a calm and orderly fashion. Down the mini steps, and sat down next to Paisley in the first row. No tears. No emotion. I think she was adamant to not faint, or lose control of herself this year. But she must been have so dejected.

Everyone cheered. But it was hard to tell if they were cheering for Parayka or Pretty. I mean Pretty was the pumpkin who won. So the cheers were most likely for her. Parayka had become the runner up in back to back years. Pretty had become the pumpkin beauty queen for the third year in a row, and it was the fifth time in the last six years. The only time she didn't win during that stretch was when she developed a scar on her face. Right underneath her left eye. A mysterious unwanted mark, on the night before the judging was to take place. Pretty claimed it was due to the excessive heat.

Pretty gave a warm speech. She thanked the committee, and her friends for their support. How she was so honored to be selected beauty queen. She was awarded thirteen sets, of a dozen roses each. Patricia placed the tiara on her head. She was given numerous boxes of chocolates. I was sure she would not need them all. So that was great for us. They would be distributed amongst the crowd in attendance.

Pretty had such soft skin. I felt it a few years back. Not on purpose. I mean, I wasn't a weirdo. Her eyes were so big. There were so few grooves on her face. And the ones she did have seemed to be so rounded and curved, to match the shape of her face and body. Her teeth so straight. And just the most beautiful, bright orange color skin that any pumpkin had ever seen. Her body so round. Her stem so green. And her movements so smooth and graceful. Since she was a senior, it was the final time she would participate in the pageant.

Pretty would leave our patch the following weekend, and travel to another patch as our representative. To the largest patch in the land, where the Grand Mr. Pumpkin lives. To compete as the most decorated, beautiful pumpkin in all the land. That must be exciting. She was probably the only pumpkin I knew of, who had travelled in an airplane. The winner of that pageant would be invited to the peoples' version of the same pageant. Not to compete, but only to watch. I was not sure what they called their contest. I had seen bits and pieces of it on television though.

Wanda Witch would want her to compete though. As well as other ghouls. All species. And she wanted the winner to be crowned Ms. Universe. But it was believed that people were resisting the idea. I don't know for sure. Like I've said. I had never really been interested in the pageant until this year.

Many pumpkins were eager to congratulate Pretty, and the other finalists. But Petrina wasn't so interested. She wanted to exit the arena as quickly as possible. She was repeating 'It's over now' and 'let's go.' We could sense her frustration with the whole event, so we agreed to leave. Besides, Pavneet thought it was very hot in the arena. There was very little circulation of cool air. All we could feel was the hot air coming out of pumpkins' mouths. None of us wanted to stay any longer than necessary. And there were far too many pumpkins waiting to congratulate Pretty, that it seemed hopeless to do that.

As we were making our way to the arena exit, I noticed Precious. Sitting in her wheelchair. Off to one side. It seemed that I had lost touch with her since her accident. We had become really good friends over the past year. We had gotten really close. But it seemed that we had drifted apart. Which was a shame. It was like I hardly ever saw her anymore. She would sometimes spend the night at my house. Either sleeping on my bed, or with Plouffe and Patrice. But now, she rarely left her hospital room.

I wanted to stop and say hello. So I let my friends leave the arena on their own. I wanted to wait for Parson and Patrick to leave her side. They were talking to her. Or trying to communicate with her anyways. But it didn't seem like Precious was in the mood. When they finally did leave, I greeted her before anyone else appeared.

"It's great that you came Precious," I said.

"I'm only here because Ms. Pumpkin wants to talk to me. So I'm waiting for her to finish whatever she is doing."

"Ok. Well that is so great," I replied.

And again our conversation stalled. She was resting her chin on a fist that she made with her hand. She was looking downwards. It was great that she came to this event. To any event really. To see her outside and in public. I was going to ask why she had a blanket draped over her, especially because of the intense heat. But I knew the answer. She didn't want anyone to see her non-existent leg. I was going to ask her if she was coming to my birthday party. But I knew there would be no such thing this year. It seemed that we never talked about any of the things we used to talk about.

"So why are you meeting with Ms. Pumpkin?" I asked.

"She wants to talk to me. It's called counciling," she replied. "It sure is hot today, isn't it?"

"Yes it is," I said.

"How is Patrice? Is she here?"

"I'm not sure. I only saw her this morning."

"I miss spending sleep overs at your place."

"I know Precious. But I'm sure you will again." I wanted to give her the confidence that everything would be better for her. "Very soon. I'm sure of it."

"So what do you think I should do?"

"About what?"

She sighed. She thought I knew what she was really asking. And I wondered why was she asking me? Because I didn't know. I didn't know what to say. I didn't know what advice to offer her.

"Maybe you should talk to Ms. Pumpkin. If you talk to her, then maybe she can help you."

She nodded in agreement. 'Maybe' she said. Then she changed the subject again.

"Didn't you want to enter the beauty pageant?" she asked.

What? Seriously? She thinks I should have entered? Wow.

"Well I thought about it."

"You could have. It might have been fun for you."

"Did I tell you that Petrina entered?"

"I think so."

"Do you know what she did? She snuck into the supply center and hid the beauty supplies from Pryanka."

"Why?"

"Well many pumpkins go to Pryanka to receive skin treatment. To beautify themselves. Right? And Petrina thought that if she didn't have any products, then those other pumpkins would suffer. Petrina would gain an advantage."

"Really?"

"Yes. Isn't she crazy?" I said, laughing.

And then Precious laughed too. With me. Which I thought was great. I mean I couldn't believe it. I thought for a while that she would never laugh ever again.

"Pretty sure looks nice, doesn't she?"

"Yes she does," I confirmed.

"So what do you think I should do?" she asked again. She seemed so helpless and lost. She seemed so much in doubt, about herself. She was looking for guidance. But I didn't know what to say to her.

I noticed Ms. Pumpkin approaching. I thought I should go, and leave them to talk by themselves. I really thought that if Precious talked to Ms. Pumpkin, that she would feel better. I mean, I just hoped Ms. Pumpkin would reassure her that everything would be okay.

"I should go Precious. Don't give up, okay?" I said.

She nodded, as we said bye.

And as I was heading out the exit door, I heard the strangest thing. From Portia of all pumpkins.

"Stay," she said.

Why? I mean was she even talking to me? I thought so at first, but then I thought probably not. She was probably talking to someone, who had just left her to be alone. But she was starring right at me. She almost made a lunge to grab my arm when I passed by her. But I tried to avoid her, whenever possible. And besides, I wanted to be with my friends.

When I first heard that Petrina had entered into the beauty pageant, I thought about entering myself. And I wasn't really sure why I didn't. I was normally not one to say no. Maybe I thought I would never win, so what was the point? It would be very difficult to maintain my body and shape like those finalists. They all look nice. They were all very talented. That they could all endure the harsh training regimen. The strict dieting and eating schedule. The exercise. Taking care of their skin and their body, at all times. All those types of things that made a fantastic looking pumpkin.

Pretty Pumpkin seemed to have mastered the art of beauty.

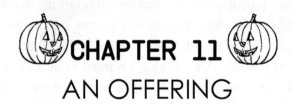

CHAPTER 11

AN OFFERING

On the next Thursday, we were all invited back into the arena. The elected elders wanted to make some public announcements. It was encouraged that we all attended.

All the commotion about the Tea Party and the green smoke, made me forget about my birthday. And my party. I felt helpless about the situation. No control. I hadn't cut my cake. Or blown out the candles. It was like being stuck in time. I needed closure. If there wasn't going to be a party, then someone should have notified me. It needed to be official. I didn't want to hear any speculation about my party being cancelled. I mean I wanted to turn eight years old. I wanted to move closer to being an elder.

My party should have happened before the Tea Party. And the conversation I had with Paradis and Patrice on the way to the arena that morning seemed to have confirmed that there wasn't going to be a party. At all.

"Did I say happy birthday to you? I don't think I did. So happy belated birthday Pashelle," said Patrice. She leaned over and gave me a kiss on my cheek.

"Same with me," echoed Paradis.

I didn't even care that they hadn't given me a present. It was nice to hear those words. From someone. Anyone. Pavneet had said it a few days prior. Same with Paxton and Pannette. Even Ms. Pumpkin had said it. She would normally bake such a beautiful cake. But not this year. It was a bit of a disappointment, I must admit. But our lives were so busy. We had so many things to do. That who could possibly even remember. And so many pumpkins were born on this day. I know Pimlico and Penner were born on the same day. They were two years older than I was. Penny and Pom Pom were born one day before me. And Pandria was born on the following day. I mean it wasn't just my birthday. It was a lot of our birthdays.

The arena was crowded. But we were able to find seats reasonably close to the stage. At least we weren't way in the back. We seemed to be late. Although attendance was optional. I mean we are not required to attend these meetings. But it was encouraged that whoever did, at least arrived on time, to prevent the least disruption. I hadn't been to a public meeting in quite some time, so I had urged Paradis and Patrice to accompany me that day. It took a while convincing them, and thus the unnecessary delay.

Anyone was free to attend, and even participate to some extent. The elected elders would respond to questions from anyone in the audience. I didn't have a question, or comment to anything that was said that morning.

Ms. Pumpkin was on the stage reading items from a list. And all the other elected elders were seated behind her. Ms. Pumpkin seemed really nervous talking to the whole audience in public, all at once. Like really uncomfortable. I guess some pumpkins were natural in public speaking, while others were not. Patricia was a natural. Her voice had always been strong, and loud. So much so, that I wondered if she really needed the microphone. And she had read the announcements for so long. For as long as I could remember. But when Pudge was given as an offering, and Patricia was elected our leader, she thought it was best to find a substitute. And many pumpkins had tried. First it was Mr. Pumpkin. And then Mr. Pumpkin tried. But I don't know what happened, because they don't anymore. Not that I know of. But then how would I know, because I didn't always come to the meetings. I thought Ms. Pumpkin was pleasant conducting the pageant.

And on that morning, it was Ms. Pumpkin on the stage. In front of the microphone.

By the time we sat, and started listening, she was in the midst of reading the new resolutions that had been approved by the elected elders.

Due to the passing of Ms. Pumpkin a few weeks prior, Mr. Pumpkin was now the elected elder responsible for fitness and athletics. And she reiterated what the committee hoped to achieve going forward. The members had the responsibility to ensure that each pumpkin did regular exercise on a daily basis. And in that spirit, a new program was announced called Play 24/7. No details were provided about the program, though. The games of summer would no longer be organized by the education committee, but now by the fitness and athletics committee. Apparently that was a big deal to some elders. There had been talk about that for quite some time. We would hear the elders in the school rooms, talking about the changes the elected elders had wanted to make regarding the games.

She also announced a resolution in principle had been agreed upon, to build a swimming pool. But no details on the implementation of the project would be available for the foreseeable future. Probably because the elders didn't know where it should be built. One possibility would be to build the pool inside the arena. I mean, there was a lack of available space in the patch for new building projects.

On another note, it was decided the lounge would not be enlarged at that time. The announcement was met by a smattering of boos. Some pumpkins were not happy. Many started talking at once. The rumblings and general disappointment of the crowd rattled Ms. Pumpkin on stage. Especially the ones in the front row, who had stood up.

"This is the worst news ever," I heard someone say in the row in front of me.

"Why?" said another.

"Something must be done."

"I want to speak on this issue."

Mr. Pumpkin was forced to stand, and asked for quiet. He reminded everyone of the proper procedures that were put in place during these meetings. That anyone was given ample opportunity to voice their opinions on any of these motions and resolutions. That objecting to the results loudly, and talking out of turn, was counter-productive. He waited for everyone to be reseated, and quietly nodded to Ms. Pumpkin, as if to say 'please continue.'

Another resolution that had already been approved and implemented was now official. That all buildings must be wheelchair accessible. Resolutions were passed to build elevators in the school, office and hospital. Those were the only buildings that had multiple floors. No time frame, or detailed plan, was provided.

It was also announced that the east end of the patch was off limits to everyone, until further notice. That no one was to go near Pashelles' Peak. Well she didn't use that name. She referred to it as the slope. That area of the patch was not safe. Well we all knew that. With the jagged rocks and sharp incline. And steep cliff. She explained that people would undergo a construction project in the next day or so. She didn't exactly state the day, or time. Or even the reason why. But it was off limits. That it could be dangerous to be near and around the slope during this construction project. But it would be any day now. She didn't provide too many details.

I wondered why everything was always such a secret? If the elected elders knew what would happen, then why didn't they just tell us? Why weren't we allowed to know then? Why did the people need access to the peak? I thought that I should stay behind afterwards, and participate in the question and answer period.

And because of this construction project, all major functions planned for the next week had been cancelled. What did that mean for my surprise birthday party? That essentially made it official. Because my party was a major function. There would be no birthday party this year. And I had to deal with the facts. No party. No cake. No presents. No candle wish. I had to accept that I was eight years old. Besides, maybe everyone was right. I didn't need a birthday party to know I had turned eight. And who wants to grow up and be old anyways?

And finally, she announced we would have a gathering for Pretty. To wish her success in her next pageant. That she was leaving the patch in the next few days.

I didn't stay after the announcements to participate in the question answer period. I didn't want to ask any questions about the construction project. I wasn't in the mood. As I turned to exit the arena, I saw Paxton. He sensed what I was about to say. All major functions would be cancelled? A party for Pretty, but not for me? He just shrugged his shoulders. He knew my party was cancelled. It's such disheartening news to have to accept. He just didn't want to tell me.

And just then, as soon as Paradis, Patrice and I exited the arena, Pandora ran right into me.

"Watch where you're going," she said. Which I thought was rude, because she was the one who bumped into me. And knocked me backwards. I ended up stepping on Peyton's foot. Pandora seemed overly excited. She was ranting about something. Like about her right to live peacefully in this patch.

She was yelling at Pickle. Which I didn't think was necessary.

"…and then some kind of rodent tried to get into my box. It was sticking its nose around the corners. Using its claws to pry it open," she said.

"I wonder if that belonged to Pikachu?" asked Pickle.

"I don't care whose rodent it was. It has no business coming into contact with me. Or my box. That thing has been following me around for days. This is my box. It's my personal property. I should have killed it by now," Pandora continued.

"There is no such thing Pandora. Everything is shared. You know that. Even your box," I interrupted. And I took a lunge for her valuable box. I grabbed it with my right hand, but couldn't take it away from her, as she had a firm grip on it. And instead, she lunged all her weight forward, and ended up tackling the box and me, to the ground. She fell on top of me. I landed hard on my right elbow, and let go of her box. When she rolled of me, she immediately stood up.

"Ouch," I said. "Are you crazy?" I was still on the ground.

"Hey. What's going on here?" I heard. It was Mr. Pumpkin.

"She tried to steal my box," she said.

"No I didn't." I said.

"Pashelle. Is this true?"

No. It wasn't true, I thought to myself. I wasn't looking for trouble. And I doubt she was either. Patrice helped me up off the ground.

"I don't care about that ghastly creature," added Pandora. "You tell that thing to stay away," she said, as she scurried away.

Strange pumpkin. She wasn't that way before. Ever since she found that box, she has become so weird. It was so difficult to have a normal conversation with her. Why bother saying anything to her at all? All I got was a sore arm for my efforts. Not only did I hit my elbow on the ground, my entire arm became twisted around under the weight of her body, when she rolled of me.

"Come on. Let's go get some lunch," I said to Patrice.

And we found my friends in the dining hall. Seated in our favorite spot in the back. Three rows from the kitchen. And Precious was there too. Which was really nice to see her outside the hospital room, more and more. Pumpkins were talking about the people and the Olympics. The Olympic committee had completed their investigation. All the medals that had been taken away, had been re awarded back to the athletes. The committee believed it was some kind of intoxicant in the air. Even though the athletes tested positive for an illegal substance, they deemed that since there were so many for the same intoxicant, that it must have been something beyond their control. The drug was not consumed on purpose. They concluded it was not their fault. We wondered if it was the green smoke. We all thought so. I mean what else could it have been? It was near the stadium, floating around the air. We all had seen it first-hand, and the damage it could do.

The unfortunate part, though, was the committee was unable to scientifically differentiate the substances in the green smoke, with other common illegal intoxicants that athletes had used in the past. The green smoke contained such a variety of unknown chemicals that they could not derive their origin. Further investigation needed to be done, to fully understand what they even were.

Precious began talking about the green smoke herself. And how her life had changed because of it. How she was having difficulty using the wheelchair. How the wheels would sometimes get stuck in the grass and dirt, and how frustrating it was to get it moving again. How much of a nuisance it was to use. How she had to plan every trip before-hand. Every physical movement was no longer natural. Everything that she took for granted was gone. Nothing was second nature.

"The doctors want to talk to me. About my life," she said.

"Are you still thinking about going to the city?"

"Yes. I have no choice but to think about it. I have to think about all the options in my life now. I have no control over anything anymore."

"Take your time. Don't be hasty."

"It's not about being hasty. I just don't want to live my life like this."

"Because what you are saying is so permanent," I said. I had missed the beginning part of the conversation. It was still so hard to think of something to say to her. To cheer her up.

I wondered how my friends managed to get their lunch so quickly. They must have missed the meeting. After we had lunch, Precious asked for help.

"Can you help me?" she asked. "I need help to return to the hospital. That is where they are waiting for me. Dr. Pumpkin wants to explain all the options in more detail to me."

We all helped Precious to the hospital. And it was difficult pushing the wheelchair over the grass. I saw myself how difficult it really was, and how much exertion she had to use to move that machine. To manually move the wheels forward.

We wished her luck, as she was greeted by Dr. Pumpkin at the entrance.

When she left our view, we continued to talk about her situation. About her options. I mean no one volunteered themselves as an offering, did they? I have heard stories. But who knew if they were even true.

"I heard Pagano gave himself as an offering. He became blind. He lost his eyesight when a witch thru some kind of powder in his eye."

"Petrov was crushed. In the city. He was hit by an oncoming bicycle. He was in so much pain. He was given medication, and was put to sleep. Permanently."

"But wasn't Pinilla deaf? I heard she lived her whole life while not being able to hear anything at all. Not a single thing. And I heard she lived a long life. She probably had all kinds of difficulties coping. Both physical and mental."

"Someone told me that Pelonia starved herself, after her sister Paloma was kicked by a person. She was hit by a steel-toed boot. In the city," said Petrina.

"Aw!" I exclaimed. That was disheartening. I didn't know that.

Just then, as we were lingering near the activity center entrance, we saw people enter our patch. They were accompanied by Mr. Pumpkin. They walked right past us. It looked like the construction project would begin. Whatever it was. I had to explain to my friends what it was all about. Because they missed the morning meeting. But since I didn't know very many details myself, I wasn't able to answer their questions. I told my friends what I knew. The things Ms. Pumpkin told everyone during the public announcements. That we were told they needed access to Pashelle's Peak from our patch.

There were four of them. Maybe five. They had cables, wires and other small machines. We followed them east. And we just watched. Many pumpkins stayed to watch, despite repeated requests from the elders to vacate the area. But the elders were just as interested as everyone else, and vacating didn't seem such a priority at all. The people were up on the peak for a few hours. We could see them, doing their work.

And at the same time, since people didn't have a direct access to reach the other side of the peak from New Surrey City, we saw a man, leaning out of a helicopter. He was lowered downwards. He went so far down on the other side of the peak that he completely disappeared from our view. It was difficult to determine exactly how far down he was lowered. All we could see were the ropes that the man was tied to, that were dangled down from the helicopter. And after a short period of time, he was lifted back up into the helicopter, and left. And soon after that, one of the volunteers yelled 'it's quitting time'. They packed up all of their stuff, came back down the peak and left our patch.

The whole thing was so mysterious. No one knew what type of work they did. Or why it was necessary. And none of us knew why it was necessary to stay clear of the area. I didn't know what all the fuss was about.

But we all found out soon enough. The next morning, in the early hours, as soon as the sun came up. When we were all sound asleep.

We heard a loud Boom! Like wow. It was like a bomb went off. Like we see on television. It woke us all. It was as if a huge explosion occurred. A loud bang that I had never heard off before. By the time I realized that we might go outside to have a look, Patrice had already jumped out of her bed. And I saw Pascal running down our hall. He opened the front door and took off outside.

I was in shock. I was thinking of something to say to Patrice. I wasn't exactly sure what. And before I had that chance, Boom! A second explosion.

"Aw!" we exclaimed.

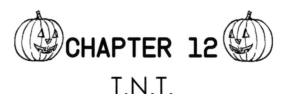

CHAPTER 12
T.N.T.

The earth shook underneath me on that second explosion. I could feel my bed move. Plouffe, Patrice and I left our house and raced towards the blast. And we knew where it came from. It was from Pashelles Peak.

The whole patch seemingly awoke at the same time, and we were all racing towards the explosion. We were headed for the smoke. It could be seen for miles. It was part white, and part black. It was as if a fire was lit to the clear white clouds, if that made sense. And this time it wasn't green. The black smoke was drifting upwards, further into the sky. And the westerly wind only made it worse. The smoke had created a blanket over the patch in no time.

The smell was totally gross. It was sickening. It smelt like burnt seaweed. By the time we made our way to the gardens of the eye, the smoke was seeping into my mouth, like some kind of intoxicant. It tasted like burnt marsh mellows, like I had eaten in Squashland. I could hear the frantic desperation in pumpkins voices. Was it an invasion? No it couldn't be. We knew people were going to do some kind of construction work. That's what we were told.

It didn't take long for hundreds of pumpkins to arrive in the gardens of the eye. Too bad I didn't see what happened first hand. That would have been cool. But what was not cool was the actual result. Once the black smoke had cleared, we realized what had happened. The people destroyed Pashelles Peak. The hill had disappeared. From our vantage point, we could now see the tall buildings of New Surrey City. They blew up the peak.

"Did you see the blast?"

"No."

"I did. It was crazy. A big ball of fire raced up the sky. It was awesome."

"And the whole cliff just fell into Caswell River."

Caswell River separates the patch from New Surrey City, to the east. That's why we go thru an underground tunnel to arrive at the city transit depot. The tunnel is actually surrounded by water.

"The smoke is getting in my eyes."

"Did we allow them to do that?"

"Ms. Pumpkin said. Don't you remember?"

"She said some kind of construction work. Not an explosion."

"That was such a nice hill."

"It was such a cozy plateau."

"The view on the slope was incredible."

"Is anyone hurt?"

"The smell is gross."

"Why is all the dust flowing this way?"

"Why did they blow up our mountain?"

"Look at all those witches. And ghouls."

We could see Wanda and countless other ghouls up in the sky, hovering over the people, examining the destruction of the peak. Wanda was screaming out at the top of her lungs. With eerie laughs between each sentence. She had the loudest voice.

"You people are so stupid. If this smoke enhances your performance, then why don't you use it? You should be begging me for it," she said.

I wasn't even sure what she meant by that rant. Or what she was raving about at all. I mean she was screaming at the people. Maybe she was upset that the peak just got blown to pieces. I don't know.

"Is this a new war?" someone asked.

"Did people declare war on us Mr. Pumpkin?"

"What was Wanda talking about?" I wondered aloud.

"She seems upset."

"Why is she yelling at people?"

"Everyone, the show is over. Let's get back to our business. There is no point lingering around here," Ms. Pumpkin requested. She instructed security to clear the area.

"We should investigate the physical changes to the slope, and examine how it will impact the landscape of the patch," suggested Plato. "After the dust settles."

Probably a good idea. I noticed Preakness was crying. 'Oh, what's wrong,' I thought. But I knew. The dust was getting into her eyes. The blast had blown so much dust from the city into the patch, it was getting into all our eyes. It became quite a nuisance. That was a time when we needed a good pair of sunglasses.

We could see rats and other vermin scurrying. Some escaping into holes through to the underground. Many were racing towards the east tunnel. There are a million rats in that tunnel. But not all the vermin vanished. One emerged. It vacated the masses and flew down the peak. It came racing towards us, thru the gardens of the eye. It was darting around pumpkins. And then it leapt and landed right on Pikachus head. She had her back turned from the blast site. It didn't take more than a split second for Pikachu to recognize her friend. Her pet rodent had come home.

I guess the rodent didn't want to live in a strange land afterall. Or it was tired of hanging around other vermin. It didn't want to live with its own kind. Or maybe it just missed Pikachu. It was probably so used to being with her. No creature needed that much of a lifestyle change. I could see tears of joy streaming down Pikachus face, while she cradled her friend.

My friends and I sat in the Rose garden for hours on that morning. And the morning turned into the afternoon. We were basking in the sun. There was less and less daylight each and every day. Summer was coming to an end, even though that day was just as hot as the others. I laid down and had to close my eyes, so I didn't stare right into the sun. The excitement of the blast must have taken all my energy. I must have dozed off for a few hours. Because when I re opened my eyes, there were much fewer pumpkins in the gardens. And the sun had shifted much further west.

My friends were talking about the explosion.

"We can see the city buildings," Petrina said.

Which was true. And kind of strange. The peak had blocked a direct view of the city. That was no longer the case.

Plato was explaining why the people blew away the peak.

"It was the green smoke," he said.

"What do you mean the green smoke?" asked Polo.

"Oh. Everyone knows about the green smoke. Like you really don't know?" I said. Polo could be so slow to pick up news. I had to explain everything to him. But I said it, as if I was bragging that I knew. Because I really didn't know why they blasted our peak. I was forced to hear the news from Plato.

"I know about the green smoke. I just don't understand how it's related to blowing up our hill."

"Well that is what Plato is saying," advised Petrina. "Just let him explain."

"Right. So underneath all that rock, on the other side of the slope, there was a mineral. The witches were extracting this mineral."

"What?"

"They were digging it out."

"So they used a magic spell?"

"Yes. In a way. Once they extracted this mineral from the rocks, they used a melting and fusing process."

"A what?"

"They melted the mineral into a type of gas. Then they inhale the gas. And by breathing in the normal air at the same time, the mixture of the two created a type of smoke."

"Why is it green?"

"We don't know. It could be just a witch color preference."

"Or maybe because their own breath is green."

"It could be."

"It is?"

"Isn't it?"

"What did this green smoke do to us?"

"This green smoke caused us to lose gravity."

"Gravity. What is that?" asked Polo.

"Don't you know?" I asked Polo. But I was actually glad he asked because I wasn't exactly sure myself.

"Gravity is what keeps us grounded. It keeps us attached to the earth. A physical connection to the ground. So when we lose it, we float up into the air. As if we can fly."

"That is weird."

"Like the type of gas that's in a balloon. Because they float."

"Well yes. And no. That's true. That balloons don't have any gravity. Because they are filled with helium gas. But we think the mineral was creating a different type of gas, to lift us upwards."

"That conversion process must be part of a magic spell. Converting the mineral to this type of gas has to be some kind of witch science."

"Exactly. That's what happened to Precious. As soon as she was sprayed with the green smoke, she lost gravity, and started floating in the air," confirmed Plato.

"Is that why people were spraying the water. To get rid of that smoke?"

"Well, I'm not sure. I don't think people knew what the green smoke was all about themselves. They were probably just spraying the water to get rid of the witches. Like we are told to do," Plato said.

"Why do we even do that?

"What?"

"Spray water on witches?"

"No one really knows. It could be a myth more than reality. That witches are afraid of water. They don't die when it's raining. Do they?"

"Maybe they do."

"Have you actually seen a witch die when it's raining? Like on Halloween?"

"Maybe they don't die. But they sure are afraid."

"Or maybe they can survive bits of water falling on them. Like drops. Maybe it burns their skin, or something. But maybe they cannot endure mass amounts of water all at once."

"They probably never take a bath."

"Is that why they always smell? Because they never take a bath?"

"Probably."

"Then they shouldn't have sprayed the water. The water mixed in with the green smoke gas, and then it disappeared. That's why Precious fell down afterwards."

"I mean people had to do something. If they didn't spray the water, then the witches probably would have grabbed Precious. And besides, she would have fallen anyways. Even if the green smoke disappeared by itself. Someway or another, she was going to fall to the ground. It was a lose-lose situation," I offered.

"We could have tried to catch her when she fell. So she wouldn't have hit the hard concrete floor."

"Maybe. But we didn't know what was happening to her. I mean it was all happening so fast. How could we have thought of that, so quickly?" I wondered.

"I know right."

"And the whole witch spell came from a mineral that was buried inside those cliff walls?"

"Yes. It looks like it."

"Why do witches want creatures to lose gravity?"

"Because everyone knows witches are better fighters in the air. They can out manoeuvre anyone on their fancy broomsticks. It's a strategic advantage for them."

"Peter told me that Wanda wants to organize an all species competition. To prove witches are the most superior," added Plato.

"How does Peter know this?"

"Victor Vampire told him. That Wanda was testing the smoke on people. To examine the effect it would have on them. And I'm not sure it had the desired effect. The news said that it acted more like a stimulant, and actually enhanced their performance. Unlike the effect it had on the werewolves. It made them weaker."

"So that's why she was yelling at people earlier today? Saying things like 'why don't you use it?'"

"Probably."

"How did the witches know about this mineral? It was like they knew what it could do."

"Yeah. It's like they knew it was in the mountain already. How could that be possible?"

"Who knows? I guess that's a story for another chapter."

"So people blew the slope away, so they could get rid of the mineral?"

"Yes."

"How did people find out that witches were using this mineral?"

"Peter told them," confirmed Plato.

"Aw!" we exclaimed.

"How did Peter know?" I asked.

"I don't know. You'll have to ask him. But…"

"Well I will. Wow. That is amazing that he found out."

"Wait. What?" asked Pannette. She was still confused. I could tell.

"Peter told people that the witches were gathering more frequently on the slope. That one day, when he was on the hill, he overheard the witches talk about the texture of the smoke. He claimed he didn't see them, but it sounded like they were undergoing the conversion process right then and there. So he told the elders that the witches might be creating the smoke on and around the hill. And Peter said he responded from a plea by people to come forward with new information regarding the Olympics drug scandal. He said exactly what he told the elders earlier that morning. He suggested to people to conduct tests on the contents inside the hill. To determine if they could find the same substance that created the type of drug, or gas, that was found in peoples bodies."

"And?"

"Well I can answer the next part. People didn't feel the need to do any testing did they? They had a better idea," I said.

"Like what?"

"Like excuse me? Seriously? You didn't see what happened this morning? People probably decided the testing was going to take years. So they figured 'Let's just blow up the peak. And find out if the smoke reappears'," I reasoned.

There was a pause in our conversation. A rare break. We needed time to digest all the information.

"So. You guys are coming, right?" Peekaboo asked. He appeared out of nowhere.

"Yes. Yes we are," my friends replied.

"Good," replied Peekaboo. And then he continued walking thru the eye gardens.

Where were they going? No. Where was I going? Where were we going? How could I have not known what was happening later? Where was everyone going?

"Where are we going?" I questioned.

"To Pretty's party."

"And to say good bye to Precious."

"She's decided to go to the city after all. She is leaving tomorrow morning. You didn't know?"

"No," I replied. I mean I didn't know.

Going to the city? That could only mean one thing. The only reason why Precious would go to the city, would be as an offering.

"We're all meeting soon. Later."

"Maybe Ms. Pumpkin told Paxton. And he was going to tell you."

Maybe. Probably. Seriously? I couldn't believe it. My heart sank. I didn't know what to feel. I looked at my friends faces, and for the most part, they were expressionless.

"Well. I'm gonna go home. Get ready. Maybe have a quick bath."

"Same with me. So why don't we all just meet back here?"

"For sure."

"No. Wait. Where?" I asked.

"Here. In the gardens. This is the best place to have a gathering for them."

"Right. I guess so." I had to agree.

I got up off the ground and started walking home. We all did. Polo started walking with me. He looked sad. About Precious, probably.

"Are you okay?" I asked.

"Yeah. I'm fine," he said. And then he added "Do you mind if I walk."

It's odd how he says that, but I knew what he meant. He actually hadn't said that to me in a while. Polo loved to walk me home. Even though it was out of his way to his own home. He liked to come over and hang out. And I knew what he meant. When he wanted to walk home with me, and come inside my house, he would say something like 'can I walk' or 'do you mind if I walk'.

And I never said no. Well sometimes I had. If I was super busy, or extra tired. Or something private was going on in my house. Or I don't know. But I had no reason to say no on that day.

I hadn't spoken to him very much that summer. I mean it had been a busy and hectic few months. I used to talk to him quite often. But not so much these days.

He always tried to stay to my right. I was not sure why that was. Force of habit, I guess. I examined the side of his face. The indentations were disappearing. He took quite a beating from Perses in his martial arts match a while ago.

"I wish you would have told me about the horses. I wanted to see them too," he said.

"I know. It was just that you were walking so far ahead of us. With Ms. Pumpkin. And we left the group so abruptly," I said.

"What? Abruptly?"

"Quickly. I mean it wasn't planned or anything. We just left. Almost on a whim," I explained.

I wondered if he was disappointed in me, leaving him behind like that. I'm sure he was.

After only a few steps, he pointed out Ms. Pumpkin. Up ahead. She was just getting up from a bench near the West Gate. He said he wanted to ask her something. Something about school.

"Okay. I will just wait right here then. I guess," I replied.

"Yeah, I mean there she is. Right there. It's only going to take one second. Oh by the way. Happy Birthday Pashelle," he said.

And off he went.

I started to take baby steps thru the West Gate. Pacing myself in super slow motion. Knowing that he would race up to me, once he was ready.

School. Wow. I couldn't believe that school was right around the corner. I still had to write my mandatory essay. About how I wanted to volunteer, when I became an elder. Usually I didn't hear 'happy birthday' and 'school' on the same day. I mean normally they occur at complete different times of the year.

It had been a real weird summer. With all the commotion of the green smoke and the destruction of Pashelles peak. That area looked so different now. It was unbelievable how Peter found out that was where it was created. And Precious getting hurt because of it. But I couldn't believe how she had decided on that. I think it was a decision made in haste. One made without proper thought. Life could be so strange. It was ending for Precious. And it was just beginning for Pandion and Pericles. While I seemed to be stuck in time.

All these thoughts were going thru my mind, walking along Column CD03, when Polo had finally caught up to me.

"Wow. That was a long time," I said. "What was so important?"

"Yeah. Sorry. Nothing really. It was just about my essay."

"Okay then. Maybe I will just go home, and wash my face, and brush my teeth. Put a new red bow on my stem. And then we can come back here," I said.

And we continued to walk very slowly. It didn't seem to be such a happy celebration. But we all wanted a chance to say good bye. And as soon as Polo and I veered onto column CD04. I heard numerous pumpkins scream out.

"Surprise! Happy Birthday!"

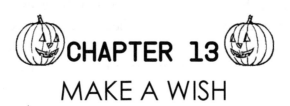

CHAPTER 13
MAKE A WISH

Oh my gosh. What? What's going on? What a surprise. I couldn't believe it. Everyone did remember my party. There were so many pumpkins scattered across, up and down the column. I was positive my birthday party was cancelled. I mean I had already accepted i was eight years old.

I saw Pebbles, Picasso, Patience and Prima. And I saw Porter and Pekka. Everyone seemed to be there. All my friends and family. Wow. I felt so honored. So special. My face must have turned all red with excitement. Even redder than my bow. I mean I was blushing. I'm sure of it. I couldn't believe the moment had finally arrived.

"Happy birthday Pashelle," said Paxton, as he kissed me on my forehead. He was the first to greet me. And so many followed. Giving me hugs, and wishing me all the best. Pascal, Paradis, Pimlico and Pony. As if there was some kind of a line up.

Everyone had smiles on their faces, and seemed in such a festive mood. The constant chatter of pumpkins, interrupting each other as they spoke. Screaming into others ears. After a while I wanted to abandon the line and join in on some conversation. I didn't know where to go. To join my two sisters, or to go ask Paxton and Payne how they managed to plan such a terrific surprise. Or to join my friends and talk about nothingness. Which was always fun. I mean I was so wired with excitement.

I just started to mingle around the column. Many pumpkins were headed for the tables full of drinks, and food. Appetizers. Sandwiches. Desserts. Elders headed towards Mr. Pumpkin, who had his usual assortment of alcohol drinks. He was always prepared for every celebration. Polo had left my side. He began stuffing his face with food.

We were in the center of three adjoining columns. CD04, CD05 and CC01. Which seemed to provide us with some space. We were near Star River. But we were still crammed together in such a small area. And each time I managed to move a few steps, I bumped into a pumpkin, who would wish me a happy birthday. I found myself listening to conversations. I ran into Peter again. He was at the party. He was chatting with Pretty.

"Yes. I know. Palak and Paneer should eat more spinach if they want to be strong like Popeye. But some pumpkins will always be kind of soft and ..." Pretty was explaining.

I wondered if my birthday cake was on the food table.

Since I had spotted Pavneet, I decided to get within ear shot of my friends.

"Well at least she seems happy," said Pannette.

"She must be so scared," said Petrina.

"But they will do it. I know they can. They have the technology," Plato added.

"What? To do what?" I enquired. I mean, what were they talking about?

"We're talking about Precious," confirmed Petrina.

"I know," I said.

"Stop daydreaming about your party. It's here already," said Pavneet, with a big smile on her face.

I really wasn't daydreaming. It was just that so many pumpkins were still grabbing me by the arms, and shoulders, to scream happy birthday in my ear.

"About the testing she will do in the hospital this weekend."

"So like hopefully she will be a candidate to be fitted with an artificial leg."

Right. Wait. What? She was getting an artificial leg? Oh my goodness. What a relief. She would not become an offering? Oh, it was such good news. The best news. I mean, what was I thinking? Why did everyone keep saying she was going to the city? I mean how could I have known? I have heard pumpkins use that phrase all the time, because no one wanted to use the word offering. So we said 'going to the city'. I don't know. Maybe not? I mean I loved going to the city. What was I thinking? I must have been so confused.

"Precious looks up to you Pashelle," I heard someone say.

She did? I found myself pushed out of the middle where my friends were standing, and out of the inner circle. My back found its way leaning against one of the bushes.

"Like a role model. She wants to be like you. Always doing things and keeping yourself busy. She enjoys listening to your adventures and stories. She always has."

"I didn't know that," I wondered aloud.

I mean I didn't know how to react. Not just because of the content of the message. I mean all of that was inspiring, in some way. But it was from Portia. Of all pumpkins. I hadn't noticed it was her until she appeared right in front of my face.

"You should go talk to her Pashelle," she said. "I've been trying to tell you this for quite some time now. She values your opinion more than you think."

Portia had a good point. I mean we were all there to say goodbye to Precious. And to wish her the best. So I pushed my way thru the crowd, back towards Column CD04. I had seen her there, right behind me, when I first heard surprise.

And there she was, talking to many pumpkins. It looked like she was demonstrating all the things she could do in the wheelchair. Backing up. Stopping. Turning. She was showing all the moves to Plouffe, Peekaboo, and Ms. Pumpkin. There were so many pumpkins around her.

I wanted to spend a few private moments with her. As I neared them, I thought if I started talking to her, then the other pumpkins would just go away.

"I'm so glad you made it to the party, Precious."

"Same to you Pashelle. I'm glad you made it too."

"Yeah. For sure. I don't think I would miss my own birthday party for the world."

"Never. I wouldn't miss mine either."

"Are you having a birthday party too?"

"Yes. Always. I want to have a party every year. Just like you."

"Did you know about the surprise?"

"Yes. I knew you wanted a party. Patrice mentioned it all the time. And the elders asked me about it. And I told them that we should. That it would be fun."

I really didn't care that it was my party anymore. I was actually pleased this gathering was really for Precious. And to wish her the best.

She had a smile on her face. Maybe not the way she used to smile. With her mouth so wide and her gleaming eyes. I hadn't seen that smile in weeks. But now it was more of a nervous type of smile. But a smile nonetheless.

Of course Precious was happier. I mean, if she had decided to be an offering, she wouldn't have been. No way. Never. We wouldn't have had the party.

"I thought that having a real party on the same day as my going away gathering, would make it easier for me," she said.

"Why?"

"I don't know. I have received so much attention from everyone. Maybe I didn't want everyone feeling all sorry for me. And being sad themselves. That having a real party would cheer everyone up."

"You seem so brave. Are you scared?"

"I'm not brave. I just feel like I have no other choice. Either I feel sorry for myself and my situation. Which makes me feel even worse. Or I try to have a more positive outlook. I know my situation may never improve. But at least I can try to feel better about myself."

"That is great to hear you talk this way Precious. So when are you leaving for New Surrey City?"

"No. I'm not going there. I'm going to a city further east. To Madison County. It's still near the Grand patch. I'm going on a plane. They said it was a helicopter. Pretty and I will be on the same plane."

"Wow. So how long are you going to stay there?"

"They just said for a couple of days. So they could run some tests and take some pictures. There is a doctor who is interested in my situation. So I don't know what's going to happen. Really."

"Okay."

"And I may never get a new leg. But I'm not going to let it bother me either way. Because life is too short. For any pumpkin. No matter how healthy we are. Life is short for all of us. So even if I'm not fitted with a new leg, I'm still going to fulfill my life. With my dreams. There are far too many other important things to worry about, than to worry about deciding to be given as an offering. Like what I'm going to do tomorrow. And the day after. And the day after that," she said. And she said it with so much determination and passion.

"You're right Precious," I said.

"I wouldn't miss any events or functions or parties. I want to live my life," she said. With such a gleaming face. And yet she seemed so scared. And nervous. And so excited. And full of hope and with the fear of despair, at the same time. She was half crying, half smiling. There was so much emotion in that one little phrase, that I could tell it would guide Precious for a lifetime.

And just then Ms. Pumpkin appeared.

"There you are, you two. Come on now. Let's not keep everyone waiting," she said.

"I think we're going to cut the cake now. You can push me if you want."

"Sure."

I grabbed the handles on the wheelchair and pushed it forwards. Thru the dirt and grass. It certainly was difficult.

"Maybe you should learn how to use the walking sticks," I suggested.

"They are called crutches. And yes. I will. There's no way I'll be able to move this thing by myself when it starts to rain. In the mud."

"Or you could ask for a chair with a motor. That would help," I suggested.

As I approached the cake table, I let go of the wheelchair. I positioned myself behind the table. I knew where I was supposed to stand. I saw another table with all the presents. Ms. Pumpkin took hold of the wheelchair and moved Precious right next to me. Which I thought was odd.

I saw the cake. It looked beautiful. So delicious. So nice. It was one layer. There were ten candles. Two in one vertical row, and eight in another vertical row. I leaned over the cake. There was a giant message reading 'Happy Birthday'. I was so excited. This was my moment.

And I wondered why Precious was stationed next to me. I wondered why there were ten candles. And she seemed to know my question without me asking.

"It's my birthday today Pashelle. I turned two this morning."

"Of course it is, Precious. Happy Birthday!" And I thought about it for a second. She was right. She was the only pumpkin born that whole summer. One week before I started my second full year of school. I mean this was great, I thought. We both got to celebrate our birthdays. It was a special day for her. And for me.

All the other pumpkins were crowded on the other side of the table. And on either side of us.

And just when it got a little quiet, as if everyone was waiting for me or Precious to say something, Ms. Pumpkin said, "Ok. Shall we all sing?"

And when she started singing, everyone else joined in.

"Happy Birthday to you. Happy Birthday to you. Having Birthday dear Pashelle Precious. Happy Birthday to you." But everything got jumbled up when our names were said. Pumpkins weren't coordinated to know which name to say first. It made for a confusing song. But it was all in good fun. It was music to my ears.

Everyone started clapping and congratulating themselves on a job well done. They all sang beautifully. I think. Well I was sure most of them did, anyways.

Then Ms. Pumpkin squeezed in beside me and lit the ten candles. And then moved out of the way.

But as she moved away, I unnecessarily backed up in the table behind us, with all the presents. And a couple of them were knocked to the ground. I was going to bend down and pick them up. But Precious spun her wheelchair around. Moved it forward slightly and to the left. She parked it right next to the presents. So close that she was able to bend down and pick up the presents, and lob them back onto the table. Then spun the wheelchair around on its wheels, so she was facing the cake table again.

"Not bad Precious," I said.

"I think so. But I still need to use the crutches though," she said with a smile.

Then out of the blue, I heard a pumpkin use his mouth to whistle. Which was kind of strange. And funny. It broke the temporary silence. I thought everyone was waiting for us.

"Are you ready Pashelle. Are you ready to blow out our candles and make a wish?" asked Precious.

"You bet," I said.

But I still needed something to wish for. I had thought about it for quite some time now. But just like in past years, I was so undecided.

I looked at Precious. I thought how she almost lost her life because of her fall. And even so, I still feared the worst. I mean I really thought she had decided to give herself as an offering. And I thought of Puff. He really did lose his life.

A million thoughts raced thru my mind. Just like they were on the way to the party, only a few moments ago. I thought about life and death. And birth. I saw Plato holding his two young brothers, mixed in the crowd. And I remembered the pumpkins who were given as an offering, when I was in the office last month.

It made me realize how short life could really be. And that we had to make the best of it while we were here. And that meant taking care of our body. And exercising. Not drinking alcohol. Nor inhaling any drugs or illegal substances. Like witch crafted green smoke. It meant eating healthy.

And how it was inevitable that one day, we would all be given as offerings. The thought of becoming old and unhealthy created an unnecessary tension.

"Oh Pashelle. Come on. Stop daydreaming and blow out the candles already," shouted a pumpkin. I didn't know who.

"Let's get this party started," I heard another scream out. It snapped me out of my deep thought.

And I still didn't know what to wish for. I would have wished for the moon and the stars, if I could.

I glanced at Precious again. And thought about the new adventure she was about to embark on. And how brave she had to be. And how she was probably just fortunate to be alive. And she was probably thinking that very thought herself. She said she wanted to live her life. Well, I wanted to live my life too. It was all in front of me.

I inhaled a considerable amount of air. And I blew it out very fast and straight. Wiping out the fire on all eight candles, at the same time as Precious blew out her two. And afterwards I looked out at every one, yelling and screaming. And cheering. For me.

I couldn't have imagined what Precious wished for. And I couldn't ask her either. Because she knew it had to be kept a secret, if it was ever going to come true.

But I felt like telling her my wish anyways. And I did.

"I wished I stayed eight years old for the rest of my life."

To Lindy,

Peter Nanra

CPSIA information can be obtained
at www.ICGtesting.com
Printed in the USA
LVHW01s0130150518
577203LV00005B/23/P